Additional Acclaim for *There Is Room for You*

"A beautifully wrought story . . . The book is beautifully written, filled with descriptions which capture both the essence of India and the personal relationships of the family."

—Islander

"Through the eyes of these two different women we see both a fascinating macrocosm—India as it was and is—and the internal microcosm of the personal. Each component of *There Is Room for You* is equally intriguing."

—Pages

"The book provides acute glimpses into India of the 1940s as well as the country it evolved into in the 1990s."

—Mantram

"Bacon does a wonderful job of creating beautifully complex characters and exploring the nuances of their attitudes and actions. Bacon's words and scenes will tug at the heart."

—Foster's Sunday Citizen

"*There Is Room for You* brings out India's spirituality, but it does so without resorting to tantric chants."

—India New England

"In *There Is Room for You*, the relationships are complex and true, and the atmosphere, especially of India, intoxicating. . . . An elegant, beautifully written novel about the ineffable bond between mothers and daughters and the powerful pull of place."

—Curled Up with a Good Book

"Two of the best-developed characters a reader could hope for . . . Bacon writes beautifully about the mysterious and misunderstood territory of modern India and the equally mysterious territory of mothers and daughters."

—The Sunday Monitor

Also by Charlotte Bacon

A Private State

Lost Geography

There Is Room for You

Charlotte Bacon

Picador
Farrar, Straus and Giroux
New York

www.picadorusa.com

Picador® is a U.S. registered trademark and is used by Farrar, Straus and Giroux under license from Pan Books Limited.

For information on Picador Reading Group Guides, as well as ordering, please contact the Trade Marketing department at St. Martin's Press.
Phone: 1-800-221-7945 extension 763
Fax: 212-677-7456
E-mail: trademarketing@stmartins.com

Designed by Jonathan D. Lippincott

Library of Congress Cataloging-in-Publication Data

Bacon, Charlotte, date.
    There is room for you / Charlotte Bacon.
        p. cm.
    ISBN 0-312-42384-5
    EAN 978-0312-42384-1
    1. Mothers and daughters—Fiction. 2. Americans—India—Fiction.
3. British—India—Fiction. 4. Loss (Psychology)—Fiction. 5. Fathers—
Death—Fiction. 6. New York (N.Y.)—Fiction. 7. Divorced women—
Fiction. 8. India—Fiction. I. Title.

PS3552.A27T47 2004
813'.54—dc22   2003059579

First published in the United States by Farrar, Straus and Giroux

First Picador Edition: April 2005

10 9 8 7 6 5 4 3 2 1

For Edie

There is room for you. You are alone with your few sheaves of rice. My boat is crowded, it is heavily laden, but how can I turn you away? . . . The travellers will land for different roads and homes. You will sit for a while on the prow of my boat, and at the journey's end none will keep you back. Where do you go, and to what home, to garner your sheaves? I will not question you, but when I fold my sails and moor my boat I shall sit and wonder in the evening, — Where do you go, and to what home, to garner your sheaves?

— Rabindranath Tagore

Contents

Prologue

I have suffered and despaired and known death
and I am glad that I am in this great world.
—Rabindranath Tagore

Anna

June 1992 ❖⊂⊃❖ En route to India

My mother, Rose, was born in Calcutta and lived there until she was seventeen, when she came to England in the middle years of the Second World War. She arrived in Boston five years after that, but she pretended she'd known nothing but London's blandest neighborhoods and affected steely boredom, especially if needled about life in Bengal. "India," she'd mutter if my brother James or I pressed her. "When I was a girl. So dull, Anna," she'd say, closing the spigot with a tight turn. An entire childhood cordoned off like a diseased town.

We knew little more than that her father was a botanist who'd studied the mangroves growing at the mouths of the Ganges, and that Rose had attended a convent school. On occasion, she'd recall the marble top of a bureau crashing to the floor, the wooden drawers below it riddled with termites. A nun hurling a globe at a rat that darted through the classroom. A tiger shot in the swamps when it tried to kill a cook. Yet these incidents were never offered as a way to delight or distract, given like a candy to soothe a bad mood; they were mentioned only when some bit of daily experience called them unexpectedly to mind. Despite her best efforts to keep us fixed in our brisk American lives, the past would arise and insist on its presence.

As with a reckless or harmful relative, it's almost impossible to erase all mention of a charged history, and Rose wasn't able to keep the country entirely separate from us. It could and would erupt at any time. A mongoose might pad through the backyard, Barrackpore or Howrah become neighbors of Acton or Belmont. When she smashed a finger or broke a vase, she swore in Bengali, her first language. All this was contained in the tall woman heating leftovers for an early supper on our balky stove. James and I would stand there, shifting from foot to foot, wondering what to make of her and of a world that could have produced her. How was it possible that the word "cholera" could crop up on a January afternoon in Massachusetts as we thawed our toes after skating? Had she had it? Known people with it? What was it like, a cholera outbreak? But she wouldn't say, and instead she turned to squint into the last of the sun, deepening the fans of wrinkles at the corners of her eyes. Snowmelt from our heavy coats puddled on the floor as the kettle reached full boil. Not listening to us at this point, she was caught somewhere fierce and important, inside territory she'd defined as not suitable for children, which made it all the more unnerving and gave it that much more allure. We quickly learned not to try to cross any of the bridges between the girl who'd found lizards in her shoes and the woman who ran our baths and shoveled the walk. Even so, once India or its links had entered the day, she'd retreat somewhere dim and cloistered. She'd bash off to the shed or the garden and restore order with a vengeance.

My father protected her silence with his doctor's sense of discretion. "It's her choice," he'd say, small hands raised in a gesture of mock helplessness. I assumed she'd told him everything, one of the conceits I have about their marriage, which was strange but solid. They were so different, David Singer and Rose Talcott. He was a Hungarian Jew, as precisely made

as a jockey, and there was Rose, as tall and English as West-
minster. They made no sense in Concord, yet they'd managed.
A wide scratched table with a delicate caned chair pulled up to
it. It didn't look right, but it worked. "Life, liberty, and the pursuit of privacy, Anna." Hands back down and leafing now
through the paper.

Rebuked, I cataloged the few remnants on display. A comb
she said was her mother's, which was made from a spine of hol-
lowed ivory that held a ladder of silver teeth, a knot of initials
carved at the center of the handle: *A*, large *T*, then *B*—Anna
Talcott Balfour. She died in childbirth, the woman I'm named
for, a woman Rose says she knows little about. A dramatic gap
masked as something ordinary, a stain on a carpet, a chip in the
paint. I found a book in the library, *Glimpses of Indian Birds*, in
which Rose had scrawled notes on sightings in a child's uncertain hand. On the piano, she'd placed a photo of Grandfather in
a topee, and one of herself in tennis whites that came down to
her ankles. That was it. She'd learned to play the game as a girl,
but there wasn't time now, she said, her fingers holding a length
of twine, a box of tulip bulbs propped on her hip. She tossed
me the barest scraps of information from which to build a
story—all of it, both what Rose and my own mind supplied,
fraught with imperial trappings, outmoded, musty, redolent of
something gloomy and creaking. The Raj as old armoire. Slight
whiff of cedar and mostly of mothballs. But you still wanted to
open the door.

When I told James I was planning to go to India, he said
right off, "Rose'll be livid." By the time he was ten, he'd chosen
the sensible tactic of ignoring what he couldn't understand or
wasn't invited to, and had taken up with airplanes from kits.
Balsa wood, rubber cement, and instruction booklets were his
means for lifting himself away from our house and the tight-
lipped people there. It was a hobby he treated as gravely as if it

were an important public service. Perhaps it was. Of all of us, James did the best imitation of a normal person, a good American. Now he's an international banker, with none of my qualms about traveling to poor countries that have uneasy relations with the fat and pushy West, though he's never been to India, either, both of us aware that it would irritate Rose.

"Of course she will," I said. "Maybe I don't have to tell her," I added, though how I might explain some four weeks away wasn't clear. Our reflex was fear, as if Rose were still part of a tyrannical culture that could be expected to behave coldly and without explaining its motives. To defend ourselves, James and I had used her first name since college, hoping to turn her into a kind of artifact, a statue of alarming proportions who happened to be our mother. The device kept her at a remove, where she could do less damage. We'd wanted to since we were little—Rose is that distinct a person; she occupies space that fully—but we hadn't gathered the authority until I was twenty, James eighteen. "So it's Rose now, is it?" she'd asked, which implied she liked it. If she hadn't, her mouth would have puckered, the dogs been ordered from the kitchen.

"James," I said, looking at the layers of tickets I had on my desk, eight hundred bucks' worth of jet fuel and bad food, "we're still scared of her."

"Why wouldn't we be?" he asked. "You're going to go and dig her up, aren't you?"

"Want to come?" I was suddenly aware of how much I would have liked his company.

"Why do you think I work in South America?" he said. "Anna, do you know how many miles Santiago is from Calcutta?" But I was sure he'd thought about it. He probably could have told me exactly how far Chile was from India, what the plane's route was, and on which island in the Pacific you'd have to stop to refuel. And I knew he knew that people still spoke Portuguese around Goa. And that Rose had received her schooling at the hands of nuns from Lisbon. No matter how he tried to distance himself, our family's history grafted onto his sleek and modern life at small, strange points.

This is true even though he's a man committed to the aerial view, the perspective that makes landscape an array of geometric figures and the people so small as to be hardly visible. He spends as much time inside real planes as he did building models when he was a child. Yet he sent me a special pillow to keep my neck from getting stiff on the long flight and a note that said only "Mazel Tov." We're just eighteen months apart. We'd played old games on old boards for hours without talking: Chinese checkers with cloudy marbles; chess with nicked bishops, knights without manes. When we did have conversations, each could finish the other's sentences. Alike. Then, after college, something altered in James. A rigidity came over him that I suspected was fear of trying to know himself in greater detail. His quickness with numbers and Spanish led to a job with the bank, and it concerned me to see how abruptly my brother blended into a world of men in somber clothing, men who felt they knew things to a certainty. But he sent the pillow. He didn't tell me not to go. Even after crafting all those models, he hadn't been able to rise entirely away from his own wonder.

I was glad for the kind gesture. I knew Rose wouldn't or couldn't offer much help. She'd left in 1943 and hadn't been back. She'd told me once without hesitation that she wasn't planning on returning, ever. Another slammed drawer. Another tool used for a violent task in the garden, then hung back in its appointed place. Rose. Such a smasher of options. Of course I'm going for her. She's the last uncharted territory around. She's also just about what's left.

Here on the plane to India, my neighbor's a guy from Gujarat named Amit Patel. Born in Ahmadabad, raised in Baltimore, he runs a chain of Comfort Inns. He calls to relatives a few rows back, sliding in and out of his languages with the ease of a born actor, émigré, entrepreneur. He's returning to attend a cousin's marriage, and to search, I'm guessing, for a wife of his own. "Do you miss India?" I ask. I'm intimate with missing these days; within the last year, my father has died and my husband, Mark, has left. It's a bit amazing that I've summoned the will to arrange for a month away from work, New York, and what remains of family. Grief can serve like a dead bolt across a day.

But Amit Patel doesn't think about my question or hear its echoes. Nope. Not a chance. He might want his mate to know Indian ways, but they won't settle there. "Promised land," he says, "that's here," touching the tray table littered with plastic wrap and miniature cutlery. Yet we've just crossed the Arabian Sea on a KLM 767, and we're angling toward Delhi. He's patting airspace. He's groping international time lines. He's fondling just about nothing and he knows this. What he means is that he doesn't need an actual location to tell him what's home. He carries both his countries lightly; double loyalties aren't a burden. He just chooses the most resilient version of each place to hang on to. It's clearly worked. Amit Patel laughs at something his brother tells him in Gujarati and says, with a Baltimore sway in his accent that I can hear above the engines, "Yeah, don't you wish." His transitions are spotless. He seems to manage everywhere, Amit Patel.

In my mind I've been a thousand times to India. Assembled it from fragments of news, novels, glossy photos, the UN reports I read for work that are full of bleak statistics revealing the thinness of the country's skeleton, its likely shattering points. But none of it has prepared me even for being on the plane, which is louder than any subway car I've ever known, bursting with talkative women, wailing babies, men sneaking into the galley to light cigarettes although the bossy Dutch flight attendants scream at them. Hundreds of clamorous people on their way to the already crowded subcontinent, which is about to receive a fresh load of passengers, including a hollowed-out grant writer who has collected pictures and stories of this country most of her life.

Amit has left his seat and gone to chat up another relative, and the images I've collected over the years have time to unroll. Apart from the fragments Rose gave us, my vision of India starts with the Taj Mahal, its dome floating like a double miracle, once in the air, once in the span of the reflecting pool. When I was little, I imagined only animals, exotic ones: tigers, cobras, and elephants adorned with emeralds that could span a palm. Later I learned about cows so holy they could lounge in the middle of roads, placid in their certainty that motorbikes would swerve. Later than that I read about Brahmins, princely states, Moghuls, nabobs, the Mutiny, successions of maharajas and viceroys, Gandhi, the Salt March, Jinnah, Nehru, the Gandhis. Cyclones, earthquakes, border skirmishes on the Sinkiang Glacier, troops sliding from China to India and back, shooting at each other in the thin air with rifles of another era. The population's doubling time in the 1970s predicted at twenty-nine years. Nothing in India done by half, not its numbers, ambitions, potential. Nuclear arsenals and not unserious threats to use them. Then, the seekers. A berth for Sai Baba, the Maharishi, the Dalai Lama in exile, blessed springs and holy caverns. Visible rivers that flowed on top of mythic ones, strata of spirited water. Penitents swinging from hooks, flaps of skin pulled from their backs in the shape of a tent. But most of all, people—spread across the plains, hills, towns, and coastlines. Buses and trains with arms and legs sprouting from windows and doors, room always made for one more body, as accommodating as the slums of Delhi, Bombay, Calcutta. Or not. Beggars rolled in swatches of burlap, pavement claimed and divided. Thinness. Dust. Democracy. And none of it still.

When friends found out I was going, they said, "India? Why? Aren't things hard enough already?" Women suggested healing teas, acupuncture, retreats, solutions intended to promote a graceful inward consultation with my dark luck. Men kept trying to set me up with their brothers and colleagues. I was supposed to learn something from the bad spell, extract its lessons in familiar surroundings, then move forward into a set of strong arms. India looked like wallowing. India looked like the deep end.

What I had a harder time saying was this: I did want difficulty, a new sense of what I could stand. I wasn't hoping to volunteer for the Sisters of Mercy or find instant solace among the enlightened on the ghats of the Ganges. I wanted movement, even of a tricky or frantic kind, in some of the world's largest cities, near bodies of water where people had been settled for thousands of years. The cheapest ticket took me to Delhi, where I'd get acclimated to time and temperature, an India that actually existed and not one that rattled around my brain. I slated a day in Agra to see the Taj Mahal, followed by ten in Varanasi for the temples, and another ten in Calcutta, for Rose. More generally, I wanted immersion in places that were profoundly old and complicated. Places that had devised ways of handling ancient woes that few other cultures had come up with. Places where sadness and anger like mine, surely not the worst the world had to offer, assumed the correct proportion. "Brimming with charlatans, and they all look like gods." That's how Mira, a friend from work, described Varanasi one night over drinks. "But watch it. You can catch the karma bug there. For a moment you think you've actually grasped the nuances of reincarnation."

I told her she didn't have to worry. It wasn't searching for

some Hindu balm to my troubles that had made me decide to
seek out the holy city. It would be interesting to visit a community that had staked so much on its beliefs, but I wanted,
mostly, to walk the ghats and write postcards from a balcony.
Mira eyed me steadily, and in a bubble of alcohol truth I said,
"Fine, then, I'm thinking about people believing in a river, I'm
thinking about faith," and she looked down and stirred the last
of her vodka. "Faith" is a hard word to get away with in a bar
in Greenwich Village.

"Oh, that," said Mira. "Oh, that little problem," and ordered
us another round.

Still, it was useful to have admitted it to myself. I was trying
to determine where or in what to put my trust once two cherished connections had failed. Love seemed the shoddiest of
investments when, after five years, a husband could say, No
children, no more marriage, no more you. Which was followed
eight months later by a father who wrapped his car around a
tree on an August afternoon when absolutely nothing else was
happening.

I believed most firmly these days in total reversals of luck,
and sorrow deep enough to crack bone. And I'd have more to
reckon with than fresh grief. A day before I left, a parcel came
for me. The second the postal clerk handed it to me, I knew the
bundle wrapped in serious quantities of brown tape had to be
from Rose. No one else would make it that hard to open something. It took a pair of scissors and minutes of hacking at the
envelope to extract her present, a cardboard box that, when
opened, revealed a sheaf of typewritten pages with a large rubber band around them—the kind that binds stems of broccoli
together, the kind she was now saving in a large ball James and
I had found rolling around a drawer. There was also a note:
"Dear Anna: These recollections are for you. Read them if you
like; if not, please dispose of them properly. I wrote them years

ago. I hope you enjoy your trip. India is so hot this time of year." I wondered why she hadn't sent them earlier. If what was in here gave Rose pause, what would it do to me? I tugged the rubber band around the papers, stowed them back in their box, and called James.

I had only glanced at the first page, which made it clear that she'd typed it all on the old Royal up in our cabin in Maine one summer more than twenty years ago. I could imagine her there in the unheated house, pecking at the keys on the machine she used for her gardening column in the Concord *Journal* and for letters to her father. But this was different. James didn't speak for a moment. Then he said, "Don't take them with you. Don't even think about them," and he sighed. "You know? I just don't want to hear it." As much as we complained about her reserve, we were unready for what Rose might have to say. It was often wiser to pull back from her; not that she often dealt in blows, but the news she delivered was never cushioned with half-truths. Rose was the kind of woman who knew exactly how mice died after they'd been poisoned. It had made me seize up with nerves when I first realized that I had been harbored inside her body. It was disconcerting that someone so stern had carved a protected space for something as curled and fragile as a baby. My pictures from infancy show her smiling cautiously at me, a cigarette stashed in the V of her index and middle fingers. Me, the first baby, grasped as if I were a large packet, a slippery pile of books. But she'd had two of us. Twice, Rose had submitted to the screaming, the dampness, the need.

"Where're you going next?" I asked him. It was too much to try to decipher Rose and her murky motives over the phone. We were both relieved that I shifted the topic. He was leaving from Boston for Bogotá in eight hours and he started to describe the deal, the shady players, their dubious intentions for the money. But I found I couldn't focus. Outside, New York honked and whistled, and all I could think about was a time soon after Dad died when James and I found ourselves in my brother's old room. Enough air should have passed through the house to carry away the smells of being little, but it hadn't. Wood polish, lemons, and, strangely, doused candles. James's map of the world, stuck with pins to mark the sites of earth-quakes, was still on the wall; he'd tracked them for years, start-ing in the same period as the model planes. That day, he was standing in the sun, a mug of coffee in his hand, peering at the crumpled smile of the Himalaya. His hair was spiky and his socks had slumped, alarming traits in a banker. "A lulu's due up there," he said, tapping at Nepal with the cup. "A humdinger." I got the sense he liked using funny words in English. After speaking borrowed languages, it was a way to come home.

"You still follow them?" I asked. I really didn't know. I love James. I see him when I can, but his politics dismay me. Change, according to my brother, occurs when a few rich, entitled men decide that it should. It happens with factories, highways, the reweaving of debt so that an economy's chaotic shape appears intentional. It isn't so much a conservative view as it is a world-weary one, though those terms might well be interchangeable. "From the top," he would say when he came to Thanksgiving, "slowly, slowly, from the top," as my father and I tried not to look appalled and James piled stuffing on his plate. When I challenged my brother, he'd say he worked for a good cause, too, just one well-supplied with capital and no apologies about it. When I spluttered and said that wasn't so, that the nonprofit where I wrote grants could do wonders for three years on what his bank spent in a month, he'd ask pointed questions about how we measured our success, where we got our numbers, whose data we were trusting. None of it, he implied, and no one involved in jobs bound to struggling countries, was stain-less. Who was off the hook when it came to a cleanly moral course through the world? Who was exempt from involvement in the world's complexity of motives, the dirtiness of its cash? There was this, too: as Americans who tried to stay alert, we knew we still had so much more than we had earned.

Still, James's immersion in the old privileges was troubling to me. Rose was more comfortable with imperialist ethics than the rest of us. How things are, she'd say. Corrupt and difficult. Haves saying what the have-nots can and cannot do. At least it's James and not some venal middleman who's coping with it. As a boy, he had a reputation as a lion of fairness when it came to sharing toys and candy. But none of us had expected that James would traffic in nets of statistics with bureaucrats in shades.

"Yeah, on the side," he said about the earthquakes. "I don't make charts, but I keep up." I imagined him in his office, looking at a *Globe* photo of a pile of rubble that had once been a village near Teheran.

"Seeing anybody?" I asked then, because scrutinizing a picture of wailing mothers seemed such a lonely pursuit. He was thirty-three, handsome, well-off, and smart. Proprietarily, I thought he should have been married years ago. "Just dating," he said, shutting the subject down with a finality worthy of Rose. Then he put the mug on his desk and unpinned the map. Thumbtacks sprang out around him. He held the paper as if it had the weight of a boulder. Yet when I went to take it from him and lay it on the bed, it was so light that I nearly ripped it.

By January he'd almost become smooth and polished again, poured back into a grown self and tied up in new deals, shouting at borrowers in São Paulo and Buenos Aires. Work tangled in coils of Spanish and Portuguese, and phrases like "diminishing rates of return." He was never home. He was talking about moving to Argentina. Heading on a clear runway to the palmiest version of Latin America, its troubles compressed into columns of figures. He finished telling me about Colombia. "Anna?" he said just before I hung up. "Throw the papers out. It's not worth it, what you're going to find." Safer not to ask too many questions. Safer not to know too much or look too close. But that wasn't true. I hadn't asked Dad near enough. I also should have looked more closely at my marriage. If I had, I might have spotted the early cracks and tried to mend them. Circumspection hadn't been that helpful.

"Jimmy," I said, "give them the loan this time. Give them everything they ask for."

I tuck the pillow James gave me more firmly behind my neck, but it shifts from its comfortable spot when I move to make room for Amit, shooed back to his seat by an exasperated flight attendant. They've been telling people for the last fifteen minutes to close their tray tables and buckle up. We're on our way down. "Almost there," he says, and closes his duffel with an authoritative zip. "Ready?" he asks as he straps his ample belly in, as if India were a feast, a fabulous restaurant.

"Oh yes," I say, and know that I'm a liar. I'm not ready for it at all. I'm not ready to read what Rose has written. But I've brought what she sent; the pages are still in their box, sitting in the carry-on bag wedged below my seat. The jet shakes through the sky. A baby howls. Pressure builds in my ears. We cut through layers of cloud, and the vast orange bloom of Delhi appears below, its roads and highways, apartments and housing blocks. But there are also large pockets of darkness inside the sprawl, and I know that in those unlighted spaces there are probably houses of bamboo and plastic sheeting, and inside them, armies of Indians—breathing, muscled, living—are stirring in the dark. It doesn't matter if I'm prepared or not. I'm here. The ground surges up below the plane. "Happy landing," says Amit Patel. He smiles, and his incisors are packed in gold that sparks even in the muted light of the cabin.

Part One

Imagine, mother, that you are to stay at home and I am to travel in strange lands. Imagine that my boat is ready at the landing fully laden. Now think well, mother, before you say what I shall bring for you when I come back.

—Rabindranath Tagore

Anna

June 1992　✦c✦　New Delhi and Agra

The next evening, I set out from the Hotel Diplomat to walk through the great Indian heat my mother had warned me about. Even at eight o'clock the air was as slick and heavy as oil. No one was moving quickly. I found a phone exchange a few blocks away, failed to reach Rose, but left a message for James saying I'd arrived safely. My mother refuses to buy an answering machine—too much of a bother getting back to people, she says. Thinking about Rose's rejection of technology, still blurred with fatigue, I realized I'd wandered off the crowded boulevard near Connaught Circle and down a side street. A bright light at its end drew me on. I had to pick a path carefully; the way was pitted with holes and oddly quiet after the roar of the large road, though still thronged with people: men, women, and children walking slowly in the deepening night. The light became, as I drew closer, a metal barrel with fire rising from its center. A second one behind it echoed the flame. Triangles of orange through a chemical haze. Two small men poked long sticks into the drums. Then I smelled the hot tar. I wondered which part of the street the workers were repairing, since all of it was crumbling. The sidewalk was uneven and broken, too. They lifted the sticks and leaned to spread the

tar onto the pavement. Behind the men, a blue tarp was strung
over a length of wire, and below that, I saw as I got nearer, a
small gas ring and an aluminum kettle. The men rose, dipped
their sticks in tar, bent again. Their arms were dark and shiny
with their work. Their faces were splattered black. They were
deliberate as they eased the dripping stuff from their tools, using light from the flames to spot which piece of the ruined
street they would deal with next. They wore rags around their
waists and around their heads, and they were laughing. Then
one looked up and gestured at me. Tall white people are pretty
hard to miss here. There aren't many of us this time of year; nor
do we walk the streets alone. The men stopped and watched
me, saying nothing. I turned back. It did not seem right to disrupt people doing work in rags and laughing. I had a late supper at the Diplomat and went to bed, too tired to look at the
few books I've brought—the Lonely Planet book on India, a
couple of volumes of Tagore, and the Upanishads. It had been
hard to choose reading. You could bring the Boston Public and
it wouldn't be enough to help you fathom India. I put Rose's
pages back in their box, too, and tried to sleep in the hot, poor
country where my mother had been born.

As I'd explored the city today, I thought about her as a baby
in India, listening to its music and din as she grew, knowing its
temperature in her bones, becoming familiar with the difficulties it offered its people. She would know how complicated it
was just to walk a single block. But it was hard to imagine her
doing this. I couldn't see her in this country. I couldn't picture
any of the English, much less Grandfather and Rose, finding
their way in this huge, smoky city, with its compounds and
mosques. Rose had such fragile skin, but she never wore hats
or creams. She just rushed bluntly into the open, letting her
freckles widen to splotches of cocoa-brown ink. It would have
been vanity for her to care, and that accounted for the severe

skirts, the men's pants, the tennis shoes where her pinkie toes rubbed holes and the skin bubbled through like a blister. It seems improbable that this country was where she became so tall and quiet. One reason I don't want to start reading her pages is that I'm nervous about finding something unlovely in her attitudes.

I've also been thinking about the English who preceded her. To last here as long as they did means that they curbed what it was they actually let themselves see and feel. They must have entertained a muted range of options. It's a stratagem I'm familiar with in Rose's life. Plants, dogs, children, chores. Keep the focus tight. If the English had wanted to look more widely, they would have had to cotton on to the real problem for any conqueror of great civilizations. It's my guess that nothing but the collective habits of its 880 million people controls this place; not empresses, Congress politicians, Asokas, Shah Jehans, or Hindu nationalists. It's just too big. The sprawl I saw from the plane was real, it seems: even a taxi ride across town to the Red Fort could tell you that. So it's got to be the small, daily decisions Indians make about food, family, love, and work that maintain its restless stability. That, plus thousands of years' worth of a broad and subtle way of thinking about God, might have kept the English presence, no matter how onerous, in perspective. According to the Hindus, we've spent the last few millennia in the Kali Yuga, the black age, a cosmological prediction whose accuracy seems apparent given the woes of the twentieth century alone. World wars, famine, and profound disenfranchisement would certainly qualify as components of a dark time. Yet Indian myths have a penchant for capricious change—the slide of a ruler from power, the promotion of a humble man to wealth and grace.

They must have behaved, then, as if they knew they'd eventually be rid of the foreigners, even while Victorian and Edwardian functionaries plotted train routes, sentenced criminals, and schooled soldiers, saying Indians think this, Indians always say that: retreating to the general to avoid seeing the particular, the human. Trying to brush off not just myths but politicians, marches, uprisings. Indians themselves probably didn't often bother to differentiate among district officers, judges, and memsahibs either, except as potential bosses or oppressors. Everyone trying to cut each other down to size, as all around them India just grew and grew.

That's what struck me on the early morning train to Agra from Delhi. Every inch of land has someone on it, though that was just in the cities, Mira said. Unfortunately, I had to peer at the passing landscape in quick glimpses. The conductor pulled the shades in our compartment to keep the heat from stunning us. When I tried to lift the one nearest my window, the Indians traveling with me grew upset. "Do not be steaming us with the sun," a man cried.

Nonetheless, he was quite friendly. "Where is your homeland?" he asked, and nodded, not quite approvingly, when I said, "United States," with that odd combination of pride and dismay I'd come to acquire after being raised by Rose and Dad. My father often used to tell the story of how his parents had obtained three of the last visas out of Budapest. He also had tales about Grandpa the physics professor and Grandma the opera singer. Walter heard Isabella practicing at the university for months before he worked up the courage to find out who she was. But from the instant he heard her voice, he knew he wanted to marry her. "Isn't that incredible?" I said to Rose, who said it wasn't entirely true. Their families had known each other for years and approved the match. That part was left out because it wasn't as charming, and I was angry at Rose for not letting me make romance too pretty a destination.

Still, it was hard to link that beginning and those elegant professions with the people I knew. They were so fixed inside dense recollections of their old life, they barely seemed to have arrived in modern times. For them, the real world was still in Europe, and what they lived in was a platform not for life but for memory. The only concession they made to America was to speak English and use its schools to help their son learn skills to showcase the superiority of their culture. Their apartment was a reservoir of music and knowledge that found no outlet anywhere else in the country, or so they implied, and that was what fed their hearts. Visits from boisterous children who hoisted open the windows to stare at the suspended wonder of the George Washington Bridge provoked a kind of puzzlement. We were something they had never expected.

Isabella was tiny, and she creaked under her clothes in ominous but comforting ways. Liszt. Violins. Walnut furniture. The slump of Walter's shoulders, his hands so like Dad's. Hands of those who've never touched earth, hands meant to roll and squeeze the ends of cigarettes. Men who slouch in small chairs in cafés and argue. I didn't know that that was where he should have been until I saw people like him years later in Central Europe. The men with the caps, wearing knitted vests below their jackets, men worn into deep grooves of community that I did not mistake for satisfaction. Grooves that were simply grooves, worn by habit and history.

I don't have many memories of Rose there. She looked ill at ease in that apartment which smelled of cinnamon and bleach, where you could hear the neighbors' radio broadcasting the Yankees, an assault Grandpa fought with higher volume for Mendelssohn. Isabella and Walter were always kind to Rose, but I could sense they resented that Dad had used the American gift of choice not only to become a doctor, but to pick a gentile from England as his wife. A woman with crooked teeth and large bones and no experience handling proud and shat-

tered people from a part of Europe that had tossed away its
Jews with ruthless speed. At least the English had Disraeli,
Walter pointed out diplomatically.

Even so, they treated their grandchildren gently, with great,
intimate affection, though I think we baffled them. Looking at
James, you'd never know that half his blood was Hungarian.
He inherited Rose's size, and he's as blond and polite as an
English prince. He also moves like Rose, which makes it curious to hear such lovely Portuguese from him: it's a sensuous
language, perfect for ballads, even when you used it, as James
did, to pick apart debt schedules. All I acquired from our
mother was height. I'm as olive-skinned as Dad, and have the
black hair he got from Isabella, a woman veiled in flour and
disappointment. She wore bobby pins like the withered digits
of a witch. Everything about her appearance was pinched, except that hair.

"Hard times, small bones," Dad sometimes said, holding out
his delicate hands, often red from all his washing in the ER. Hungary, the 1930s, then New York during the war—he understood in his body what it meant to have to scrimp on light, food,
room. He was nearly as quiet as Rose about the past, though
kind enough to lessen the terror of his childhood by turning his
experiences into actual stories. Dad's recollections were often
harsh, but they managed to include cousins given to practical
jokes and stickball play-offs. Still, he grew hunched when he
talked, as if memory could diminish you. He looked like his father then, and I knew it wasn't just bad eating that had kept
him small. Walter, too, was as sparely built as a house on stilts.

Dad used to look at me and James in his parents' home and
say, "Behold the conquering heroes," amazed and a bit horrified his children had grown so big, so conclusively American.
He was thinking of Russians and Nazis. Of Rose and the English and India and of his new country's strident, interfering

ways. By the time we were seven and nine, he'd made us learn the preamble to the Constitution by heart and had read us *The Grapes of Wrath*. "Remember your strength," he yelled when we got rough with the dogs, with each other.

Stop it, Anna, I told myself, the heat of grief beginning to rise, the memory of his hands on my shoulders as he told me that anger was temporary but scars were not, preventing me from ripping James limb from limb during a stupid fight. I was thinking of this, I realized, because two small children in the compartment started to whinge and squabble, as Rose might have said, and the father, like Dad, restored calm with baleful patience. To compose myself again, I leaned forward to peek past the shade and glance at an upcoming station. Music blares everywhere in this country, and I forced myself to listen to its bouncy edges, the tremolo of the women's voices pressing high, then higher. Every time we pulled into a station, the loudspeakers were going. I recognized a few words now and then, and they also helped to pull me away from thoughts of my father. Love, house, mother. *Prem, makan, mata.* I had my Hindi phrase book handy and the list of words and curses Mira assured me would be useful on train rides. "Just don't say 'thank you' all the time. Americans are profligate with it. In India you only say it on important occasions. Getting someone's son a job. Finding a husband for an ugly girl." Use it, she said, when you really need it.

Two girls stepped into my compartment and settled themselves shyly across from me. They shared a Walkman, the headset spread wide to make room for one ear each, their cheeks pressed close. It was probably a sound track; they looked dreamy and a little scared, the way fantasies about men make you when you're fifteen. But they were older than that. They had bridal magazines and a pharmacology textbook with them. Eventually they turned off the music and began to quiz each other for an upcoming exam, though they kept stealing looks at the pictures of new wives. "Very hard," one girl said to me, nodding at the heavy volume she held in tiny hands, though it was really marriage I wanted to warn her about.

The word "hard" made me think of Rose, and what my father had said once about Grandfather when I asked if he loved his daughter. "Of course he does," he said. "But he was awfully hard on her." I wondered exactly what that meant. I knew Grandfather had helped Rose and Dad buy our small Concord house and the cottage in Port Clyde, where we spent happy, fogbound summers. I'd even seen his checks, bigger than American ones, signed in what I always thought of as India ink, documents that Rose whisked off to the bank without discussion. My father, when pestered, said it was money her own mother had had, money for which I should be grateful because it allowed us what he called, with no irony, "the good life." He was right. We had our modest yet well-located real estate. Dad worked at a public hospital but told us to attend the best colleges we could and our tuitions would be paid for.

Still, I also knew that in other ways my childhood was a single bed of a place, stingy with warmth. Rose set lights on timers, recorded gas mileage, and bought books and snow boots secondhand. Her own clothes were worried at the hems and sleeves by brambles and puppy teeth. At bottom, she was ashamed of her privilege and did not want any of us, herself included, to grow accustomed to soft living. Good fortune, her thrift implied, could change at any time, and what a horror it would be to have acquired tastes one couldn't sustain. Better by far not to develop them in the first place. You'd never risk disappointment that way.

With Dad's pension and God knows what she's hoarded in savings or from Grandfather, she could afford a couple of luxuries. Yet she still fills the days as she has for years, treating them like droppers full of precisely measured medicines. She writes her column. ("Forcing bulbs too early only leads to weakened plants later in the season. Wise gardeners are never greedy." James and I howled at these through high school. But it turns out that Rose is really good; her advice works, for plants.) She reads mysteries, tends the dogs, weeds the flower beds, drives to Maine on weekends.

Then, after Dad died, the saved rubber bands began to appear. "Jesus," James said one afternoon when we visited, "she's stopped using the dryer." Sheets were flapping on a line in the yard, and we found her, mouth stuffed with clothespins, clipping up socks in wet pairs. "Shame to spend so much on electricity," she said when she saw us, the English lining to her accent more pronounced for a moment. She's lived in Concord forty years, and there's still no question she's not from there. When she's particularly unhappy, the English notes grow sharper, as if that nationality could better handle grief or irritation. Since Dad's accident, she seems like a person caught in a bad winter, brittle with cold, aware that it has settled in her joints, as if she were preparing for chronic discomfort.

I didn't know how my thoughts had drifted to that house, those damp sheets, on a bumpy train ride through countryside I saw in stolen glimpses, being watched by the pair of Indian girls. The magazines and textbook had been abandoned, and it was clear they wanted to say hello. I asked their names, and they said Shakti and Sita. Sisters on their way to meet cousins. Nets of family. They asked me in shy English where I was from and if I was married. But "New York" and "no" stalled them, and the words made me miss both my adopted city and my husband. What did I do? they ventured next. I doubted my small dictionary had the translation for "I write for a nonprofit," so I said, "I write," and they cried, "Stories?"

I was startled. I did write poems, which I'd fit in during lulls at work, but I was uncomfortable making a private pleasure out to be more than that. What I did was more like nonfiction, I said, but they gestured to my notebook, excited. "Articles for the newspapers, then," pressed Shakti, and I still had to say no. Work about women, I said, from around the world. I'm the cleanup person at the office, provider of finishing touches on applications and proposals, crafter of opening remarks for higher-ups. My colleagues are specialists in places and problems, but I bounce from country to country, grant to grant. The young women said then, finally satisfied, "Feminism!"

"I am a student of pharmacology, but I love the poems of Alfred Tennyson," Shakti admitted, and to my amazement, she and her sister started to intone the first stanzas of "The Charge of the Light Brigade." " 'Half a league, half a league, / Half a league onward, / All in the valley of Death / Rode the six hundred.' "

The man who wouldn't let the shade be lifted chimed in from across the aisle, "Oh yes, Tennyson, a master," as the thumping English rhythm made light by high Indian voices filled the compartment: " ' "Charge for the guns!" he said; / Into the valley of Death / Rode the six hundred.' " I'd seen copies of Wordsworth and Eliot for sale in Connaught Circle bookshops, along with Marx, Gandhi, and Hegel. Mira, too, had told me about the poems she'd had to memorize as a child. "Reciting bloody 'Tintern Abbey' while staring out the window at the Siva temple." Then the porter trundled in, and the girls were distracted from the doomed soldiers by his offer of boxed lunch. "Pure veg?" asked Sita, and he nodded. We lifted the flap of the container, and inside sat a flat brown patty. "Cutlet," said Shakti. "Put on the sauce, and it will taste marvelous."

She was right. A splatter of Sri Guru's Chili Sauce Special made all the difference. Munching on her cutlet, Shakti said, "Even more than poetry, I like Sri Guru's." For the first time, it seemed like a good idea to have come, despite the tiny men spreading tar, the broken sidewalks, Rose's package, memories of my lost family. Camus said once, so French and austere, that the greatest gift of travel is fear. Maybe. It makes you alive to what you're trying to absorb, certainly. But the creaking old Tennyson, the hot train, the spicy sauce, those giggling young women with their magazines and their textbook, that was gift enough. Distinct from Rose, Mark, and Dad. Something I alone had seen and been invited to join. It was the odd pleasure of those girlish voices saying, " 'Someone had blundered. / Theirs not to make reply, / Theirs not to reason why, / Theirs but to do and die,' " then offering up a spare packet of seasoning. Of looking at green-eyed brides with nose rings and listening to the sisters invoke contraindications for amoxicillin as lustily as they had a poem about the Crimean War, all while laughing. Feminism. "Good-bye, Miss America," they called as they left a few stops before mine, bent double at their daring, loose pants held high so as not to catch in the door.

But none of that lightness prepared me for Agra, where it was 110 degrees by the time I returned to the station for the express train to Delhi after my visit to the Taj. It seemed by then that 110 hours had gone past since eating veg cutlet with Shakti and Sita. Partly it was the heat, which had the weight of wet, clinging silk. The Indians who shared the platform examined me closely, as if I were a large and slightly unusual bird. I wondered what the mother in the gold sari thought as she stripped an orange of pith and gazed at me, her eyes as still as her lips and fingers were nimble. She rapped out an order to her child in testy Hindi.

English seems to be spoken in pockets here, words like "tip-top" and "post-haste" dashed like pepper on signs, in speech.

"What, Dilip, are you mad?" I heard someone say today. But mostly I'm surrounded by the spiky sounds of Hindi, a brash bird of a language. Bristling with *k*'s and *t*'s and spoken so fast it is as mind-bending as watching a sewing machine's needle pierce fabric over and over again.

I tried a smile, thinking to coax a response if not a conversation. The woman neatly spit a seed in a crescent of peel, handed a segment to her son, kept watching. The sandpapered scratch of movie sound tracks at full volume racketed across the station rafters and platform and on into the white sky.

Other foreigners retreated to the first-class lounge, where the ceiling fan, a mark of the extra money they've spent, sliced the hot air and sent it in ribbons to the dusty corners of the private space. An Indian family sat in a clutter of bright cloth, as if there were no room on their bench, when in fact they were its only occupants. The mother glistened with glass bracelets and lipstick. Her two sleeping children were slung across the lap of her husband, who wore a Western-style shirt and tooled leather shoes. He was half the size of his wife, and the sweat poured down his nose, but he couldn't stop it. His arms were full of his children.

I could have stayed, but the room was even hotter than the platform, and I was more interested in what was happening out there. I wanted to think about the Taj, the name as casually shortened as if I'd been in India for weeks, when it's only been three days, heat crimping speech the way it does motion. Still, something as embedded in the world's mind as the Taj needs only that single syllable. It seems a minor wonder to have traveled in the space of a week from New York to the grave of Mumtaz, dead at thirty-six from the birth of her twelfth child. In honor of love and sons, the Taj.

A mirage of the building hung in my memory, floating there in front of me, its image powerful enough to sponge away the

crowded station. Like everything beautiful, its edges were littered with muck, glitter, commentators. Reflections of reflections of reflections, wavering when an egret touched down or a
child's hand stirred the surface of the pools. The error caught
and enlarged, so the soft curves and straight towers started to
snake. Below the building spread images of blurred tourists.

They're printed in my imagination, too, as much a part of
the Taj as its floating dome. Indian men, linking arms and shad-
owing solo women, corralling them into photos with their
buddies. I avoided them by attaching myself to some French
tourists, who mixed bursts of appreciation for Moghul architecture with disgust for the rest of the country. The heat and
the delayed monsoon particularly offended them, and they
spent a great deal of time fanning themselves with brochures.
Fuzzy pictures of the tomb fluttered in their faces as the real
one stood there, a monument to clarity of both grief and design.
I turned to watch Indian children—girls in taffeta, boys in
miniature business suits—play games with the shadows the
building threw, as if the heat were nothing more than a thin
sheet to rush past. Their parents bent to reknot shoes or tighten
a sash. Indians came in large family groups, arrayed in their
best. Men in suits, women in saris, children holding umbrellas
over grandparents' heads. They left their shoes at the entrance,
and their feet seemed not to mind the scorching white marble.
Most of them moved with a thrifty grace, if not in tune with the
sun, then accustomed to the limitations it imposed. The Indians
posed for snapshots, not so much of the monument, but of
themselves anchored in front of it, blinking in the heat, and
then walking forward and through it.

I hadn't taken photos, though I'd brought along my small
camera. I didn't think this country would fit in rectangles. India
was spilling all over my journal; pictures wouldn't do better, I
suspected. Mark had trusted photography, thought it held on

harder to truth than language. The camera had been his last gift to me. He was an architect who specialized in low-income housing, and he was calm and matter-of-fact, and for all that, more likely than anyone I knew to get cornered in Washington Square by the Hare Krishnas.

The young women would sweetly explain that reciting the epithets of Krishna evoked his essence and that the repetition of those names brought the divinity into their presence. To speak the word "Krishna," they said, was to speak the name of love. Their companions danced through the archway like ecstatic chickens dressed in pink. Crack dealers were knuckling down to work a few benches away. Blue-skinned, flute-playing Krishna was quite palpably absent. Mark wouldn't quite rip the girls' hands from his arm, but it horrified him, all that open focus on adoration and God in a setting so linked to grit and trouble. He'd been born in California, in the loopy, gorgeous north, and it had spoiled him for the holy. His father had turned to the right, all guns and brimstone, while his mother got swallowed by yoga and wheatgrass. New York was diverse enough to water down that sort of orthodoxy and was full of people who believed in nothing but what could be made, moved, touched. I loved how he could rig a shelf from the simplest of materials or spend an afternoon savoring wood grain in a lumberyard in Queens, absorbed in exactly what was in front of him. At the start he'd been that way with me—patient, gentle, observant. We'd woven, I thought, an excellent net: work we liked; friends; tenderness at home in a city that, no matter how we admired it, did not enshrine that quality.

Most important, what we had was separate from his father's anger, his mother's dreamy fizz, and nothing like Rose's and Dad's glaring at America, both in and out of the country at once. We had something based not in faith exactly, but in concrete acts that could be pointed to, named, and shared. We would never have called it simple; New York's too ragged for that word to apply. We painted the walls of our tiny apartment on Horatio Street, scoured flea markets, stripped off layers of varnish from tables to find the sheen of hardwood. Then, quite suddenly, we proved ourselves more complicated than the most elaborate blueprints, more attached to what we couldn't see than either of us thought possible.

But I'd come to India in part to fill the space Mark took in my mind with other images, so I pulled away from the cranky French. I was by myself, framed inside a marble arch pitted with pollution or weather, it was impossible to tell. A camel kicked the banks of the Yamuna to a moving curtain of potato-yellow dust. My first camel. It was the kind of experience many of the British had written about: the first tiger, elephant, banyan tree, funeral pyre, woman in full veil. An India of animal and natural oddities, the dead and sequestered. Looking closer at the brown ribbon of the river, I saw the flicker of a current and stumbled into wondering again how I'd let a terrible year push me so far from home.

I felt stripped bare. I couldn't handle this place. But I don't think it's meant to be handled so much as warmly, diligently witnessed. And from how far back? The view from the heavens, the royal one, is too distant, too stupid in its confidence. Too close, and you're left a vulnerable fool, which might be the point.

The train was delayed, and I sat on the bench thinking first about the tomb, then about Rose. It was late May when I told her I was going, and we were in the Concord kitchen drinking tea. The afternoon light striped our hands, and just looking at the skin caught in the sun, you'd have thought both of us were older than we were. "I've got a trip coming up," I said. She was used to my departures; I attended conferences at home and abroad for my job all the time. Saying this wouldn't make her too wary, though she and Dad were always suspicious of travel. They'd worked so hard to find a spot from which they could never be pried up that trips other than those to Maine or New York often struck them as potentially disruptive, almost unseemly. Rose treated her rare visits to England as if they were journeys to Antarctica: expeditions that required a great deal of equipment, a reckoning with mortality.

"Where?" she asked, her large fingers pinching the handle of her cup, her face in shadow.

"India," I said, feeling the shape of each of the three syllables in my mouth. Delhi, Agra, Varanasi, Calcutta. A dim vision hanging in front of my eyes, black lines connecting the cities, signaled by glowing red dots. My unfolding itinerary.

"But it's almost monsoon," she protested. She knew at every moment what Indian weather would be, its climate hanging like a curtain in her mind. "It's horribly hot. And when the rains do come, everyone gets sick. Roads and bridges wash out." She wasn't looking at me. The cup scraped against its saucer. The gritty sound of china on china. "India." She said the word flatly. I thought I saw her scrolling through my life, taking up its various pieces, examining them for weight and size, seeing that there wasn't much to keep me here. But perhaps she wasn't doing that at all, because she looked drained, washed through with an unpleasant thought. She pushed the cup back. "You'll need shots, of course," she said. Even in her American kitchen she looked so English. And she was, from her crossed sevens to the trucks she had to call "lorries," the *u* she added to "labor."

"I've had the shots, Rose," I said, pouring out the last of the tea.

"I imagine they hurt," she said as she reached for the sponge to mop some that had spilled. "I never had to have them myself, but I imagine they must be painful."

That night, a storm pummeled the garden. The locust tree

lost a big limb, and Rose decided to take it down. We woke early and went onto the porch Rose had built when Grandfather died in 1983. She'd spent three weeks in London, the longest she'd ever been gone, selling his house, clearing out his belongings, and doing whatever else it was she did. She never said much about it. Then she'd returned, bristling with grief, and had banged away on two-by-fours and screens until there it was, the porch. Astonishingly well-proportioned for something created in such a fire of sadness.

Now she held a trowel and her favorite clippers, starred with rust. "It's worse than it looks from upstairs." She walked into the steaming green wreckage and cautiously knelt to clear out the broken tulips. It always took time for her to make herself the right shape for crouching. I set to work next to her and realized that she had finally taken off her wedding ring. The skin where it had lain was smooth, almost polished from the steady pressure of the metal. My own had come off much earlier. Looking at my left hand, you couldn't tell that I'd ever had a claim to anyone or he to me. Sun had erased the thin white stripe.

"You mean it, don't you," Rose said, trowel in motion. It wasn't a question, so I didn't respond. "You're going to go." She stared at the tulips. Small lakes gleamed in their bent leaves. "Wait at least 'til the rains start. It's cooler then." She speared the trowel in the dirt and said, "It's a totally foolish plan. You can't just run off and expect to solve your problems."

"Dad is dead; Mark is gone," I found myself saying, not wanting to mention how it was taking me two hours to shower and dress before leaving for work. The desire to write had fled to somewhere cold and inaccessible; it was hard finding the right words for thank-you notes to donors, much less the poems that meant more to me than I liked to admit. The old pleasures—movies, dinners, walking the city—seemed like lucky distractions I could no longer remember enjoying. I didn't bother to mention how much James was traveling and how little she was talking. My clippers fell into the nest of thorns at the base of the fairy roses.

"Anna," Rose said, reaching in to pull them from the ground, scratching her wrist. She passed me the orange handle as a trickle of blood curled down her thumb. We sat there on our haunches, the garden dripping.

A truck pulled up then, and we saw the tree man come around the corner. He was trim and pale blond, elfin, but his delicacy did not prevent him from hefting his chain saw as if it were as light as a child's plastic sword. Rose and I watched as he slowly reduced the trunk to manageable sections. An assistant helped rake the twigs that had broken from the locust's crown. I didn't even have to restrain myself from asking for a piece. Saving one wouldn't help. When they were done, it would be hard, I knew, to remember what the garden had looked like when the tree was there. I didn't know what to believe: that memory was as thick and resilient as a railroad tie or as easily spoiled as muslin. When I left later that afternoon, the men were still hard at work. "Carry your money with you," Rose said at the door. Her arms were furred in the sawdust that had been the locust's branches. She didn't reach for me.

Suddenly I was furious with her for yielding so little. I wanted to shout, I'm going for you—to find out what made you so bloody-minded. You're what's left. He left me with you. But words like that never passed between us. The dogs, as if to compensate for Rose, sidled closer to me and sighed their terrible-breath sighs. The animals were always named for characters in Conrad, a favorite of my father's. Marlow, Jukes, Almayer. Always two at once. Always grateful for their departure from the pound. A heap of dog below the kitchen table was how I felt at home. I buried my face in their coats, told Rose I

would call once I got to Delhi, and walked down the stairs. On
the train ride south, staring at the rusting port cities of Con-
necticut, I engaged in the bad and shameful habit of talking to
my father in my head. Why did you have to die first? I kept
asking, but that was replaced by an old memory, which stopped
all conversation. One night, using a model he brought from the
hospital, Dad had explained blood to me, its route through the
heart toward the lungs, the way it changed color and thickness,
and how it traced the same path again every few minutes. With
a practiced, careful hand, eager to show me the interiors, he
flicked open the tiny hooks that closed the chambers.

Dad would have admired India. The noise, the press of people, the way even in a crowd the feeling here is personal.
Everyone bumps into one another and assumes that there is a
self there to be noticed, talked to, inspected. I made myself look
around and listen to the hum of the station. It was full of squab-
bling families and shops the width of lockers where men sold
gum and soap and a stoned and blinking sadhu looked at me
even more directly than the young mother.

I trained my eyes toward the edge of the platform, where a
man stood at a battered cart, its wheels held together with vines
of wire. He bent down to adjust the kerosene so the flames
banked from tiger-orange to blue. A pan sizzled as he ladled oil
into its center from a tin at his feet. His motions had the grace
of a dancer whose stage happened to be the verge of a railway
station, whose medium happened to be the dough that he
slapped and spread between his palms. He was making *poori*.
Once in the hot fat, the puffs of bread rose like battered gilt
moons, lifting above the pan's horizon. When they were done,
the man slid a slotted spoon below them, shook them free of
grease, and set them in a dish where their skins retracted, turning brittle as they cooled. He sold them quickly, the clink of
coins and singing clicks of Hindi part of the exchange. After

each batch he dipped his hands in a plastic tub of water and rubbed them dry on the towel tucked into his trousers. He had a helper, a boy who squatted by the cart and mixed the dough, whose knees were gray with flour, which also striped his hair.

Watching them, I felt the weight of the day, the weight of watching and trying to watch well, to catch the details and the person below the activity. It was too much right then. I didn't know enough. I couldn't presume to guess a name, a caste, a history. Beyond that, I was still ten and a half hours away from my regular zone of sleep, my regular season. Not just a simple ten, because that would put India in the same time slot as Pakistan, suggesting other sorts of disruptions. My solitude descended as abruptly as the twilight. I shifted on the bench, trying to nudge my body toward alertness. The women with stars of gold in their noses and children smeared with holy red between their brows moved closer. The sadhu in the pink shift and the Brahmin's thread around the wasted muscles of his upper arm came nearer, too.

I pinched a flap of skin on my hand, but even the tug of pain didn't jolt me. Pulling my bag to my chest, feeling the wet square of the money belt slide at my waist, I closed my eyes. In spite of the wail of Hindi, the jostle of children, the rush and pull of people speaking and buying and laughing, I was asleep. In the magical way of some naps, it was a deep sleep, a tumbling into brief, black peace that made me feel as if I'd rested well all night. Despite the heat, the smell of shit and grease and curry, when I woke, I felt like myself again. For a second at least. As I slept, the crowd moved closer, and I had the sensation of seeing their faces clearly for the first time. At least as clearly as the burned-butter light allows. I saw the wide gap between the teeth of a young woman, proud of what looked like a new sari, eyes fringed in lashes of an improbable length. I saw the sadhu's eyes staring at me, and their deep color made me

glance away. They seemed to fill the whole socket, except for
crescents of white in their corners. A smile slipped around his
face and sometimes widened enough to reveal the red gums of
a *paan* chewer. He was nearly naked except for his thin pink
wrap, yet despite his ragged clothing and the horn of his heels
and toes, he managed to make his own appearance seem appropriate and my long skirt and loose shirt as indiscreet as a lacy
bra. Sitting with deep ease, his vertebrae strung like neat beads
of bone around the vital thread of his spine, he stared and
smiled and wagged his head, speaking softly and jerking his
chin toward me. The woman with the long eyelashes laughed,
her hand stealing over her mouth.

I folded myself closer, the way men in subways turn newspapers to narrow rectangles. I feared that these people who
saw me drop into unconsciousness would assume that I was as
unknowing as when I was asleep. They would start to finger
my clothes, make an earring spin in my lobe, discover my
money belt. Yet strangely, as I watched the Indians watch me, I
recognized that part of me would not mind such an invasion at
all. I imagined myself on the bench as leaf after leaf of old and
present life peeled away: hotel key spirited into a palm, braid
unwrapped by the agile hands of the *poori* man, passport floating to the pleat of the sadhu's robe, the flour spreading a
comet's tail through my hair as it had the boy's. It was then that
a hand did reach out to assess the edge of my skirt.

The jump of my skin and the flash of my own hand to twitch
the fabric back were enough to tell me that no amount of fatigue or dreaminess could open me to that patient discovery. If
my skin's response wasn't enough, then the hiss I made certainly was. It was a sound that escaped from Rose when a
plant's root snapped or a tool broke, an annoyance that looked
small and felt large. The hiss gave me away. I'd swatted at a
child.

The balance shifted from something oddly neutral and speculative to a situation in which I began to lose ground. Something must have sprung from me, some smell an animal gives off as it tries to flee because instinct had told it to, just as instinct has told it that flight is hopeless. That's what pulled the beggars.

I'd seen them in the hotel courtyard, around Connaught Circle, anywhere I had gone, really. They had begged as my taxi was stuck in a traffic jam of cows and Tata trucks, as I changed money, went out for meals. Women rub bellies and lift fingers from their throats to their mouths. Men put their hands together so they resemble bony cups and proffer them to me. Children cling to knees like drips of wax on the body of a candle, until they puddle at my ankles and can be gently slipped off. They had found me when I was standing, able to root out the small rupee notes Mira suggested I keep tucked in a front pocket. But now I was planted there on my democratic bench, and they were on me.

A man who was a torso and a pair of arms skittered toward me in a bowl equipped with rollers. His shoulders were sheaves of muscle, his knuckles twin ranges of callus. A tiny child led a blind girl, her eyes as densely white as glue. A boy of twelve or so, with rubbery, seemingly boneless feet hugely out of proportion to the rest of his frail, agile body, stood there mutely. The *poori* man continued to fry his perfect golden spheres. The sadhu stared. A new sound track began. The mother split another orange with a painted nail. "Please, miss," said the boy with the monstrous feet. The lights flickered. The music drooped, then returned to normal. The beggars were still there.

"Do you speak English?" I asked, and my voice sounded hollow, surprisingly high.

"Please, miss," said the boy with the flapping feet, "rupee." He rubbed his belly. That was the sign for them all to start.

Their gesture, scripted and effective, provoked mine, which was to fumble with my money belt and to pass out notes in awkward fistfuls. The beggars came in close, and I saw the bowl man's single tooth, the shell of the boy's ears, the dirty curls of the blind girl's hair. I felt their fingers on mine and smelled their skin.

The station crackled with an announcement on the loud-speaker. Families started to gather baggage. The sadhu sprayed *paan* to the floor. It was my train. The white tourists and the rich Indians staggered out of the first-class lounge. They were a kind of bell, calling me to attention, making me remember how I was supposed to behave. I rose, the beggars scattered, and I watched the train sway into its berth, doors opening to reveal proudly bored conductors. The *poori* man sold his last pieces. I felt the edge of a fingernail graze my palm, and I turned to discover that the woman next to the sadhu had placed a small un-peeled orange in my hand. The lights in the rafters blinked again, yet I saw that the woman was barely taller than a girl. She carried her bags and children, her walk curled to a near limp, making her way toward the second-class compartments. She did not look back.

The orange was sweet, dense with juice and full of pips al-most as sharp as thorns. I ate it slowly on the way to Delhi. The passengers on this train were more interested in one another than in me, and everyone was tired from the heat. At least the shades were up and I could peer at the dim landscape of dusty towns and the people walking through them. I wondered if one reason Rose hadn't mentioned India much was that once you started talking about what you'd seen or experienced in the course of a day, it might be hard to stop. She might have been frightened at how much she'd actually have to say and how separate it was from what she'd mapped out for her daily life: her cropped lawn, her efficient mothering, the hedges she trimmed with such vigor. Silence, she might have decided, bridged the oddness more gracefully than words. But how strange for her to have had all that Indian life, all that Indian sound jostling around her head as she raked leaves and drove us to swim lessons. No wonder she'd looked ill at ease in the Concord photos. No wonder she wanted to marry Dad: another person who didn't quite match his surroundings but shouldered his burdens and was useful. I was doing it again: filling holes in the story with bits I was imagining. I didn't even know if Rose had been to Delhi, much less seen the Taj. I would start reading what she'd sent when I got back to the hotel. Not that her pages would soothe me—I wasn't expecting that—but they might tell me how she managed here. I put the orange peel in a small plastic bag, knotting it in just the way Rose would have, tight and neat, though there wasn't a trash bin anywhere on the train. I'd have to carry it with me, the bundle of sharp seeds and fragrant skin, the leavings of a gift.

The stain of light on the wall of the corridor was the first sign of something wrong: a yellow block of brightness startling when I'd expected the Diplomat's usual nighttime gloom. But it was the sound I heard as I stepped off the elevator that made me run toward my open door. The clatter of pages in the numbing whir of a fan turned too high. Paper seems so quiet, but channel air toward it and even a hundred sheets can mimic a cloud of insects, riled and organizing for a swarm. It was Rose's story, scattered and in motion. Someone had found the box that had housed her manuscript while he searched my drawers for more obvious valuables. The jewels that I hadn't brought; the money, passport, and tickets slung around my waist. Advice my mother had given me.

Panic met rage as I ran. I could have told the thief that my room and what it holds would disappoint him. What I've got he can have: old clothes, a battered suitcase. He should have nailed the Korean guy the next door down, with his Cartier watch, and his suits dense as armor that he wears despite the temperature. He even had whiskey. A lot more promising a target than the story the thief had scattered. Bending down to pry a few sheets off the tiles, I imagined the man who'd ransacked my room. Coconut oil in his hair, narrow fingers. Hissing in Hindi at my poor offerings. If he'd stormed in and held me at knifepoint, I would have stammered, Look, I write grants to build clinics for prostitutes in Nicaragua; I'm professionally uneasy about being an American. I can barely wear leather, much less gold. I'm a tall divorced thirty-five-year-old, the one who got dumped. I have no child. My father died last year, and I miss him so much I feel like I'm breathing broken glass most mornings. I am not the one for you. I have nothing left worth taking. I wished I remembered the curses Mira had written down for me.

But he wasn't there to swear at. And it wasn't true that I had nothing to steal: he'd taken all my clothes and my suitcase. But he hadn't taken the pages. Even though I ought to have darted straight to the lobby, I wanted only to stop the fan from whirling, to put the story back in order. Several pieces had spun down the hall. I peeled off others pressed against the door's lower hinge. A funnel of paper spiraled by the bed—an untidy, miniature hurricane of white rectangles that collapsed the moment I shut off the fan. But not before I'd fingered some wrong switches. A single panel controlled everything in the room that used electricity, so the TV flared, catching a video starlet mid-piroutte against the Alps. The bathroom light burst on. I plunged myself into darkness with the next try, a bad moment, hearing the unsettled movement of the pages, seeing how they fluttered like hands.

The second I managed the proper combination—lights on, fan off, door closed—the Delhi heat descended. A sign hanging near the window told guests LIGHTS AND FANS WILL MAKE YOU JOYFUL IF IN USING THE CURRENT YOU ARE ECONOMICAL. Paper blanketed the room. The air thickened. I heard the clang of pots from the hotel kitchen, someone shouting, the skitter of claws on the window ledge, pigeon or rat, I didn't know. Beyond that, horns from rickshaws, taxis, bicycles. Indian traffic hurtling onward. I sat on a corner of the bed. Pages lay on the spread, under the desk. Others stuck out from under a chair. Some had probably blown behind the curtains. I knew this was the moment to raise a stink. More practically, I should have checked to see if there was someone cowering in the tub; it was clear I'd missed spotting the culprit by a few moments. The pages flying around the room were the clue—if I'd arrived even two minutes later, the pressure of the breeze would have pushed them all to the walls or floor. I wondered if the thief had been dashing down the stairs as I'd waited for the elevator, too tired that night to walk as I'd done the three days I'd been here. It was lucky I hadn't caught him in the act.

I started to gather the sheets, following Rose's neatly penned numbers in the bottom right corners, careful not to read them just yet. I wanted to do that slowly, not while my heart rang in my chest and sweat poured down my neck. Nothing appeared to be missing. I found the rubber band under the bed, then rolled the pages into a tube that I brought with me to the front desk.

Kamala, one of the Diplomat's clerks, saw me, smiled, then frowned. She'd helped reserve tickets for the trip to Agra and then my train to Varanasi, which left the next morning. I'd given her a pair of barrettes she'd admired and I'd looked with pleasure at her jewelry. She wore saris of improbably beautiful patterns: pink dotted with yellow, midnight blue with tiger stripes. The exchanges had given our conversations the air of friendly conspiracy, and when she saw me trotting toward her, she came to greet me.

I explained about the fan, the thief, my clothes being gone. "And on your last night with us!" she said, appalled but careful. She wanted, above all, to avoid trouble with the police, with the manager. I'd learned she was the youngest of four sisters, all of them "working girls," she told me, the connotation so different here than at home. She was saving money for her wedding. She needed this job, which was why when she suggested that she take me to her tailor for new clothes, I agreed. She dispersed the gathered clerks, barked out some orders in Hindi, which included, I suspected, making sure a new, good room was prepared for me. Then she handed over a ring of keys to a shy young man named Rohan, unpinned her own name tag, and said, "Madam, we will go to Miss Radhika's."

Which was how I found myself packed into a cab on the way to the bazaar with Kamala, Rose's pages stashed inside my satchel. The thief was probably the kitchen boy they'd just fired, Kamala said. They'd caught him stealing *samosas*, and he was getting his revenge. "When we return, you will have the best suite," she said, patting my hand, reassured that I'd gone along with her plan, grateful that I hadn't said the words "boss" or "investigation." Sitting there with Kamala in the taxi, it was odd to register the whole experience as both violation and good fortune.

It was not enjoyable thinking about an Indian man holding my underwear, but if the robber hadn't taken everything I'd brought, I'd never have seen the women on their way to the evening bazaar, women so completely veiled they wore gauze over their eyes—a group of black tents on the move, quick and potent, short pyramids of flesh. Their hands were the only part of their bodies left fully uncovered, holding shopping bags full

of okra and detergent. It was a shock to take in the regular outline of fingers next to all that dedication to vagueness of shape.
I'd never have had the chance to go into Miss Radhika's Ladies'
Tailor, whose sign said FINE STITCHERY PROMISED FOR ELE-
GANT GALS. It was a pleasure to see Miss Radhika use scissors
from a fairy tale, made of brass and steel, the blades as wide as
a carving knife. And to hear her assistants clucking, "so tall,
such a pity, no one to be trusted," Kamala talking in Hindi,
making sure, she said, they did not charge too much. Even to
have their fingers poke my ribs while their mouths were fringed
with pins as they tugged, pinched, and told Kamala to tell me I
should gain some weight and maybe then I'd find a husband—
all while we chattered about New York, high prices, children,
hairdressers. Women's talk, in mime, English, and Hindi, and
all of it strangely comprehensible.

In an hour the three tailors made three *salwar kameez* in colors bright enough to blind: robin's-egg blue, fuchsia, and a
lime green that seemed a good idea only in India. "No saris?"
I asked. Too complicated for Western women, Kamala explained. Always falling off in awkward places. "*Salwar* covers
more, too," she said sternly. When we were done, Kamala
whisked me through the alleys to purchase underclothes, a new
suitcase, and a flashlight for "electrical inconveniences." She
also stopped to buy a necklace of beads made from small dark
seeds, which she put around my neck. "You need an ornament," she said. Hardheaded, unruffled, and totally versed in
the ways of bargaining and movement through crowds, she
held my wrist loosely the entire time with a grip that was strong
and gentle.

We left the teeming market and stood on the street looking
for a cab. It was late, we were both tired, and the heat had
barely lessened as night fell. I was leaving the next morning for
Varanasi. A twelve-hour train ride in which to read Rose's

pages. A ride that could, I'd been warned, easily take double that time. We were both ready to return to the hotel, but a group of boys surrounded us, taunting me with "Madam, madam, what is your native land?" ignoring Kamala's rough orders to leave us alone.

"*Nahin, nahin, nahin,*" I kept saying in my cribbed Hindi, and they laughed, spilling the word back toward me, their voices sharp and nasal. Finally a taxi came, and the boys pressed their palms on the closed windows. The driver reversed as if they were not there, and they scattered like a flock of cocky crows, expecting the insult of the moving car, knowing exactly how to swing their hips from its fenders, fluent in the ways of rejection and intimate with the state of the car's engine, its possible velocity. All the while, streams of Hindi filtered through the glass. "Filth," said Kamala.

"Just boys," I said. The good tourist, not the snob, refusing to be bald in my assessments, even though the boys had frightened me a little with the furled edges of their anger, their thievish grace.

"You are not understanding, madam. What they are saying. Filth." The mood shifted. Confident in my ignorance of Hindi, I knew they called me names they'd toss only at whores or foreign women, and the distinction there might be slight. I glanced at Kamala and saw circles under her eyes, though her sari was just as crisp as it had been that morning. "Thank you for everything," I told her ten times, but she brushed away my gratitude. "You would do the same in your country," she insisted as the cab lurched forward. I tried to imagine a hotel clerk taking a guest to a mall to replace stolen goods and make sure she had an ornament. The picture was hard to conjure up.

I wondered which god might be considered responsible for kindness, but I decided not to ask more questions. She was so weary. On the dashboard were pasted small pictures of deities

smeared with vermilion. Kali, Hanuman, Ganesh, and Krishna,
I thought, though I wasn't sure; the images were well-tended,
hard to make out, except for Ganesh's curled trunk. I'd have
loved to know more, but the driver was busy avoiding bullock
carts and auto rickshaws that kicked up clouds of exhaust and
noise—the danger being less that there were hundreds of vehicles on the road and more that there were all kinds, moving at
different speeds, all of them converging: men on bicycles, men
walking, SUVs with tinted windows, and an elephant. During
my Delhi taxi rides I've noticed a tacit commitment to honking
and agility, a respect for the momentum that travel required.
HORN PLEASE was painted on boldly decorated trucks; no one
used blinkers to suggest a shift in position, which was signaled
with a shout and a series of piercing beeps. The trucks had a
majesty, all orange and silver, their cabs glistening with tinsel
and small lights. But the elephant was the most beautiful, his
trunk held at a distance from the pavement, a scarf of dust
floating at his knees. He was led on a chain by a tiny old man
with a switch. The animal's ears were tattered and spotty, palm
fronds suffering a blight. He wore a bell on his neck, and his
tusks had been painted red. Then our driver accelerated. We
arrived at a new spot in the road, caught in a fresh segment of
all this ragged forward motion, this press toward somewhere
other than here. Mostly men, but some families, too, children
awake or asleep, crooked in arms, on the back of motorcycles,
the tenth person tucked into the back of a wagon. Along for the
ride.

Music rang out from loudspeakers hung near roadside
stands. Tubes of fluorescent light in green and red and white,
the colors of the flag, balanced against buildings, glowing near
restaurants, auto-parts shops, the occasional gas station. India
was on. I suspected that it did not turn off, that this was its permanent condition. I wondered which god protected you from

car accidents. I knew from earlier rides that these cabs didn't have safety belts in the back, but it didn't prevent me from searching for them. The driver wasn't wearing his, and it flapped in the breeze from the open window, the buckle clanking against the door. The windows were made of regular glass that was easy to imagine shattering in sharp and faceted chips. Kamala had fallen asleep. Her shoulder bounced against mine. I could smell her rosewater perfume and the mild ripeness of her sweat. I tried to settle us in the center of the seat, as if that position would afford us greater safety. I placed the plastic bags with my new clothes by our feet. A long day. An oddly lucky day. But looking at the traffic and hurtling along in it, it was easy to be conscious of how many people moved through this city and that they did so at considerable peril. What I mean is, I could envision many ways in which people might die here, and that they did.

Rose

June 1969 ❖❖❖ Port Clyde, Maine

In my first clear memory of India, I took a string of Ayah's beads and held them in the late-afternoon light. The lumpy bits of glass were the shade of emeralds, rubies, sapphires—rude, even, but pretty. We were sitting on the verandah, and she'd unwound them from her neck and made a ceremony out of wrapping them around mine. I was watching the sun travel through the colours when the string snapped. The beads bounced underneath the canna lilies, rolled next to an anthill and all over the garden. "Gulab," Ayah chastised me—it means "rose" in Bengali. "Gulab, gulab, what a load of work you've made for us today." We put the ones we could find in the watering can, where they fell with echoing pings. We were quick about it. We wanted to be done before my father returned and asked us why we were so dusty. None of us in that household liked being asked to account for ourselves. We kept looking the next day and found a few more, though I suspect the magpies were there before us, or a rat who liked the shine. When we strung the beads back onto a stouter piece of thread, the necklace was somehow not right again. Its pleasing alterations of colours had gone muddy in our reconstruction. I never enjoyed playing with it after it was repaired. That Christmas, a holiday she did not celebrate, I gave Ayah a new piece of finery, made of silver, that I found in the bazaar. She wore it for as long as I knew her. She put the old necklace away.

Memories are suspect, naturally. They put roads in the wrong places, rearrange furniture, distort proportions of trees and rooms, put houses where they do not exist. Yet they feel as real as one's own hand. Sometimes they are shockingly right. The bridge arches as it does in the mind's eye. The remembered voice is the real voice.

The smell of the ocean here in Maine is just as I recalled: a mix of salt and seaweed with a strong note of pine from the trees that line the shore. It is my first time up this season. James and Anna are at camp. It seemed a good idea for them to do something geared entirely toward children after such a terrible year. It's partly why I came earlier than usual: to enjoy the lack of telephones, radio, contact in general. I doubt I will even buy the paper. David's working hard and may drive up for the weekend or not. We are giving each other rather a wide berth. Not exactly avoiding one another, but not seeking out each other's company. It started earlier this spring, with each of us distracted by the war and our jobs, but it has happened before. We'd survived complicated events by the time we met and were grateful to find Concord, this house, our occupations. Mostly we've agreed to keep difficult pieces of the past stowed where they belong, which is easy enough to do when the present seizes all of your time.

Then, when I sat down this morning to write, up surged the memory of Ayah. I sat for a few minutes after typing it on the back of a medical questionnaire—David brings back old forms from Emerson for me to use. Anna and James would smirk. They think me miserly, which I am to some degree. My hatred of waste is one reason I find it so hard to fathom the expense of the war, the dollars thrown at trying to reach the moon.

But I've just squandered both time and paper myself. The sheet should have been filled with information about nematodes or building a cold frame, but instead, there was Ayah. I know why; news came from India this spring, old news. But I hadn't realised how much I had wanted to revisit those times, to think about what happened there, the ordinary and the unusual. Even the parts that reveal what most shames me about myself. So it is disconcerting to start. I thought I'd done a good job of keeping it all tucked away. I hadn't even dreamt about India for years until recently. But I can see that the stories will return quickly. Apparently I've been cultivating them all along.

It is natural enough to begin with Ayah. She raised me after my mother died, and she's deeply involved in what happened. Blood is important, but it is not the only way to forge a connection. Ayah taught me about being a child and having a mother, and showed me how separate the two jobs are and how braided. Mrs. Shanti Devi Kumar came from a village near the border of West Bengal and Bihar, where her father farmed millet. Ayah hated the fields and came to the city with a major's family. Eventually she found her way to us. Quite tall and slender, she wore saris of excellent silk in pink, orange, and blue, which she ordered from shops that got their goods in Benares, where her mother's family was from. (Her mother was of a slightly higher caste than her father, but she had scarred her face in a kitchen fire and had to accept the match her parents made with the farmer.) Ayah's snobbery came from this disappointed woman, and no matter the source, Ayah was particular about many things, including silk, and she thought Calcutta tailors lax. She wore masses of jewellery that made her clink as she walked, which she did with a slight limp, the result of a broken ankle when she was a girl. Her eyes were a distinctive grey-gold. Her hair was fine, and she wore it in a braid that she kept pinned to the nape of her neck. She smelt of jasmine oil and sometimes of woodsmoke if she had come from the kitchen. Her teeth often pained her, and my father tried unsuccessfully to get her to visit the local dentist. When I think back to India, it is most often her high voice I recall, telling me to hurry along, my father was waiting, finish your tea, slow girl. She used to say I'd be reborn as a snail if I didn't walk faster.

Her husband, Mr. Kumar, lived back in their village. She saw him only a few times a year, during important festivals such as the Durga Puja. Occasionally she was gone for a month at a time, to assist at a wedding or a funeral or the birth of a relative's son. When she returned, she was often too thin and more sour in temper. It took me years to realise that in part she stayed with us all that time because Mr. Kumar probably beat her. I never saw the marks, but I remember that she wore *salwar kameez* after returning, arms and belly hidden, as opposed to a sari, which is more revealing. She rarely spoke of him, though I ferreted out of her that he was a Congress man and the owner of twelve cows. Shelling peas on the verandah, the pods thrown with a flick of the wrist to waiting ravens, she would say with scorn, "Mr. Twelve Cow Kumar."

Many other women would have considered her lucky: she had found an acceptable way to live apart from a husband she could not bear. She wielded unusual and considerable power in our household—over some of the accounts, over the housekeeping, and especially over me.

Ayah presided over meals, baths, the writing of letters, and the doing of lessons. She scribbled alphabets on the back sides of my practise sheet. In the guise of helping me, she would work at her own penmanship. Shanti Devi Kumar (Mrs.), ayah to the most esteemed Rose Talcott (Miss), daughter of Mr. George T. Talcott, B.A., M.A., of the Royal Survey of the Sundarbans. She invented that. There was no Royal Survey. There was barely a project there at all. Boats, mangroves, lanterns, stained maps stored in cracked oilskin, but no real survey. Ayah loved initials and phrases such as "respected" and "most admirable." She knew all of the King's honorifics, the train of his titles. She read *The Statesman* as soon as everyone else in the house was through with it and tested me on current events.

Ayah consoled, scolded, and kept me in line. She had been there since I was born and knew everything about me. Her version of history was always the one that prevailed. "No, no, it was not like that," she would say to me. "The name of the cook's helper in Darjeeling that year was not Pra*kash*, slow-witted child. It was Pra*dip*."

Ayah had little patience for imprecision or needless fretting. The world was full of trouble; it was best to be informed about it and move on. That attitude perhaps explains why she decided one evening, when I was seven, to tell me how my mother had died. Slats of burnt-orange light came through the blinds and sliced her into stripes of light and dark as she sat in my bedroom and told me what had happened.

"You were born on August 15 at your parents' home off Harrington Street," she said. Monsoon rains had been late but heavy, and the afternoon had seen a downpour that allowed water to rise to the tops of the ground-floor windows. Everything was drenched: the streets were filled with drowned cats, cows, and pye-dogs. Temple courtyards flooded and sent the monkeys scurrying to the pointed tops of the *shikaras*. It was rather quiet, except for the rain and the shouts of stranded men and women, because the motorcars and lorries were silent. Fishermen were the only ones who profited. They made a fortune ferrying the stranded back and forth down Chowringee Road. They rowed their boats up from the docks on the Hooghly and charged ten annas per person for their services. Bands of water-taxi wallahs shouted at each other as the showers continued and their passengers hovered under sheets of gutta-percha. "Your father took a water-taxi to fetch the doctor, who lived near Dalhousie Square in a flat above his means. You were your mother's first child, and he was nervous. He wanted the doctor there as soon as you started to arrive."

The doctor was a Scotsman named Clendenning, who said that my mother had been among the bravest of women he'd ever seen in delivery. I wondered if this meant she hadn't screamed. Not screaming meant a great deal to everyone I knew: my father; Ayah; Muhammad Rashid, our khansama; everyone except my friend Veronica Browne, who screamed at everything. I wonder if my mother hadn't dared. If she was afraid of having my father or her Indian neighbours hear her. If she minded their knowing that the English felt pain. "You were big and healthy," Ayah said, and Clendenning was pleased. He went off after a few cups of tea, and my father sat next to my mother. Ayah was holding me, a big swaddled lump, she said, and then, "Memsahib died."

It must have been a haemorrhage, I imagine now. A complication as common and unstoppable as monsoon. Ayah finished, her voice a little flat. She gathered her sari in a ruffled handful, her limp more pronounced. I had always known she could be severe in the way that those who have witnessed suffering on a large scale are—pragmatic and shorn of sentimentality. I did not cry. I never did much as a child. Ayah would have thought less of me.

The salt was a damp lump at the bottom of the shaker, and I decided to make a trip to the grocery store to stock up on provisions. I've just come back with sugar, new salt, tins of soup, biscuits, tea, tuna fish. Simple food. One of the pleasures of time here alone is not caring about cookery. David, more attuned to daily pleasures, insists on decent meals. The customers were buying much the same sort of goods as I was. Their faces have some of Ayah's hardness to them and their hands are cracked and lined as hers were. They are aware of long stretches of bad weather and the complications of earning a living, but they feel no need to belabour the difficulties. That's one of the reasons I like it here. The willingness to keep one's own counsel.

It was a skill I needed to acquire while young, partly because I did not have my real mother. There were many children like me in India, thanks to malaria, sunstroke, and dysentery, many children who functioned perfectly well without anyone, and I had both my father and Ayah. Still, I wondered often about my mother and what my life would have been like if she had been there. Her name was Anna Rose Balfour. She was born in 1907. She met my father when she was eighteen and married him soon after, coming to India and dying a year later. That slight outline is most of what I know of the facts.

Occasionally my father would tell me a story about her, but there were long lapses between instalments, during which he was scathing about some blunder on the part of the generals with the sepoys or the venality of babus who had grown rich under British rule. He grew bristly with politics, as if they were a kind of hedge to keep my curiosity from growing. One of my favourite stories was of their meeting, though he told it awkwardly. He and my mother had first seen each other on midsummer night's eve at a garden party. Her aunt Dorothy had hosted it at her house in Surrey. He said that the sky was purple and yellow for hours, and when the sun finally did set, the clouds remained as blue as an opal. I remember that part particularly. When I saw opals years later in the bracelet of my aunt Fiona, what struck me was that blue was only one of their colours. Really, they blended blue with pink and gold and something milky and were hard to place in the spectrum. My

mother was wearing, my father said, a white dress. I asked him
what it looked like, but he grew impatient at that. "A dress. A
simple dress." He could glance at a cluster of mangroves and
describe with meticulous precision the thinnest articulations of
its root systems. Dogs and horses, glimpsed only once, were re-
constructed equally well. Yet he pretended to blunt impervi-
ousness when it came to clothing and women. I am quite sure
that he was just as aware of collars and flounces as he was
of botanical features, and his mulish insensibility to women
was affected, to hide how much they aroused him. He was
not someone who wanted to be seen caring for finery. "We
danced," he said, and I tried to let the picture develop: my father in khaki, my mother in white. Because I lived in India, I
added parrots, servants in turbans, and rattan chairs. "A string
quartet played. Fireflies came out. There was Pimm's cup and
little sandwiches." He stretched his legs a bit. "Your mother
didn't like them. Didn't like watercress. She wanted to talk
about books. But we didn't agree on that—she liked novels and
plays. We walked by the lake and surprised a pair of pheasant."
Curious, he said, to see them so close to water and not in the
brush. He glanced then at his watch, said, "Time for your supper," and rose to his great height, leaving me with the twilight,
the white dress, the startled birds. I imagined the green flare on
the male's head. I'd seen colour plates in *Panoramas of Scotland*.
Their disagreement about books—he read only newspapers
and science, keen as ever for objectivity, which still existed
then—hung there in my mind.

We had only one photograph of her, the wedding picture,
and it did not look like other wedding pictures I had seen. Oval
face, sunny, not drawn, as so many Edwardian girls were.
Ruddy, even in black and white. A cloud of pale hair, and small
bright eyes under triangular lids. A face that met the camera,
more curious about the technology than about how it would

make her look. A face that understood that this was not a
slowly built portrait in oils, but a new phenomenon based on
chemistry. She looked intelligent. The bouquet in her arms
seemed casually supported, as if she might as well be holding
reins or a leash. Strapping, my father said, inadequately. A person.

But she had died. Someone so fiercely herself had died.
When I was about seven, I started to fear that my father would
die as well. I lived in dread of going to an orphanage. In the
Hand-Book of India that had belonged to my grandfather, a district judge in Assam, I read that year about the Bengal Military
Orphan Institution. I copied this passage into a notebook, one
of the few that were saved from that time: "It was established to
afford a home to the orphan children of officers and soldiers
. . . Children are not, however, merely housed, clothed, and ed-
ucated; their advancement in life is cared for, and sums varying
according to circumstances are assigned as portions to girls
marrying, or as premia to set boys forth in the world." This was
a book bound in red leather and set on the same shelf in my father's study as the six volumes of the *Flora of India*. It followed
that I would not, like a boy, be sent "forth in the world," but
that I would have to be married. I thought I could get used to
the rows of beds and the people coughing at night, which is
how I imagined the children's ward, but the idea of an uncho-
sen husband chilled me.

My father was impatient with me when my fear was revealed. If anything happened to him, he said, I was to go and
stay with Aunt Fiona, who lived in Kensington with her husband, Uncle Lawrence, and their children the size of barrels.
We had pictures. Fiona, my mother's youngest sister, sent *Girls'
Weeklies* and commemorative plates printed with the likenesses
of the monarchs of Europe. Queens from Romania and Austria
with dressed hair and multiple chins. In the 1930s, when the

political situation heated up, her presents, from her perspective, grew more serviceable. Sweaters of coarse and smelly wool eaten by moths within weeks. Once, a kilt in a garish tartan with a startling blue stripe. Also marmalade, stale toffees, and bars of Pears' soap, all of which we could easily buy.

India to her was a place where one not so much lived as bivouacked. Her packages were the sort one might send to someone on a rugged frontier, not a well-supplied colonial outpost whose inhabitants prided themselves on their ability to replicate the surfaces of English life. To Fiona, India remained a place of pagan heat and disease from which people returned embittered and disabled. They needed weeks longer at the seaside than others to recover from an illness and lived with too many brass pots scattered around their houses. "All that Indian brass! Don't they have anything else to bring back?" she cried when I met her in London. My father and I agreed that Aunt Fiona was a personage of a minor sort, though she was jolly and rich. Now, however, I don't blame her so tartly for those mistaken impressions. After all, India had taken her sister.

In addition to the monthly letter she sent me, she wrote to my father alternately pleading and shouting for my return to a decent climate. By 1938, Fiona telegraphed every week. NO PLACE FOR MOTHERLESS CHILD STOP GEORGE SEND THAT GIRL BACK NOW STOP. I knew because I unballed the bits of paper after he'd thrown them into the dustbin. She died ten years ago, of pneumonia. When I came to England, she was the only person who was kind to me. She took me in and tended me through the war. She was boundless in her sympathy for us and for me in particular.

My father never liked her, however. A jealousy, at base. She had lived, and his wife had not. When I asked too many questions about her life, he said, "I am not planning on letting myself get swept away," and flicked a toast crumb to the floor, where an ant set on it.

When my father said he wouldn't die, I believed him. He proved resilient in the face of Indian disease and seemed stronger than anything I had ever experienced, except Indian weather, which was larger than anyone. Even Hindu gods fled to the Himalaya when typhoons came. Still, his enjoyment of his work and his basic self-regard gave him a tremendous solidity. Apart from missing my mother, apart from the trouble I caused him, he liked his life in India up until the very last years: the strict order he was able to impose; his sacrosanct responsibilities; the range to which his curiosity could spread in a country where his people were still nominally in charge; and the fact that there was always a new problem that needed to be solved, even amongst the mangroves, since this was indeed India, where problems bloomed luxuriantly.

From the time I was six, and enrolled at St. Angela's, a convent school, I was expected to sit with him on our verandah for an hour in the late afternoon while he drank gin and bitters. Before I went to meet him, Ayah would tidy my hair and drag a washcloth across my face. I used to watch the ground, too shy to meet his glance. His shoes were polished but, if one looked closely, quite worn. Indian cobblers were confounded by the size of his feet, and he indulged himself with one pair from Lobb's every five years. They took months to arrive from London, but the shoemakers who repaired them were always impressed with the craftsmanship.

We often talked first about his horse, Badger, and how he'd behaved. My father rode him almost daily, and they were well-matched. A snake bit the animal one night. That was when I learned that horses did scream like women when they were in pain. The stableman saved him by sucking out the poisoned blood himself. My father spoke as well about whether or not the rains were coming on time—he had an uncanny ability to read Indian weather, and people in our neighbourhood often called him Bristi Sahib, Mister Rain. He claimed his accuracy stemmed from studying meteorological records and the current science on the topic. But those volumes were home mostly to silverfish that could eat through six months of the history of Bengali cyclones in an afternoon, and monsoons were notoriously hard to forecast. Astrologers devised all kinds of ornate equations, as did the weather specialists. Rarely were any of them right. My father had more luck, but that was more because he was sensitive to pressures and fronts, I suspect. He taught me a word that I loved when I was little: "keraunoscopia," what the Greeks called divination by thunder. His work in the Sundarbans, a region renowned for its storms, informed his intuitions as well. That, and he spoke a fluent, nuanced Bengali he used with everyone he met—bicycle salesmen, barbers, old priests, people who had seen and lived through many more seasonal rains than he had.

He conversed with me as he would with an adult. One of his earliest presents was a dictionary of English, given as if it were something as girlish as a hair ribbon. I remember, too, the jiggle of his wrist as he swirled the liquor in the glass. No clanking of cubes; we didn't have a freezer. I saw my first ice at a party in Garden Reach. What also returns is the sun on his face, Indian sunset, which is bold, orange, and quick. Hot air from the fan made my hair fly about, while his, cut once a week, never moved. My father hired a punkah-wallah, a boy named Rajiv, who on nights when he wanted to go off with his friends would force his twin Sanjay to cover for him. They looked nearly identical, but each had his style of fanning. Rajiv was faster but erratic, Sanjay more steady. As was common with punkah-wallahs, they fell asleep from the boredom of their work, and my father often shouted, "Rajiv, *punkah*." When awake, they heard everything we said. They spoke quite a lot of English. I do not think the formal tone of our conversations would have changed if we'd been the only ones there.

I was aware without having words for it that he wished I were my mother at the end of the day. Wished he were saying "Hullo, Anna" instead of "Hullo, Rose." He never called me by the wrong name, but I sensed the inadequacy of my age and condition. He wanted a grown woman there to discuss the talk of the day. Germany was preparing for war. Gandhi, whom my father respected and loathed, was agitating for India's complete independence, as were Nehru and Jinnah. The Muslim League was gathering supporters. Bengal's partition seemed possible again. Dominion Status was being discussed as a possibility. He wanted someone not only to receive his opinions but to respond to and amplify them. He could not talk so critically with most of his colleagues, and it grew complicated with Indian acquaintances.

Aware of his need, like all children, I suppose, I adapted. I told him instead about bird sightings. There were birds then in Calcutta: tree pipits, tailorbirds, red-vented bulbuls, parakeets. I do not know what it is like now, but then there were sal trees by the river, and houses often had gardens full of butterfly bushes and palms that served as home to the birds.

Muhammad Rashid, our khansama, walked me to school each morning. Sometimes we left early and meandered by the river for the breeze. He was the one who would point out the birds, though he did not know their names. "*Pahki*," he would say in Bengali, shrugging. "Bird." I taught him the names anyway, and he would indulge me by using them. It didn't matter to him, all these distinctions. Knowing "flycatcher" and "white wagtail" didn't help me see the birds better, did it? He still spotted them more quickly, even ones hidden in the rushes.

I did not tell my father about Muhammad Rashid's keen eye. It was an innate skill, part of his personal intelligence, but one he'd also had to hone as a servant. He guarded us and his job with a powerful watchfulness. I revered most his ability to locate snakes from as far as forty feet away. He and Ayah were both good at killing them. Yet Muhammad Rashid could also be counted on to tell my father if I'd returned ten minutes late from an errand or had not made my bed. Anxious not to accustom me to too easy a life, my father insisted on my performing a number of household chores. In this, I differed drastically from my classmates, both Indian and English, so I jealously claimed sole responsibility for my expanding life list. It helped me feel an equal, a fellow observer of India. I didn't dare reveal the depths to which I depended on Indians to tell me about their country.

My father in turn would tell me about the mangroves he studied in the Sundarbans, a vast ring of roots tucked into the mouths of the Ganges south of Calcutta, a shifting landscape of islands shaped each year by storms and tides. Its mapping was provisional, charts from one year useless the next because of cyclones. A dangerous place, full of snakes and fevers, in which guides were not just necessary but venerated—people who could read the brown water and say that three feet below lay last year's nesting site for the egrets. The mangroves were my father's particular fascination, but he kept track of the populations of birds and mudskippers and was interested too in the tigers and crocodiles. I begged to accompany him, but he would not let me, claiming it was no place for girls. According to Muhammad Rashid, who had gone with him twice, the local people were not always happy to see my father; he asked so many questions. These were men who gave him data he needed for his studies but whom he did not credit in his publications. He would have been startled at the idea that he might have. He was imperious about the directions the boat should turn and the temperature of the tea, which he liked barely warm.

India was less a country to people like him and his colleagues than a berth for projects. Despite their infrequent

success, they were more than mildly confident, both civil
servants and scientists, out of schooled reflex, pride, necessity—not entirely out of belief in their own abilities. The faith
in their mission was not an exterior crust or a pose, nor was
it rooted in their interiors. It floated indeterminately; their
relation to India was at once thickly public and very private. But none of this I knew then or could have expressed. I
sensed little of this complication during the evenings we sat
and talked on the verandah. Then, it merely felt grand to trade
stories about the place we lived. He seemed to imply that we
were cataloguing various pieces of Indian life while the city
darkened around us. The air filled with fruit bats until the sky
grew so black you could only hear their whistles and their
wings.

The house is cold, and I've got the kettle on. Something crashing about next door woke me, and then the dogs started to
bark. I thought at first it was raccoons, since something
sounded intent on causing damage. I took the lantern and went
to the kitchen window. It was Sam Ellis, the son of the people
who live next door, a lawyer from Boston and his wife. Summer
people, too, though their house is more posh and has electricity.
A cottage much like ours had once been on the site, but it
burnt, and their far grander house was built. Sam did not blend
well with its handsome lines. He was drunk or drugged up,
stumbling. He had knocked over the dustbins. A light switched
on. An angry man's voice started to shout, and I saw Bob Ellis
loom inside the frame of his kitchen door. Sam glanced around,
looking, I could tell, for a way to escape. They both saw my
lantern and started. Sam turned and ran away up the drive.
The window was open, and I could hear his bare feet slapping
the path. I doused the flame then, not wanting to intrude fur-

ther. I saw Bob Ellis frowning in my direction. I tried to sleep, but decided after an hour to come and write. I do not look forward to seeing either of them tomorrow, to having an exchange of stilted pleasantries.

I knew a great deal about those from my childhood. Though I felt rather important during those evenings my father and I talked, I knew that other Europeans considered us inconsequential. My father's work at the Indian Museum was not treated disdainfully, but it was not well-paid. We intermittently attended church, and my father belonged to the club, but he went there only to have dinner now and then, when it was time to extract funds from trustees or directors. He wrote his articles. I dragged myself to school and tagged along with Ayah and the servants on their errands and visits around the city. Our countrymen regarded our life as excessively simple, even monastic. "Out in the bush," Veronica's mother said. I yearned for more contact with girls my age outside the classroom. But when I went to parties, I did not enjoy their games and shrieking, and I missed Ayah and our trips to the bazaar.

"Poor" and "rich" were words that meant different things depending on one's company. We had a water tank and did not use the pump that served thousands down the street. There was money for sweets and for the lepers at the Kali shrine on the way to school. We were English. Still, we lived off Cotton Street, in the unfashionable area of the city near Kumartoli, the statue-making district. We had come there soon after my mother's death, Ayah said. My father liked the mango trees, a pair of them in the garden, and the fountains, and now, I suspect, the distance from Tollygunge and Garden Reach, the neighbourhoods where the English liked to live or gather—the distance from people who would have tried to persuade him to raise me more properly, to take home leave, mingle more, study less unattractive plants.

In other ways he behaved just like the rest of the English. The walls of our house were painted white each winter when the air was driest. The muslin curtains too were replaced after they grew moldy shapes every monsoon. The sweepers lived in fear of letting one mango leaf lie on the grass, which women with handheld crescent knives crouched down to cut each week for a few coins. Muhammad Rashid would pay them. They would cup their hands to receive the change, then slide it into a fold in their saris, but not before pressing the money to their foreheads.

I recall that as clearly as the house itself, which was large and square and built of sandstone, with marble columns and wrought-iron terraces, two levels around a courtyard. We were grateful for the open space that allowed air to circulate in the bedrooms. The top was draped in a vast net, meant to keep the birds from flapping through the house. When one looked to the sky from the courtyard, one saw it cut into imperfect squares. The net drooped and required constant repair, and birds got in anyway. I woke often to the thrash of wings in my bedroom, a pigeon's shadow on the wall.

It had been an Indian's home, a button manufacturer named Mr. Rao who lost all his money in an expansion scheme. He'd had to sell it to a jute merchant, who leased it to us. Mr. Rao, however, still lived in the district, and we would see him in his suits, fiddling with the round bits of metal on his sleeve. He came by the house to read the newspaper once my father was done and to feed the carp in the fountains. I remember my father saying, "Buttons. In India," shaking his head. Only Europeans needed buttons, and there were so few of us compared to the numbers of Indians. Buttons were especially useless when Gandhi and his advocacy of homespun cloth gained ground and traditional Indian dress was seen as not just practical but also as a statement of rebellion.

In addition to the fountains, Mr. Rao's family had built walls around the grounds and an iron gate guarded by a pair of damaged stone lions. During the riots of 1905, half of the lion to the east had been pulverized, losing most of his head and a back paw. Despite the gates and the size, only my father and I and a few servants lived there. We always had servants; life there needed many people to make it work. They were paid tiny amounts. Some of them, like Ayah, stayed for years.

The district was lively, and crowded buildings pressed up against the garden walls. I heard arguments, bicycle bells, children calling in the street, vegetable sellers hawking eggplants and greens. I could smell the curries of the neighbours' cooking, thinking I knew what the Singhs were making and how fresh the Chatterjees' fish was. I could sit on the verandah among the potted ferns and listen and pretend I was not seen and only the observer. But even as a girl, I knew this was absurd. My skin colour alone meant I was always watched. The apartments were higher than the walls, and in the evening it is easy to see white skin against stone, even white skin patterned with fern shadows.

I was never not visible. One day, walking with Ayah, I saw a group of men holding placards and shouting for Indian self-rule. "Indian self-rule?" I said. "Yes," she answered. "That means the British should be getting out and leaving Indians to their own devices." I knew, though I did not say it, that that included me and my father, even though we weren't, from the European perspective, the right sort of people. Indians weren't going to distinguish among the different kinds. I looked at my hand on Ayah's brown wrist and knew that it would be there, fingers fiddling with her bangles, a finite number of times.

Yet I learned Bengali at the same time as I learned English, though I could not write it well. I craved rice and dal when I was ill. I still count my numbers like an Indian, in fours, along the joints in my fingers. I reach for food with my right hand. India was home because that was where Ayah was from. She sang me lullabies, my favourite one about waking up to find yourself a princess with rubies in your hair. I shook out my slippers because we found cobras behind the flour sack, in the washroom, in the stable. You could never assume that there wasn't a snake in the house. We woke at dawn in Calcutta, and Ayah would often come and fetch me for her morning prayers at the ghats near our house. I would sit next to her as she bent her neck and the water streamed from the brass pot to her skin and she said her devotions. My fingers were frequently stained with the vermilion paste we used to smear on the statue of Hanuman that we passed on the way to the river. Ayah used a rough brush to get it off; its bristles were stained pink. She'd stolen it from the cook, who'd used it to clean potatoes. I listened to Muhammad Rashid scolding a new sweeper or complaining to my father about his wages. The colonies of ants; the carp; the rickshaw drivers who congregated in front of the astrologer's next door, which was called Vijay's Astro-Help and advertised itself as the House of Efficient Astrologers and Palmists. Vijay was famous, and parents flocked to him when it was time for their daughters to marry. On the rare occasions when someone from school wanted to visit, I'd say, off Cotton Street, near Vijayji's, and they would know exactly where it was. Of course it was home.

England, a place I'd never been, was where I was supposed to belong. I would plunder my father's desk drawers for British coins and examine the King in profile. I often took *Panoramas of Scotland* from a shelf in the study to see what moors looked like. Foxes and stoats I found frightening. I shook the hands of my father's colleagues and wished we didn't have to touch. The Indian greeting, a tilt of the head and body as the hands tuck into a steeple and press themselves to the heart, was preferable to my mind. The feel of one's skin, the degree of one's strength, weren't for mere acquaintances to know.

A cool day. I woke late because of the clouds and the late night. The dogs nudging me for their walk finally roused me from a dream that was at least partly in Bengali. That language has sheared off from my conscious mind, a process that started in England when I was seventeen. I lost much of its grammar the first year, great chunks of its words next. It returns in anger, when I bash into something. I've met few Bengalis in this country, and I couldn't read it for my life. Writing, pieces dart back. The words for "fish" and "tiger"—*mach* and *bagh*. "Snake" and "girl"—*shap* and *meye*. More started to return when I took the dogs to the pier and back, though it felt odd to prop up the language I spoke in the vicinity of palm trees against lobster pots. It's got its romantic moods, Bengali. Love, for instance, is connected to nightingales, roses, and snow. I still know some Tagore by heart, though it comes now in fragments. "There is room for you. You are alone with your few sheaves of rice. My boat is crowded, it is heavily laden, but how can I turn you away?"

The word for love, *bhalobasa*, is also frequently connected to tragedy. Love between thwarted lovers, separated by snobbish and shortsighted parents. Gods whose consorts have been snatched by rival gods. In the Hindu stories Ayah told, love was sometimes indistinguishable from violence—in fits of passion, swords and spears flew through the air, severing bodies and hearts, sending the pieces flying across rivers and fields, where they landed and sprouted temples and wish-granting rocks. Love, then, was something with endless possibilities and manifestations. It could come from the most grisly of roots.

I understood this at an instinctive level and may well have

felt Indian, but by the time I was eleven, I was as tall as many of the men who sold Ayah our vegetables. The Great Wall, one of my father's colleagues with experience in China called me, taken aback at how much I'd grown one summer. If I'd been an Indian girl, I might well have been promised to someone by the age of ten and married by thirteen. Ayah herself had wed at fourteen. It is still a surprise to realise that when I first knew her, she was not even thirty and had been married for more than a decade, which explains in part what she did when Veronica Browne and I enacted a wedding in my garden.

I had little knowledge of these events, though I was aware that there were wedding parties at the club, which my father and I never attended. I read about royal marriages in Fiona's magazines, but no one much talked about them, except for King Edward's to the American divorcée. Ayah spoke often about how stupid he was to renounce the throne for a trollop. (She liked that English word, and threw it at women she had spats with, cackling when they looked confused.)

On trips through the city with Ayah and Muhammad Rashid, I had seen the gods and their consorts depicted on temple walls, in posters at restaurants, in the shrines that decorated every shop owned by a Hindu. Parvati, the consort of Siva. Sarasvati, the consort of Brahma. Attendant, servant, consoler, forgiver—though the myths were filled with stories of jealousy and pique. Still, it seemed a more generous idea than wife, with less of that word's English gravity. The range of motion was wider. These divinities had summer homes in the mountains, and they travelled by cloud. They made of a day a more sinuous affair than my father would have believed possible. Love became loud and glittering, something I saw echoed in the actual weddings of Indians. These were the times I gained my most concrete vision of matrimony. They were events that gathered hundreds of people and featured days of feasting, dancing, thousands of marigold garlands giving off their bitter, not quite unpleasant scent. A bride and groom with their clothes knotted together. What I admired most were the elephants, with their gilded howdahs, the mahouts thin as twigs stationed near their knees.

But Veronica and I were enacting a much more solemn, whiter undertaking and far drearier. Ayah was looking on, bored at the simplicity of our arrangements. I remember her yawning, which she seemed to do with her whole body, as if there could have been nothing duller in the history of the world than watching us steer our dolls through this ritual, yawning the way cats do, with every bone. Her boredom managed to communicate itself as the tedium not only of watching two girls, but of watching this piece of life in imperial India play itself out. I see this now, but even then something in me knew that Ayah was discontent both with our scrappy little game and with everything else about us.

We had given the bride a veil made from one of my father's cast-off handkerchiefs. The cake was dirt and water, with a scarab beetle as its top layer. Veronica insisted that the bride and groom were to sit next to each other, eating slices of the mud. These ideas flow from girl to girl almost virally; we had no idea what the inside of a real English church smelled or looked like. Ours had rafters that echoed with the fights of blackbirds, and pews with caned seats that creaked when sat upon. Not to mention plaques dedicated to soldiers dead of *coup de soleil* or a bayonet in the chest during an Afghan war, the brass kept bright by Indian hands wrapped in cloth.

Veronica asked for more cake, and I, the groom, served up another wedge. We had fashioned teacups from locust leaves, something local that we had, as usual, transformed to suit our purposes. "How happy we will be, darling," Veronica said, and Ayah snorted and muttered in Bengali, "Well, that's all very nice, all that pretty talk, but that's for when everyone's watching. What happens later, that's not as pretty. That's talk for the relatives and guests. English love. No wonder these women get so sick. It's from being stupid about love. I have seen what happens to the memsahibs once they get to the bungalow and sahib is angry and tired. I have seen what they turn into then." Ayah could get away with this because Veronica spoke only enough Bengali to order her servants to fetch cold water or a new frock and because Muhammad Rashid and my father were safely away. Not even the gardeners were there. She knew, too, that I would do nothing to jeopardise her care for me, and she could shake out her scorn like salt in my presence.

Fury with English ways would strike her from time to time. There were moments when she couldn't bear how the conditions of her service fell inside the structures that the English had established in India, how the English tried to sit on India —as if it weren't a river about to burst its banks, a tiger ten times as large as we said it was. As if we could. Often her anger was condensed to a gesture of grievous quiet, as subtle as the opening of a single panel from a woman's fan. A bit of change not returned. A slipping of fish to a friend. But sometimes it was more dangerous. She would hiss about something—a rumour of Lord Linlithgow serving pork to a Muslim nobleman, a banned meeting between Gandhi and his supporters—almost within earshot of my father or Muhammad Rashid. If she had been overheard, she would have lost the position on which her family relied.

When Ayah started to rattle on, Veronica dropped the bride in the dust and said, "What's she going on about? Tell me what she's saying." Veronica was as imperious with me as she was with her servants. Imperious as a matter of right, because she was prettier than I was and her father ranked higher than mine—awareness of status and its effect on every aspect of an

English life in India another viral transmission between children. Veronica's father was a shade more important than mine,
but more stupid, so that made it worse. Mr. Browne looked
dashing in a topee, which was quite a feat, and had a laugh like
a donkey's that servants and children imitated. He kept track of
medical expenses incurred during epidemics—not of people
who died, but of how much the Ministry of Health spent trying
to control the danger, which also meant that he was partly in
charge of keeping the disease from spreading to sepoys and
British troops. Our Man for Nasty Symptoms, my father called
him in a rare moment of lapsing into something as personal as
irritation.

I said, glancing at Ayah, cross with her, "She says the cake's
not big enough for all the guests." This is the part I remember
best, because what happened was strange. Ayah rose grace-
lessly, like a flustered chicken—not fearful, but full of a
chicken's jerky motion as she hustled herself off. She shook out
the pleats of her sari and headed to the house, a dust cloud
travelling around her ankles. "You are a bad girl," she called
out to me in Bengali. *Kharap meye.* "That is the child who needs
most to know what I say is true." I pretended not to hear her
and went on serving up the mud cake.

"I don't like her," Veronica said. "She's not cosy, and she
doesn't smell very clean."

This restored me to myself. As all devout Hindus did, Ayah
started every day with prayer and washing at a nearby ghat,
where I'd crouched with her on the wet steps countless times.
"I am not playing any more," I said. Veronica huffed off to wait
for her servant, as if to say she'd had enough of the wedding
and of me. But it was Ayah's abrupt departure that had ruined
our game. We hadn't realised it, but we had needed her tacit
approval, and when she rejected it and us, there was no pleasure left, and we soon quarrelled.

I was sitting there in the sun, looking at the remains of the wedding. The twigs were now just twigs. Even though I hadn't enjoyed the pretend ceremony and felt, as Ayah had, suspicious of the proceedings, I had been glad to be lost in something other than my life. I'd been eager to practise a piece of adulthood that I had never seen, as if it might better prepare me for being English.

Sam Ellis is back at home. While I was in the garden, I saw him sitting in front of his house, staring out at the ocean. He was watching the water, still as stone in his webbed chair. His father came out to join him. Neither of them took notice of me. The fog had blown away, and the day had grown hot. I went inside for water, tired from weeding. Sam's father started to talk to his son about going back to school this fall. I gathered, not wanting to listen, but not being able to avoid Bob's braying voice, that Sam had left without finishing his exams. Waste of money, shiftless, I heard. From the window, I could see that Sam got up and sank to the grass, his head on his knees. He curled himself tighter and tighter until he was only a curved back, with his ponytail spread out over his shoulders. More, he was like a ball that rolled into himself, that contained. I thought Bob would strike him, but then he pivoted and marched back into the house. The door slammed. Sam stayed there.

He is having trouble being a son and being a student. He's not grown, and he's not a child, and something has undone him. This year his hair is long and shaggy, and he appears to have dispensed entirely with shoes, not an intelligent choice here in Maine given the broken clamshells that the gulls scatter everywhere. He used to be a quiet, open boy. He would come over to talk to Anna and James, who are younger than he, but he was lonely, an only child, and glad for company. They played Monopoly on rainy days, and he tended to let them win.

Though I'm aware that his worries are far different from

mine, school was not a place I fit into either. I'd known how to read since I was five or six, thanks to my father and his students, who took breaks from their discussions in his study to teach me my letters. I had the run of my father's library, mostly monographs on swamps and botany, with a few exciting exceptions, so St. Angela's struck me as provincial even at the beginning. It was a shabby place into which I eventually smuggled Wilde and Scott to read during catechism. We were not Catholic, but every student had to act as if she were. The school had four classrooms attached to a makeshift chapel hung with oil paintings made by Indian converts who borrowed their effects from El Greco. Jesus and Mary had Indian-sized hands and Indian grace, as well as the dewy eyes of Indian gods. Rats were a problem in the chapel and in the classrooms, but not in the refectory, which was next to a Muslim butcher shop where cats and dogs roamed.

The nuns were a ragtag collection of Ursulines sent from Goa via Lisbon. They spoke English with heavy accents and resorted to their own language frequently, often in the midst of lessons, leaving us all confused. Most of my classmates were third- or fourth-generation Anglo-Indian girls whose fathers were ticket collectors and conductors for Indian Railways. Often their given names had a Shakespearean ring—I knew several Mirandas and Jessicas. They had surnames such as DeSouza and Pereira and protected their skin from the sun more assiduously than most of us. They were proud of their pale complexions and perfect English grammar earned in spite of the lapses into Portuguese. They were devoted to their pen pals in Yorkshire. Their mothers ran charitable societies for the relief of indigents. They would have very little to do with me.

The Indian girls were thin and studious. They ate their chapatis at lunch in a corner with one another and spoke Bengali together in low voices. Many were eager to go on to further

studies to become nurses or teachers. A few came from newly
wealthy families and were dropped at the door by drivers in
fancy uniforms. Shy and giggly mostly, and preparing for marriage. Dedicated to Indian classical dance, seeing films, eating
bagfuls of sweets.

The English girls, the most glamorous of the students, came
and went, caught at St. Angela's between their fathers' post-
ings. I was one of the only regular English students, and a
disappointment to the nuns, who could not get me to be
enthusiastic about knowing the saints' lives or reciting their
version of world history, which featured an excessive emphasis
on the achievements of Vasco da Gama. Every morning, priests
would come to perform mass, which they did with terrific slowness and soggy pomp, and we could all see what deeply disappointed people they were. Indians had a way of adopting
whatever they pleased from imported religions, claiming to be
converts without entirely abandoning their old beliefs. Most
priests, then, had little real work, for they had few real parish-
ioners. Faced with their lack of success, many took either to
drink or to anthropology. The worst were the anthropologists.
They liked to insinuate themselves into our classrooms and lec-
ture us on the Perils of Rural India. I could not bear school.

The advantages of St. Angela's inexpensiveness and proxim-
ity must have seemed slim to my father, given how many times
Dona Teresa, the mother superior, visited his study to complain
that I had been caught drawing cartoons of the Viceroy during
geography. Quite often the dancing mistress came when I refused to serve as the boy in waltzes. Ayah and I would listen,
and she would say, "He's going to send you back this time." I
would tell her, rudely, to be quiet. She would rise and wrinkle
her nose at me, and we would take a day or so to become familiar again. My father would call me to his desk and tell me half-
heartedly that I must try to behave.

But I could not. I seemed to itch for trouble. On spring afternoons or early evenings, when Ayah and Muhammad Rashid were either busy or napping, I would go down to the banks of the Hooghly and get wet up to my knees. I did not know how to swim. We did not go to the ocean, we did not take home leaves, so I did not learn to paddle about in the North Sea or in some country lake. I wasn't allowed to visit the Sundarbans, which were, after all, full of nine species of deadly sea snakes and estuarine crocodiles. Water in India, though sacred, was a terrifying element. It teemed with dangerous animals. Unboiled, it could kill you. Whipped up in a cyclone or typhoon, it could sweep away villages and overturn ferries in an instant. I craved less the sensation of the water, which was brown and warm, than the sense of escaping the square courtyard and exploring on my own. Silence always descended when I arrived on the riverbank. The neighbourhood children knew exactly who I was. Bristi Sahib's daughter. I was the only white child there. They stared at me until I said something cheeky in Bengali, insulting someone's long nose or ragged haircut, and then they would toss one back at me, and we would begin to play. Splashing each other with water or hurling stones as far as we could into the river, tearing down bamboo to build forts against the serpent queen that swam the Hooghly. I was jealous of their bobbing about, but I didn't dare get entirely wet. It was bad enough to have sneaked off; I knew that if I risked full immersion, Ayah and my father would have my head.

One afternoon, however, I lost track of time and turned in my muddy frock to see Muhammad Rashid standing at the bank. The others had glimpsed him first. The silence that gathered around them was far quieter and less inquisitive than that with which they greeted me. "It's your khansama," a boy whispered to me. "He looks like Indra," he added — Indra, king of the gods, who travelled with rainbows and lightning. He did, even though he was Muslim.

His face was grey with tension. He said nothing. I walked towards him, sopping and stained, the ribbon in my hair long gone. We marched back through the streets without talking. Women gathered in doorways to point and to stare from behind their veils. My shoes sloshed, and my knee was scraped. When we reached the gate and the ruined lions, Muhammad Rashid said softly, "You are a complete disgrace. You have made your father's work more complicated here." Ayah shouted at me that night as she washed my hair with a nauseating concoction of coconut oil and turpentine—she worried inordinately about lice. She had painted my knee with a profusion of red antiseptic, making the wound seem twice the size it was. It looked, I remember, like Australia. "If he told your father, do you know what would happen? It would be like a tiger who swallowed a swarm of bees," she said. "That's what he would turn into. Stupid girl. He caught you mixing," and she pushed my head into the basin and poured more water on my stinging scalp.

I still went back to the river from time to time but was more cautious. Both there and at the market I often saw the young boy who told me Muhammad Rashid had come. His mother sold pulses and peanuts, and Ayah and I bought from her. Her prices were fair, Ayah said. Besides, her cousin knew Ayah's family. The woman's son was her helper. He was agile and bright-eyed, but we did not greet each other. Now and then he would come with a couple of other boys, and we would play fierce, nearly wordless games of marbles in the alley behind our house when the adults were gone.

Although I appeared to be quiet and tractable, I apparently yearned to make life difficult for myself and others. One afternoon when I came back from school, the house was empty but for the cook and his assistant. This still meant I had to stay in, because someone might say they'd seen me go out, so I decided to mope about my father's study, where I found his magnifying glass on the blotter. It was something he used to read fine print in scientific journals and to examine specimens in the field. It was one of many, actually. His eyesight was poorer than he liked to admit.

I took it into the courtyard and found a pile of mango leaves the gardener had left there. I had read somewhere that one could light a fire with a glass, and I discovered now that it was true. I angled the lens to the light and within several minutes had a fine flame coming from the centre of the pile. What I had not anticipated was how quickly the leaves would spread to the grass clippings the women had left the day before. I had no idea how flammable it all was. It must have been very, very hot, however, and I had underestimated the power of the sun.

Muhammad Rashid came running into the courtyard with a towel flapping in his hands, calling to Allah to quench the flames. When he realised the fire was quite small, he changed to pleading that he not be sacked when it was discovered no one had been watching me. "Experimenting?" he asked me as he took up the magnifying glass and peered at it to see if there were scratches. His kurta was striped with smoke. He coughed, tugged at his vest, and said, "He has never told you, has he? What is it, this family, this taste for destruction?" Hands flying, still coughing, he said that soon after we had moved, sahib had burnt the dresses. A pyre, not for a Hindu wife, but for an Eng-lishwoman's clothes and artifacts. "You mean he burnt her things?" I had my mother's comb, and I suppose the fire ex-plained this lack of stuff through which to know her. Muham-mad Rashid was still stamping on the mango leaves and the grass, though nothing was left that would let the fire spread. He had been asleep, I think, and had been woken by the smell of burning. I had never seen him move so fast or seen him in such disorder.

Then he realised what he'd said. He looked appalled at himself, and his hands stopped flapping and dashed back inside his sleeves. Everything drained from his face but his officious servant look, a pose he assumed only in desperate circumstances. "This is not a story for young ladies," he said. It seemed impossible: my father in shirtsleeves, arms piled with dresses, staggering off to a bonfire around which a crowd of Indians no doubt gathered—a white man ruined by grief always an exciting event.

That evening, as I sat with him on the verandah, the story seemed to me more and more incredible. I slowly stopped believing that it had ever happened, except at times I would dream of flames engulfing houses, and it would take both Muhammad Rashid and Ayah to help me to sleep again. Still, at heart, I knew that my father had the capacity for reckless action, and I was frightened that it, too, had been transferred to me. Yet it also explained why he kept me with him. He had little left of her but me.

It came as something of a relief to understand this about him, but the awareness did not stop me from behaving badly. In part, Ayah colluded with me. When Muhammad Rashid caught me at the river and Ayah punished me with that awful shampoo, I think she was suggesting that I should have been more cunning. Not that I shouldn't have gone, but that I should have been home and dressed before my father found out. She certainly didn't think I was like the other children at the river—one way in which Indian and English societies complemented one another was that they both sustained adamant beliefs in privilege—but she also believed I shouldn't be deprived of all pleasures. I needed, she implied, as much contact with people as possible. Anything to make me less awkward.

Also, she subtly relished the possibility of annoying my father by taking me where I did not quite belong, making our situation even more precarious than it was. I did things with her most English children did not do with their ayahs, starting with going to the ghats. She also took me once to a Holi celebration at her cousin's house north of the city. My father was off in the mangroves, taking advantage of cool weather to check a diseased plantation. Holi is a spring festival and usually occurs just before the real heat descends; it's a joyful, manic celebration, part bacchanal, part New Year's. People buy new clothes, visit family members, eat special sweets. Men and children throw coloured dye at each other, and for weeks people sport magenta and green on their shirts, scalps, and hands. It was a raucous scene, with men drinking arrack in the streets and singing loud, profane songs. Cows wandered past, their bellies splotched blue and red. Pailfuls of coloured water were dropped from balconies on the heads of those walking below. Women and children tossed handfuls of powder at each other on rooftops. I was given the task of passing platefuls of sweets about. *Gulab jamun*, the rosewater treats, and *rasgullahs*, balls of cheese drenched with syrup and sprinkled with pistachios. "Don't stain the sahib's daughter," Ayah scolded all afternoon, but I wanted nothing more than to grab a handful of powder and smear it on the goblin-green face of her youngest nephew, a boy who teased me mercilessly, saying I was as fat as Ganesh and the like. Instead, I was told to ladle out tea and remove plates as Ayah directed and watch as the children streaked back and forth, screaming. We had to spend the night; the streets weren't safe the first evening of Holi. I slept on a mat and envied the children the glitter that still shone on their arms and faces.

The next morning, we left before the revellers woke or too many English people were about. Ayah was quiet in the rickshaw. All over the Maidan lay men in untidy piles of stained clothing, drunks who hadn't made it home. "You'll need to give me that frock for an extra washing," she said. "Holi colors stick," though I hadn't seen a speck of dye on me. She yawned. "They make you sleepy, too." But Ayah was tired because she had stayed up most of the night talking about politics with her cousins. Congress, Bose the Communist, Gandhiji. I wasn't supposed to be listening, but I couldn't help it. Much of it I didn't understand, either the Bengali or the ideas, though I couldn't miss the passion. I got up and asked for water, wanting to be closer to that circle of adults. I felt safest with Indians, who were tolerant of children tearing through a house, a street, a festival. Adults parted to let them pass, smiled, talking above them, occasionally sticking out a hand, not to check their passage, but to give them a candy or take a thumbful of cheek and shake it, rarely scolding or criticizing. I spent my early years travelling from one set of thin, strong arms to the next — Ayah's, her relatives', the local shopkeepers'. Anyone who would have me, really.

Ayah ordered me back to my mat. "Not talk for the likes of you," she said after she gave me the water I requested. She pushed me off with the same roughness she used to pluck at my skirt in the rickshaw. "Hah," she said when she found the smallest streak of purple. "I told you." She scrubbed it when we got back home with the same brush we used to get the vermilion off my fingers. We did not want to get caught, though for some time we continued to take those risks, which neither of us seemed able to stop.

My father never found out about Holi, the river, or the fire, but he did discover that Ayah had taken me to the Kali temple. Kali is the central deity of Calcutta, the one for whom it is named. Kali's ghat, some say. Others argue that the name comes from the word in Bengali for jute, one of the region's most important crops. No matter, Kali is Calcutta's animating goddess—the Black One, Siva's consort in a fearsome aspect. Ayah was quite devoted to her, and as soon as her offerings were made to Ganga Ma, she recited prayers for Kali. She is depicted in many ways, sometimes as a mouthful of teeth, a bony hag; sometimes with a skirt of skulls at her waist, a pink tongue, a bowl of milk, a bowl of blood. She terrified me, even in the shrines, which could be found throughout the city. I was probably nine when Ayah took me for the first time to the big temple, which was said to have been born of one of Kali's fingers when her corpse was torn to pieces. It was before dawn when we left, and my father had just gone from the house himself, to ride. He was supposed to be away all day at the museum. "Important job, gulab," Ayah told me as she hailed a rickshaw.

The temple was thronged with pilgrims. Indian temples, like English cathedrals, are usually right in the middle of a street and often have markets that abut their borders, though one doesn't usually see a bishop slaughtering goats at Coventry. That day, a priest was slicing open the throats of kids, some black, some white, and the whole scene was sticky with blood and loud with squealing animals. We got in line for darshan, the sighting of the deity, of which I only remember women singing and swaying and a smell of incense so powerful I nearly fainted. Sighting, however, is not quite right. Darshan is a chance not only to glimpse the goddess but to be enveloped in her presence and power. In addition, it's believed that she sees you: even the most ordinary of us are held in the knowing glance of the divine. Passing black-faced Kali, her shoulders hung with gold cloth, I had a sense of something reaching towards me, but it was only Ayah's hand. Ayah said her prayers, made her offerings, and we left, but I had the misfortune to slip in a pool of goat blood. My feet and hands were covered in it, though I had managed to avoid staining anything but my socks.

Unfortunately, Badger the horse had pitched a shoe, and my father decided to return early to the house. He was in the courtyard when we got there, removing his gloves as the stable boy led the lame animal away. There was no way to disguise the blood or to pretend we'd just been on an errand; our foreheads were smeared with sandalwood paste, and we reeked of incense. He sacked Ayah on the spot, the third or fourth of probably seven times that he did so. Then he leant down, and for a moment I thought he was going to examine me for marks or injuries. Surely the blood had alarmed him. But then I saw his raised palm and its swift descent as he smacked me hard on the face. I fell, and my head felt as if it had spun on my neck. My jaw clicked. The blow gave me a bruise and a black eye, which Ayah tended with a compress and herbs to reduce swelling. She knew he had sacked her out of anger, not really meaning it, though she was wise enough to leave for a few days. Not, however, until she had taken me to the bath and said, "Gulab, it was a necessity that we go. Otherwise I would not have done it." I forgave her, of course, because I forgave her everything.

I spoke tonight to David, on a reversed-charge call that I made from the store near the ferry landing. He had visited his parents in New York and was caught in the sadness that comes over him when he talks with his father. His parents are fading even further into nothing but old stories of Hungary. All they did, he said, was drink coffee flavoured with chicory and eat tiny pastries. He told me the city was brimming with protesters stalking around with signs to end the war and police milling about. But there weren't so many of them in Washington Heights, just below the bridge, which was, I imagined, sticky with melting tar and crowds sitting on stoops. The bridge is one of the reasons I don't like to visit David's parents. Isabella and

Walter's apartment shakes so from the traffic crossing back and forth. Dishes in cupboards, too, and even chairs. It makes my teeth rattle.

David asked how I was, and I told him I was well, but I did not describe what I was doing. There will be time enough for that. He is thinking of coming here after the weekend at the camp when we're allowed to visit the children. I will perhaps tell him then. Neither of us trusts the telephone. We both talk too loudly on it. We are better with each other across a table, the dogs underfoot, with long gaps in the conversation and the leavings of a meal between us.

On the way back from the store I ran into Sam, who tried to get Marlow to sniff his hand. "He used to like me," Sam said. He was just sulking a bit, I said as Marlow retreated into the lupins, and I hoped Sam would believe me. Little galls people more than children or dogs that refuse to come closer. But I knew why Marlow wouldn't approach him. He smells of depression and marijuana. I asked if he would like to come over for a cup of tea that afternoon, said he was welcome to, that Marlow just needed some time to remember him. I surprised us both with that comment. I hadn't realised I wanted company, and then I understood I didn't quite. He sensed my hesitation perhaps and didn't answer for a minute. He'd like that, he said eventually, convincing neither of us. But he didn't come to see me, to my relief. Instead, I saw him out rowing, a slim figure in a sea that was slightly too rough for a boy with problems. He looked none too steady in the dory. His parents were on their porch. His mother, Karen, who looks far too thin, said, "He's ruining himself," and started to cry. It was a choking sound, horribly private. I felt awful that I'd overheard it, awful, too, that I hadn't been more sincere in my invitation, and I closed the window, although it was still hot.

After my father had hit me, I had the satisfaction of hearing

Muhammad Rashid shout at Ayah that he was not going to sit by and watch her destroy me. Drugs wreak a certain havoc, of course, but there are other ways to hurt a child. Ayah, shamed for once, said nothing. When she came back, my father was speaking to me again. She brought me a toy elephant of carved wood painted in bright oils. I was too old for such gifts, but I saved it for years. It was as close as she ever came to apologising for anything.

Ayah was too accustomed to difficulty to give in to something as personal as saying she was sorry. Even more, she was proud of her unflinching strength. She was the only servant who did not cower when my father flew into a rage. She had helped the stableman care for Badger's snakebite, holding the animal's ears and mane. She had just nursed me through a bloody bout of dysentery a few weeks earlier, which perhaps explains why, one day soon after she returned, she was trying to get me to eat.

She had placed a fried fish on a banana leaf and was sitting next to me. We were both on the floor, on reed mats. It was noon and so hot the air assumed a form, like a large sweating person standing over me. Ayah was trying to get me interested in the food. The flesh separated into flakes on her fingers. "Eat," she whispered in Bengali. *Khaoya.* "You need to eat." I told her I was tired. I told her that I was not hungry, that I was not well, but she knew I was lying.

It was a whole fish, eyes fried to pale grey, bread crumbs clinging to the bones in its spiny tail. "Take it, take it. It will make you healthy," she said, gesturing. She smeared a bite with mango chutney and lime pickle. The banana leaf was frayed. The soles of her feet were the colour of ash. A gold button decorated her nose. "Take it, take it," she said in her high voice. Then she recited one of Kali's pronouncements. "Whosoever eats food, eats food by me; whosoever looks forth from his eyes, and whosoever breathes, whosoever listens to whatever is said, does so by me." She gave me a glare.

Still, I wouldn't. I was dizzy with hunger, but I did not want to take what she offered. The flesh around my eye was dark yellow. I hadn't been allowed to go to school, which I'd rejoiced at, but I hadn't been let out of the house either. When Ayah had returned, she caught her breath when she saw me, then hurried to her room. I thought now about asking her for ice cream or curried vegetables or dal, about making things complicated for her. But I did not want to touch this creature, which had so obviously been alive. I imagined the fish Mr. Rao fed each morning. Lazy carp who took bread from my fingers as if they were birds or horses. "No, Ayah, I don't want it," I said, and pushed the leaf off the mat.

Ayah said to me then, looking at the flakes of fish stuck to her fingers, "My own children would make a fish last three days, would never eat it all at once." My face burnt red. I hadn't even known she had a family with Mr. Kumar. A bitter jealousy spread through me: there were children who had her as their mother. There were children she no doubt loved more than me. I could not stand the thought of sharing her affection, thorny as it was, with anyone else. I yearned to take the fish and slap it across her cheek, see its skin stick to her sharp jaw. She yanked the leaf back towards me. "Some people are not as lucky as the daughter of curator sahib." And, in a rush, she said we had gone to the Kali temple because her girls had been ill with cholera. We had made a sacrifice for them.

Her girls. "Ayah," I asked, "are they better now? Did they recover?" She rose then and walked quickly from the room, sandals slapping smartly on the tiles. Flies buzzed near my hands. I heard the pigeons flapping against the net that covered the roof. I took a mouthful of the fish and chewed. I ate it down to the transparent bones, though my stomach clenched and I had to swallow a mouthful of water for every bite of flesh I ate. Only later, with much prodding, did I find out that Ayah had given birth to five girls who lived in her village with her mother. Five daughters, only three of whom would live to be adults. The children with cholera had not survived.

Sam has come back. His clothes are dripping wet, and he is shivering. He was standing on his parents' doorstep when he turned and looked at our cottage. The dogs barked, and he came over. At first I was quite irritated. He expected, naturally enough, that I would open the door and make him tea. I sensed a bit of entitlement on his part. But once he was settled, I was oddly grateful for his presence. Marlow finally wormed his way towards the boy and let his head be stroked. It started to rain. I lit the lantern, made more tea, and gave Sam one of my old sweaters to wear. One of David's would have been too small. He told me about taking a biology exam at Williams in the middle of May, looking at a question about mitosis, and the next thing he knew, he was in a car with four friends driving to San Francisco. He just couldn't sit there and write about cell division when bombs were dropping on Vietnamese children. I did not ask him how driving to California changed anything for the Vietnamese children, but he recognised the incongruity himself. He was slumped and huddled, and he knew he was making a hash of it all. He hated making his mother feel awful, and he hated feeling so at odds with himself and his family, but he couldn't pretend everything was all right. I let him talk, and I didn't say much in response, which I sensed he did not like. He wanted to hear he'd be fine, that it would all work out, but he and I both knew that this was not necessarily true, and I wouldn't give him the easy satisfaction of platitudes. Near suppertime, he took off the sweater, thanked me, and left.

It is easier to listen to the troubles of someone else's child. There's no recrimination, no regrets over past behaviour. Yet it also feels quite strange to hear all this from Sam. I don't have much skill at this sort of listening. Anna and James have always been rather self-contained, and when they have talked, of rivalries at school or misgivings about friends, they have chosen David. Now, on the brink of being teenagers, they seem to find us both cumbersome and dull and are drawn instead to classmates. Still, I don't think they've ever confessed very much to me, and I can hardly blame them. I haven't been a model of free exchange. My only excuse is that I never had any idea that this was possible between parents and children. After Sam left, I opened a tin of soup and sat down to think about my own unruly behaviour. My father had been quite as upset with me as Bob is with Sam. My father's solution, curiously, was to require me to attend church more frequently. It had been Mrs. Browne's suggestion. Occasionally she would descend on the house in a tumult of bad Bengali and perfume to pick up Veronica. I heard her pointing out to my father my overly competent use of that language (the swears I learned from Rajiv and Sanjay), my unnecessarily large collection of marbles, my desire to be barefoot at home. For some reason it shamed him to hear this criticism coming from her. I think it was because she was so pretty; he was susceptible to her.

Mrs. Browne wore ropes of pearls and fluttery skirts the colour of sherbets, pale pink and minty green. Thinking India a wretched place, she erected as many distractions between the country and her home as possible—she was a great giver of teas and sponsor of theatricals. She and Veronica called for me in their motorcar the next Sunday morning at nine-thirty. My father mysteriously absented himself. Mrs. Browne was full of plans for Veronica's return to England. "A lovely school with lovely girls. You're awfully excited, aren't you, Veronica?" I was pleased to see that Veronica did not look awfully excited. That she in fact was looking out at the market we were passing and staring at mangoes in a basket rather longingly. We both knew that mangoes would be hard to come by at her lovely school for lovely girls.

The service lasted for hours at St. Paul's. I tried to absorb myself in watching the way the sun came through the stained glass and daubed the floors with splotches of colour, but I found I could not sit still. This was where I saw the greatest concentration of white faces and heard more English being spoken than any other place. The shuffle of feet, the coughing of English coughs, the large moustaches, the suits and skirts. I went for weeks and weeks, and each time the service seemed to grow longer. I was starting to feel that perhaps even going back to England would be preferable to this tedium.

Then one week in the midst of the sermon I saw that Mrs. Browne had gone to sleep. Veronica noticed as well, and tried to jog her mother awake, to no avail. She snored lightly, her mouth only partly open. I glanced back to the doors and saw four Indian boys in shorts and untidy shirts standing at the threshold. In my mind's eye, they are all on one foot, the other tucked up next to a knee, leaning on the doorframe, watching the English. One of them had a bag of marbles in his hands. I knew immediately: the bag was like one I had, and it pouched and bunched in just the same way. Without thinking, I got up and darted back to them. Veronica did not follow, although she did hiss, "Rose, come back. Mummy will be in a rage." I did not care. I saw those boys and their bag of marbles, and my allegiances were clear. I knew I'd be caught; it was what happened to me. Adults fell upon me, reminded me I was naughty, but I preferred that to sitting there, comparing my rather worn clothes to the fancy silks of the other girls.

The boys were, it turned out, the sons of the caretakers of

the church. Nominally Christians, they said, shrugging. Really, just boys. I was better at marbles than they were, which did not please them. *Vagyoban*, they told me. I was just lucky. *Valo*, I told them. No, I was good. I had played with Rajiv and Sanjay and the boys from the market in quiet, competitive games in our alley. Now we squatted on the ground below a banana plant. They had no shoes, and mine were quickly filthy. We were so absorbed we did not hear Mrs. Browne approach. Her shadow, all grey spikes and angles, fell on us, and then we looked up to see the angry woman in her layers of voile and her large, absurd hat. What a waste of energy, we seemed to be thinking. She's going to get hot, getting so angry, moving so fast. Our knees out to the side, haunches high, the glint of our marbles in bright contrast to the dusty circle we played in. Mrs. Browne's dainty foot kicked the glass balls and sent them spinning. She screamed at us in English. Bloody children, you bloody awful child. That one intended for me. The boys looked at her not so much with fear as with disdain, and they rose and darted past the range of her small feet. "I'm sorry," I told them as she dragged me off. *Ami dukkhito*. They looked at me with scorn and pity, and I felt thoroughly confused, not at peace in any context. They stared at us for a long time, not even bothering to go and fetch the marbles.

Mrs. Browne, of course, refused to take me to church any more, and my father had to bring me instead. But the duty grew onerous after a couple of weeks. He got coughing attacks and had to excuse himself. At that time in his life he did not seem able to sit still for long.

When the war broke out, he did reconnaissance work south of Calcutta, terrain he knew well, which also allowed him to monitor his projects in the swamps occasionally. Later, he could not avoid more direct military service, and he did mapping in Burma. He spent the last two years of the war in and around that country, a time he still will not speak of. When he came to London in 1946, he took up with moths, partly out of necessity. Jobs were scarce in his field then. He was offered the chance to deal with Asian insects at an entomology journal based at the University of London, and he had no desire, I think, to continue with work that had been brusquely cancelled. He knew, of course, a fair amount about Indian bugs, but it always saddened me how completely he turned away from the swamps. Perhaps he had seen too much of that sort of landscape by then. He certainly was never as restless once he got back to England.

In India, he was a man of terrific concentration. His colleagues shared his focussed energy—the English and Indian scientists and students who came to the house with pockets full of fossils or handkerchiefs holding buds of plants that they did not recognise. They seemed calm in the face of so much evidence of evolution taking place. They were readers of Lyall and Darwin and Huxley, who wished science to be sheared of politics and nationality. But my father knew this was never possible. What you found, where you looked, who helped you, who didn't—all these issues determined the extent of your research and its objectives.

During those last years in India he had to spend a fair amount of time in his office at the museum, negotiating with officials about budgets and equipment. He was less happy there, but I enjoyed it. It was magnificently separate from the other worries of the era: a white classical fortress with wings devoted to exhibits of zoological monstrosities and less daunting statues of dancing Sivas. It was a place where knowledge was paramount, more important at least from my perspective than who controlled which faction of the Congress Party, what sort of concessions the Indians had won from the Viceroy, or what the Nazis would do. In my father's small office in the back, its window looking out on a courtyard where a fountain played from time to time, it was possible to imagine that all that would pass, and what would endure were the black stone Buddhas, the cases of gemstones and coins and pottery, even his specimen mangroves. He had had glass tanks specially made so that their intricate system of roots could be studied and marvelled at. I think it was a blow to him to learn that most people thought they were hideous—Indian muck and trouble at its worst.

The sheer variety of the plants could rouse him to volubility. Mangroves could alter the saline level of the water they were immersed in. They were the most stalwart of creatures, buffers against cyclones, home to colonies of fish and birds. Some of his favourites were ones he claimed were grown with success in the Philippines, where they were used as natural enclaves for prawn farms. Others could be used to manufacture soap. Still others yielded good building wood, while some species were especially suited for paper.

He didn't want to see the Sundarbans stripped for industry, but he thought it sensible that the local people should profit a bit from this easily exploitable resource. Volumes of letters flew back and forth between him and possible investors in various schemes that would let the mangroves be managed as a crop of one kind or another, but those plans interested him much less than simply being there to carry out his research and watch the terrain. "Flamingoes, Rose," he said once. "Quite marvellous." Trusting, I think, that I'd know he meant it was beautiful. Pink wings, black beaks, the sun staining the water at dawn. Another time, he returned from an expedition with a jagged cut on his arm, rudely stitched in coarse thread, a monkey scratch that had gotten infected. But I knew he was almost proud of the wound, as it was evidence of the close contact he'd made with the Sundarbans and its animals. He loved, too, how hard it was for superiors to find him there and how the newspapers he saw were usually weeks if not months old. If the mosquitoes were enormous and the tigers had a taste for human flesh, so be it. Life in the Sundarbans had been simple and dangerous for centuries, and even with its chronic difficulties, it was still more predictable than life in India's volatile cities.

I used to believe that he would have liked to live there year-round if he could have. But he had his students, his articles, and he needed to be close by for trips to Delhi to secure his funding once the capital moved from Calcutta. He also apparently felt he needed to keep at least one eye on me. Once church had conclusively proved a failure, he signed me up for tennis lessons at the club. If religion wouldn't work, perhaps sports would. He was practical like that, but Ayah thought it was a terrible sign. She feared he might turn me into a repulsive little memsahib if he let me spend too much time with those women. She also thought more exposure to the sun would further damage my already flawed complexion.

I was as worried as she, but not for the same reasons. I had never felt comfortable at the clubs in the south of the city—the studied ease, the refusal to speak reasonable Bengali, the slicked-back hair of the men. Sam this afternoon talked of power and authority with shame and ardour. He wants to become vegetarian and work on farms where they use no chemicals. He's ready, he claims, to renounce all his privilege, his private schools, his wealthy family. But inherited good fortune isn't so easily shucked. It leaves its marks in the most curious ways. It forms tastes, habits, and speech in ways that inevitably shape one's possibilities. You can't help who you are, yet he seems to think that with the proper attitude, the right amount of drugs and long hair, he'll have effected the transition. I was not so radical or perhaps so observant. I didn't mind the animal heads on the walls, the Asian deer, the boars, or even the tiger skins on the floors of those clubs.

I knew that India was headed for some form of independence, but I also had every sense that it was a decent thing that people like my father had run the country as long as they had. It was impossible to imagine that the English wouldn't be there, even though I knew from the time I was very young that we weren't going to last. I didn't see the club, then, as some ghastly political symbol. My views were far less grand. What unstrung me about it was my drastic inability to be charming and decorative: I was so bad at the talking and social niceties. The formulas fell apart in my mouth. I felt inept next to women whose skirts were pressed and whose shoes were polished to a high gloss.

But it turned out that I was good at tennis, and to my surprise, I enjoyed it. I spent many afternoons there for three or four years, and though I still did not talk much, I got better at understanding how the English girls did what they did. It was certainly simpler to concentrate on that than on the troubles of those years, which confused and frightened me: the mass jailings of Congress supporters, the increasing divisions between Jinnah and Gandhi, the railway strikes that convulsed the nation every few months. I saw the protests on the Maidan and read all about the country's agitation in *The Statesman* once my father and Ayah were done with it. Mr. Rao had stopped coming by. We had a telephone installed in the house—it had taken years for the permit to come through—and I heard my father arguing loudly with his superiors about funding. Mangroves looked exceedingly unimportant next to the prevention of unrest and the suppression of demonstrations.

He was preoccupied and glad to have me distracted by something, even something as insubstantial as tennis. He might even have been relieved that I was learning more about how English girls dressed, curled their hair, talked to boys. I tried some dark lipstick, loaned to me by a girl named Joan Cartwright who took pity on me. There was a young man named Ronald I grew fond of when I was fourteen. He was tall and blond like me, much older than I was and in his first years with the Civil Service. It barely mattered that the only time he was polite to me was when he needed my services as a player. I was treated as a secret weapon. I liked playing well, and when I returned home, I told Ayah about every shot I'd made and how Ronald had poured me lemon squash and congratulated me on a volley.

Ayah, at this point in my life, seemed almost to have lost her appetite for risk. I didn't follow her to the ghats in the morning any more. She wouldn't even bring me to Calcutta's famous street fairs, where the Ramayana was reenacted for days at a time along the boulevards and alleys. Too dangerous, she said, and they were: every year people were trampled to death. But for years I had gone, thrilled by the wild makeup, the wooden swords, and the long scenes devoted to bloodshed. I knew, without her saying a word, that the problem now was that I was too white, too English, to accompany her. It was too complicated for her to be seen with me outside the courtyard.

Oddly, this made our relationship at home easier, unless the subject turned to boys and love. We would sit on the verandah and trade stories until I would say something admiring about Ronald, and then she would tut, "Come inside. You are turning the color of a hibiscus." Ayah was voluble on the subject of the superiority of arranged marriages and the stupidity of the European system. That lower-class people were allowed shocking amounts of freedom in this critical area seemed to her a grave folly. She thought it far wiser to rely on the tangible features of a prospective spouse, such as the status of a family and the catalogued obstacles set forth in an astrological chart. "It gives things their proper shape," she would say, biting at the tail end of her mending thread. From her perspective, arranged marriages did not encourage false notions that in this world were certain to lead to downfall. Marriage was for making and raising children, she often said, for keeping men and women connected to the tasks they did best, and away from too much contact with each other. Women were, she suggested, the harder workers and the more reliable, but also, sadly, the less lucky. Given her history with Mr. Kumar, it makes sense that she wanted to convince me that a precise assessment of reality was a saner virtue by which to order a day than love, a better way for framing a life. It provided a sturdier skeleton than the sort of romance stumbled into at parties or on tennis courts, which depended so on chance, not sense, to grow straight.

As she talked, she picked out the stones from a bowlful of lentils or sewed up a rent in some piece of clothing, her thin fingers clacking along at the task as her mouth ripped apart a piece of local gossip. Did I know that Mrs. Lal's new daughter-in-law was having a baby in March? That Mrs. Bose had bought a new and expensive sari from Patel the corrupt tailor? I would still be in my tennis clothes, hot, ready for a bath, but she would keep me in the courtyard until all the Indian news of the day had been told. It was, I see now, her way of welcoming me back to the house, to our unfashionable district, of helping me bridge the gap between the club and our daily lives. She did all this while she engaged in chores that cooks and maids were responsible for, but Ayah needed to establish competence in realms not entirely her own. She liked to be in charge of at least small parts of other people's lives so that she could criticise them when they fell short.

I gave in, mostly. I let her chatter about the neighbours and the ridiculous prices the knife sharpener was now charging. I would sit next to her in the shade, drinking cooled tea and listening, while I dreamed about Ronald's legs and hearty laugh. Eventually it would be time to go inside and get ready for my father's return. Ayah would position the bowl she'd brought out on her hip and then head to the kitchen while I went to tidy myself. "Comb your hair with the pomade I brought you," she would shout as I climbed the stairs, and I would call back down, every time, "Not that awful one that smells like pomfret." She would say, "What I must stand from this overgrown girl," and I would feel happy to be home. We were careful to preserve the ritual of my return from the club. We knew it would be over sooner rather than later.

I drove to town for more groceries today. Flags are starting to appear outside gas stations and markets. It's not the Fourth for a couple of weeks, but it's an anxious year, and people are apparently ready to declare their simplest, most easily named feelings. Americans are always scrupulously polite with me during this holiday, as if I still had deep ties to England and minded the separation of the colonies or had something at stake in their loss, as if I weren't thankful to America for existing. It is worse in Concord, hotbed of the Revolution. At least here in Maine people mind their own business. No one even asks where I come from. They know in a glance that I'm from Away. Whether it's Boston, London, or Calcutta hardly matters.

On the way back I stopped to phone David, but he didn't answer. In front of the hardware store some local boys were playing baseball. A pickup game, James calls them. I saw Sam standing under an oak tree, watching. He wore sunglasses but no shoes. The boys didn't appear to notice him.

They were slightly younger than James, who would have been tempted to go out and play, if only to organise their pitching. He has recently started tracking earthquakes on the Mercator projection on his wall. The pins are clustered in Iran and China, with a few in Turkey and in South America. He collects clippings—photos of women staring at mud where their husbands, crops, and furniture had been. "So glum, James," David has said to him. "Can't you keep track of fledging democracies?" But earthquakes provide more data. He is starting to hunch into himself, as if curving preemptively under what he senses will be the weight of manliness. Moving towards that moment when to give up more than a few syllables to a woman will feel like an affront. Sam is on the other side of that time in his life. He's discovered girls, but he misses being one of those boys, too.

A ball was hit and bounced near Sam. He leapt towards it and caught it in the middle of the street. He obviously wanted to join, but the players left, quickly grabbing their equipment. I didn't think it was Sam's glasses or his bare feet that put them off, but the T-shirt he was wearing that said FUCK THE PIGS. Their mothers have probably warned them about dangerous or extreme people like him. The shirt probably horrifies his own mother, and it's my guess his father hasn't seen it, or he wouldn't be let out of the house. The boys disappeared almost instantly and certainly unnecessarily. It is obvious looking at Sam's drooped shoulders and untidy hair that all he is is young and lonely. India is one of the world's most complex countries, but it's also not simple being from anywhere, and of course America is as unintelligible as any other place. Just the last six years here would be enough to tell you that. Sam walked off, the baseball still in his hand, though from the way he tossed it up and down in his palm, I suspected he was going to hurl it somewhere.

I came to this country in part because I knew it had a short history and I thought I wouldn't have as much to learn and be responsible for. I thought political nonsense and conflict would bother me less in a country that wasn't so old. I thought Americans would be less tolerant of repetitions. Sheer foolishness, though seeing people starving has proved rare. In India there were food shortages every few years, and I never wanted to see

the effects of those again. Spring was the season of crop fail-
ures and riots. The one I remember most vividly occurred in
1941, before the terrible famine two years later, when rice and
grain were harder to come by than usual, since so much was
being diverted to troops. Between one and three million people
died in 1943, not to mention countless animals. Yet the event I
recall most vividly was not even considered an actual famine,
just a bad period for certain farmers on the Deccan who came
to Calcutta to search for sustenance and work.

It was the first time I remember cheekbones like the corners
of tables, the buoyant stomachs of malnourished children. The
wrong sort of angle against the wrong sort of curve. And this
not from pictures in newspapers, but from places in my memory where those images are riven with clarity. On the way to
Hogg Market, our rickshaw lost a wheel, and Ayah and I had
to walk to find some special thread she liked to use to hem her
cholis. We rounded the corner to the market, and they were
there: several dozen very hungry families. I remember most the
women's hands and the slack arms of the babies. No men in
sight; perhaps they were out trying to find food or jobs. They'd
left the women with not even water to drink. Dried mud
stained their mouths. The holes in their ears and noses that had
once been filled with gold were now small pits in the skin. The
jewellery had been sold for rice. Ayah did not try to keep me
from seeing them. Our walk was hitched with pauses as she
gave money to the dusty families. She fished her change purse
from her sari. The women pressed their palms together and
raised them to the centre of their foreheads.

Ayah said nothing. We walked all the way home. Though
rickshaw drivers tried to flag us down, she appeared not to
hear them. I was also quiet. At our gate, she said, "I am tired.
Go ask cook for your lunch." We usually ate together, but that
day, neither of us found our way back to the well-stocked

larder. We went to our respective beds, where I suspect we both tried to will ourselves to sleep and away from what we had witnessed. Ayah knew that I would be overwhelmed, but that I would be able to survive the sight of the starving alone. I wasn't starving, after all, myself.

Perhaps it was also a kind of challenge. Look what you and your people supervise. Look what has happened to the women in the care of those white men. She was daring me, in her way, to tell my father about what I'd seen and so forge a link between English rule and the hands from which the flesh had fallen away. Hands turned to nets of bone covered by thin layers of skin. I lay there and felt the opening of an emptiness, the start of an awareness of how others really lived. I'd lived around hungry people my entire life, but for the first time, I was shocked by them. I sat at dinner that night and picked at my food. My father did not notice, and in part I was glad for this. I did not want to talk to him about the starving women; he would have made of them a statistic, a cycle, something that could be understood and so tolerated. That was his way, how he'd been trained, how he saw everything. But it wasn't tolerable.

The next morning, I helped Ayah when I found her raiding the pantry for sacks of rice. Muhammad Rashid was disdainful of the hungry people. He managed to imply that it was their fault for being poor and unemployed and that if they had thought harder or planned better, they wouldn't find themselves so badly off. "Narrow-hearted man, you sleep with rupees in your pillow as if Yama doesn't know exactly where you live," Ayah hissed at him. Yama, lord of death. Even worse: "Don't you remember ever going hungry as a boy?" To which Rashid responded with one of his vacant looks while he fussed with the toggles on his vest. In a voice several notes reedier than usual, he said, "My parents provided for their family with unfailing generosity, you woman who has forgotten her place."

When he had swept out of the house to avoid "her lizard's tongue," she hoisted the rice to her hip, and I went to hail a passing bullock cart. She took old saris to cover the food so it wouldn't be stolen on the way.

My father found out, of course, and garnished her wages. Not only that, he lost his temper badly. "You disrespectful woman," he called her in Bengali. This was an important decision, because it meant everyone could understand, not only the servants but the neighbours. He punished her in the courtyard, and the sound travelled to the windows in the apartment blocks that surrounded our house. I stood behind the largest palm on the steps, riveted and ashamed. In a way, this display was what was expected of him. He had to stage a scene to let everyone know that he was not a man to be taken advantage of. But still there were choices. He could have spoken in English. He didn't have to yell quite so ferociously. He could have dressed her down in his study. The pressures of the war were upsetting him. He knew we would be leaving soon, and he did not want to go. There was work to be done. This was, for both of us, as close as we had gotten to having a home. He turned brick red. Spittle flew. "Thieving disgrace of a woman. After all we've done for you." Ayah covered her face with her veil, but she did not bow her head.

She did not say good-bye to me, either. The next morning she was merely gone. The cook said she was caring for a sick relative. But she'd left to recover face, I knew. Although I heard neighbourhood gossip that criticised my father for the public way in which he'd lost control, he was also perceived as foolish for not sacking her altogether. She hadn't implicated me, but she had gotten one of the cook's assistants to help with her rice-distribution scheme, and he was let go. He was expendable if Ayah was not. Even though we were nearing the end of our usefulness to one another, I still needed her. I think my father knew that.

When she came back, her face looked thinner, her eyes were blank. She knew Muhammad Rashid or one of the sweepers would tell my father of her return, so she sat at the threshold of her room and sewed and waited for him to summon her to the courtyard. His approval was necessary for her formal reinstatement to the household, but she was not going to seek him out. Her sari was pink. In the light of the late afternoon, she seemed to glow as the sun caught the glint of her needle when it dove through the thin fabric of her handkerchief. I was very glad she was home and realised I'd feared she wouldn't want to return at all after what he'd done to her.

People have the image of Indians as being above suffering, as if Hinduism resigns them to the cycles of life and death. But this is nonsense. No one is resigned. Some traditions insist on more courage and silence than others. Some regions have seen more of horror and have a different sense of danger. There is no less value placed on human lives, no less attachment to them. Perhaps, though, Indians deal in different kinds of solace. Perhaps they don't share our desire for the more obvious manifestations of happiness—in part because they can't afford them. Perhaps their faith has been tested more frequently, and they have had to try harder than most people to stay alive and keep their families solvent, healthy, schooled. Perhaps when you live in full, specific awareness of pain, disease, injustice, and violence, and they have been visited upon you and those you have dared to love, you live more starkly. Your figure cuts a more defined outline against the horizon. It is not an arbitrary fact that you can stand tall enough to cast a shadow, and you know this.

Sam knocked on my door this evening. I was tired from writing and hadn't yet walked the dogs. He asked me if he could go with me, and I was irritated, but then I remembered the way the boys had scattered. He was wearing a normal shirt now and no glasses. It was a breezy night, and clouds were gathering. I didn't say much, and I was glad that he was quiet, too. We went to the ferry landing to watch the Monhegan boat come in. The air smelled of seaweed and engine oil. People were addled with sun and exhausted from their day. Children were weeping with need for supper and bed. "A couple of years ago," Sam said, "you told me that you thought I'd make a good scientist. I was patient with plants." I had no recollection of having said any such thing, but it was a familiar enough experience. James and Anna often haul back bits of conversation or comments that I've made, usually something disparaging or cruel. "Well," I told him, "it's a lovely thing working with plants. You might want to try it." His own mother hired local people to weed and dig their borders and beds and then sat watching them from the terrace. He leant over the railing and looked at the parents and children more intently. I wondered if I should expressly invite him to come and help me, since I planned to work in the rock garden. But he's not my child, I keep telling myself, and even if he had been, I don't think I would have pushed for more contact. Bob and Karen already hectored him. I decided, as we walked back, not to interfere.

I remember that when I was his age, I both wanted to be fussed over and needed space to call my own. Ayah did not share my views about privacy and closed doors. According to her, daughters withheld nothing, not their fears, sins, daydreams. They were an extension of their mother, and their words and deeds and musings were, in a way, hers, or at least she expected access to them because they could alter the fate and fortunes of the family. In some respects it was a deep relief to be treated this way: I counted enough for her to peck and pry at me. Still, I knew this old-fashioned view would not control me forever. I was in Ayah's sphere for only a short if significant span of time. I was English; I'd be leaving.

Yet Ayah's influence was deep: she might be shocked by

how much I believe in the very Indian idea that the accumu-
lated pressure of our actions pushes our lives into their particular shapes. In some ways it's a comforting idea. We want to
know that we have weighed enough on our environment to create an impression. As if our words and actions lodged deeply
and rang there, mattering. It can be positive to think that we're
solid enough to create such an effect. But at the same time,
faith in karma is a tremendously difficult idea to live with. Obviously, if we were always good, kind, and thoughtful as we
proceeded through our days, we could congratulate ourselves
for all the happy consequences that flowed from us. Mostly,
however, when we stumble into the world, we are forced to
reckon with complication: daily life isn't simple, and neither are
we. More often than being good or kind, we are sad or jealous
or lazy. At times the words we've spoken do return to us, and
we're ashamed. So it grows tempting to blur the edges of real
events. To recall a cutting remark or a thoughtless action as being not quite as hurtful as it was. We manage to persuade ourselves that our lapses and oversights, lies and insincerities were
not quite as bald or stinging as they were. Even more, we trust
that people won't remember what we said and how we were,
and we edge towards the childish belief that nothing counts,
that people can't hold on to what they hear, because they hear
so much. Current events, commercials, popular songs. Who has
room to retrieve one person's past or the way someone held a
cup? And if no one remembers, all the poor decisions couldn't
really add up, could they? But I think everything registers:
whatever we've handled, whatever we've touched. We are
much more responsible than we feel.

Part Two

The road and I are lovers. I change my dress for her night after night, leaving the tattered cumber of the old in the wayside inns when the day dawns.
                                        —Rabindranath Tagore

Anna

June 1992 ✦⊃✦ Varanasi

I read the first segment of Rose's story on the train to Varanasi, a trip that consisted of seventeen hours of swaying cars, vile lavatories, and families who traveled with suitcases of food. It was often hard to go where she was taking me. Somewhere near Kanpur, the site of what the English call the Mutiny and the Indians call the First War of Independence, a woman plumped herself next to me and offered a handkerchief that was embroidered in a corner with a tiny Donald Duck. I said, no really, I was okay, in awful Hindi. She said, in English, "Madam, I am thinking you are not quite so fine," and she passed me her little girl, a child of nine months, as she poured tea from her thermos. Manufactured in China, she said—not the tea, the thermos. Those Chinese, unpleasant people that they were, made the best ones. A cousin in Nepal had sent it to her. I was careful not to spill any on the baby or my new blue *salwar kameez*, which had already wrinkled into deep untidiness. The child fell asleep in my arms, nonchalant about being held by someone she had never seen. I appreciated the tea and the conversation, but even more, the dense, milky weight of a child whose name I didn't know, passed to me with the implicit belief that of course I would know how to hold her. I napped myself and woke only when the woman pried her still drowsing girl from my arms to get off somewhere past Allahabad. "Wishing you a good trip," she said. "Wake up now. It is not safe to sleep whilst traveling so solo."

I haven't stopped thinking about the marbles spinning in the dust. Mrs. Browne's tiny feet. Ayah's hands plucking at Rose's skirt. The fire in the garden, that black eye from Grandfather. I knew that tendency to violence, I had seen it in her. Once, I'd crawled down the stairs to wait for Dad to come back from the hospital. I liked to watch him stand in the doorway of the kitchen and listen to him talk to Rose about his shift. He would be upset about a patient with a botched set of stitches, a nurse with too nasty a tone, and she would listen. But that night, by the time I got there, they were shouting at each other in the center of the room. Grandfather had written to ask if Rose could come over to England that summer. Rose's hair was a blond tangle. "I don't want to go," she kept saying. "I just don't want to."

"You should," Dad said. "You can't pretend it didn't happen." I don't remember much more than that, and I can't be certain about those words, but he was challenging her and she was angry and frightened. Then she threw the letter on the table and, with a closed fist, hit him hard in the face. Neither of them expected what came next—that Dad's slender jaw would drop from its hinge and swing, stretching the skin in a way that skin was not meant to be stretched.

"Jesus, Rose," he shouted, running to the mirror in the hall to reduce the joint. "It's okay," he kept saying, "it's all right," angry but trying to reassure her, too, as she stammered, "I am so sorry, David. I am so sorry." Horrified at herself. Hands clamped together over her mouth, to prevent herself from doing more.

I ran to my room and lay in bed, tingling with fear. Eventually I slept, and woke to the smell of breakfast being made. I came down to find Rose at the toaster, prying a slice from the machine with a fork. "You should unplug it," I said. She had told us that a thousand times. She glared. Dad walked in. He had a large bruise on his cheek. He looked exhausted. "I hit your father last night," Rose said, and her voice was ragged. "That is my fault," pointing at his jaw. "I am terribly sorry. I should not have done it." Then her fork touched the wires, and she jumped back. "I am so stupid, such a stupid cow." Dad pried the fork from her fingers and examined them as the kitchen filled with the smell of burning bread.

I've never found a place for that scene, much less Rose at ease with cobras, which she suggested she'd seen killed on a regular basis. Another of Ayah's specialties. Scoldings and cobra smashings. We had no idea what lay below those occasional Bengali curses, the brief, vivid pictures of tigers and lizards. I am certain James and I would have listened to everything. I am trying to be fair, to respond carefully, to make my way toward what it was like to be an English girl born in Calcutta, raised in its heat, its language. With no one in her household who quite understood her, the largest, whitest girl around. Seen but not known, a fearful combination.

I've only read through a bit of June 1969, when I was thirteen, off at Camp High Pines, the place I first kissed a boy and smoked marijuana. The usual sorts of initiations for girls then, though Rose was right that it was a good idea to send us there. It was far from Nixon but not exactly from worry. We remembered the killings. We knew about the war. We talked about it with hemlock needles patterning our toes as we rowed out to watch the loons. But all that's less important than the picture of my gawky mother waking up beneath mosquito netting to be hauled off to the ghats. I haven't even gotten to the Fourth of July yet. Rose, losing her ribbons in an Indian river. It's like staring through a door I never thought she'd open.

Curiously, Varanasi will be a good place to take in these stories. It seems like a city that has room for damaged people:
from my hotel balcony I can watch pilgrims, lepers, and old
women hobble each morning to the water, which shines in a
wide blue band below me. I arrived late yesterday morning,
and the train station was all dust, horns, and chaos. But when
the taxi rounded the bend and crossed the pontoon bridge, the
highest points of the temples caught the sun and flashed, a
brightness the river reflected as well. The city curves along the
water, a rather narrow strip of buildings and shops, markets
and temples pressing as close as they can to the banks. Only
two million people live here, and it seems easier to breathe
than in Delhi. "Sacred Ganges," the driver said, gesturing with
his thumb as we bumped across the bridge. He delivered me to
the Hotel Most Welcome in Assi Ghat, at the southern tip
of the city. The Most Welcome is on the second floor of a
family house and has copious amounts of cold water, geraniums
in mustard-oil canisters, and a fierce proprietor named Mr.
Dutt.

Once I was clean, I was tempted to keep reading about
Rose on sheets of paper that were, on one side, her single-
spaced account of a rather terrifying childhood in a dying
colony and, on the other, questions followed by blank spaces.
Previous surgeries? Current medications? As I'd turned the
pages, the Deccan Plain that the train was crossing faded away.
Grandfather, Ayah, Rose spotted in fern shadow surged up to
take its place, as did the neighborhood kids, Muhammad
Rashid, those starving women, and her almost casual mention
of lepers. She never once talked about leprosy, not out of for-
getfulness or disdain, I don't think, but perhaps out of some
odd, cramped form of concern. The disease and those who had
it weren't to be taken lightly.

Then, as I lay on my bed and watched the fan spin slowly, I

found I wanted less to read ahead than to think about what I'd just learned. Rose had been so lonely, not just in India but with Dad. The coolness between them was wounding to me. Something was amiss there that I'd not exactly sensed. I have no idea if they mended that breach or if I hadn't seen it because I hadn't wanted to. Children are eager for continuity, always so affronted when parents actually behave like human beings. But her loneliness was a practiced skill, I'm coming to think. I kept hoping to hear about a companion, a partner in crime. Not just furtive games with tough little boys. Maybe that's for later, but I doubt it.

It is disorienting to have both Rose and India to try to fathom, both of them fantastically hard to keep in focus, elusive even when they appear to reveal themselves. I have no idea if she knew this city, where she might have stayed, what kind of clothes she wore, what she might have heard on a radio or in a street. All those precise, fragile details that make us real to each other. And those missing bits are nothing compared to the other topics she didn't like to talk about when asked: her college years, coming to the States, meeting Dad. I think of her in Port Clyde, wearing a heavy sweater, hunched over the typewriter. Dad came up on Fridays, and we feasted on lobster and corn, then roamed the countryside for yard sales. Salt and lamplight and doors that swelled with rain. We argued, fished, collected rocks. Sunday nights, Rose would heat an ancient iron on the woodstove and press his shirts for the rest of the week, something she did badly. Dad's sleeves were always scorched. I don't think he noticed; if he had, he wouldn't have said anything. It was just how Rose tried to be a housewife, ruining his shirts.

Then I heard cymbals crashing and went to the hotel window. A procession of Sivaites was strutting along on the street below, thirty men with small tridents in their hands, their dreadlocked hair piled in high, thick ropes. It was a relief to be in a city that reminds me at times of New York at its quirkiest. Delhi was all smog and grim realities, profoundly overcrowded and commercial. There's something festive in Varanasi, something spooked and marvelous. A sign advertising life insurance has just been nailed on a telephone pole near the Most Welcome: DO NOT WAIT UNTIL THE 11TH HOUR: DEATH MAY COME AT 10:30. The river glimmered, and I decided that exploring the city was enough to take on for the moment. I dressed in my least crumpled outfit and went downstairs to see where the holy, mostly naked men with forks were heading.

On the one hand, Benarsis are obsessed with Siva; on the other, they are acutely conscious of where I'm from and what my country's all about. During my morning walk along the ghats, I was stopped by strangers at least ten times to be asked about my native land. Once I admitted to my nationality, I'd been harangued about our South Asian policy, the Gulf War, President Bush, sanctions against Iraq, the lack of intervention in Yugoslavia. Really, people were just trying to say hello and welcome to India, but they also expected a position, a response. DeLillo once said that in traveling he learned you could never forget you were American, because the actions of our government would not let you. Much as I might want to be perceived as my own particular, peculiar self, to have only my story counted—one of the ways in which I'm most American—my citizenship stretches out in front of me like a flag made of flypaper.

But Benarsis are also used to us. Americans have come to Varanasi in droves since the sixties, all bushy-haired and thirsty for inner peace. Australians, who seem less interested in purification and more in sampling local hash, provoke more interest, as do Swedes and their pixie children allowed to run barefoot through the dung-smeared streets. In any case, the people of Varanasi have plenty to pay attention to on their own doorstep. The newspapers are filled with the unrest at nearby Ayodhya, where a mosque has been built on the remains of a temple. I have stumbled on a couple of demonstrations, Muslims in green sashes, Hindus holding placards, and I hope to keep my distance from their hoarse anger, their strict intensity. The fury may be local, but I had the queasy sense that it could spread if given an opportunity.

Instead, I've got the luxury of choosing a different way through this place, an older narration in which to lose myself. I'm going to try to focus on the Kashi, the City of Light, that appears in the old texts. This is the earthly abode of Siva, who is described in a book I bought as the Beneficent Manifestation, the Destructive Manifestation, the Vagrant Mendicant, the Lord of Dancers, the God with the Moon in His Hair, the Supporter of the Ganges, the Slayer of the Elephant Demon, the Lord Who Is Half Woman, the Lord of the Peak, and the Destroyer of Time. In the same book I read a myth that involved a woman swimming in a river, then returning to land as a man, no closer to enlightenment but glad for the exposure to another way of being. A quick dip and a sex change was all she needed, and it didn't seem to affect her self-esteem. Perhaps Hinduism's a little more tolerant of shaky selves. Perhaps there is even power here in giving up one body for another.

This line from my new copy of the Upanishads is interesting on the issue, though I suspect I'm not reading it correctly: "Even as a caterpillar, when coming to the end of a blade of grass, reaches out to another blade of grass and draws itself over to it, in the same way the Soul, leaving the body and unwisdom behind, reaches out to another body and draws itself over to it." Caterpillars are creatures I understand right now. The sticky quality of their motion, their vulnerable skin, even the sprouting tufts of hair. But not the transformation to a butterfly, all jeweled panes of orange. I'd come back as one of Grandfather's moths that could poison birds and monkeys. Gray, powdery, toxic.

I can't read more of Rose's story yet. There are just so many memories I can make room for right now. The rickety cottage, the whiff of ocean, Sam Ellis. But those images are nothing next to being the girl in that large bird-ridden house with a father who'd torched her mother's clothes. She seems to feel embarrassed about something, to be preparing the way for another, more difficult piece of her story. Maybe if I tell her some of what I've done that shames me, she won't feel as bad, though stumbling mea culpas aren't our style. Nor does one mistake cancel another. Maybe she felt that talking about whatever it was that happened to her wouldn't have changed it. She was just trying to move on.

Maybe she should come back. Not in the grip of soupy nostalgia to pick through the relics of the Raj, but to see what's become of her old country. Not so much to put it into perspective—India seems to resist that kind of framing—but to help her get on with the next step, being widowed, having children without Dad as a buffer. The pared-away realities here shove you into contact with what it is you're made of, the stripes of contradiction, the true reactions. I'm tempted to ask her to come, yet I also don't want her anywhere near me. She got those quick, violent hands from Ayah and her father, and they still frighten me. Though Rose's temper isn't even what's preventing me from calling to invite her. I'm beginning to realize how much I've counted on my mother to stay solid, to never reveal the weak, sad pieces I knew in some way were part of her. I didn't tell her about school or boys because I didn't want to hear how she had or hadn't coped with similar troubles. But now she's rearranging herself in front of me, and I both want her to cut it out instantly and to say, Don't stop talking; sit down and tell me everything.

In the morning I drink tea on the balcony, then walk the length of the ghats, a journey of about two miles. The ghats are the steep stairs that lead from the water to the temples and then on into the city itself. Some are painted in red and white. Some are tall and narrow. Others have steps wide enough to sleep on, which people do, despite the din of pilgrimages. It's a trip that can take one hour or ten, depending on whom you encounter and if you stop to sit and write or eat. Yesterday I met a young Israeli named Lev Frankel on Tulsi Ghat, not that far from my hotel. He was shaking his Bic to coax the last bit of ink from the cartridge when I offered him mine. He bought me *chai* to say thank you. It's served here in cups made of clay scooped from the banks. Often people smash them on the steps when they're done, and the fragments are tossed back into the water. The tea itself could well be some of the Ganges, filtered or boiled, you hope, the whole experience a chance to be involved, in a humble and modified form, with the great river. Benarsi *chai* tastes of cinnamon and earth.

Lev spoke very good Hindi, and I asked him, stupidly, where he'd learned it. He looked at me, said "Haifa," and we laughed. He wears Indian clothes and has his hair cut very short. He smokes English cigarettes. His skin is tanned enough for him to look almost Indian, but his eyes are dark blue. He came here five years ago, after his army service, thinking he'd stay six weeks. He's been studying Sanskrit, working in a local clinic, living in a room above a cookware shop. He goes to sleep to the sounds of the owner clanging lids on pots and of ladle displays falling over. "You're busy," I said, but Lev said it wasn't so much with the clinic or with Sanskrit, though the language gave him endless worry, but with watching what hap-pened right in front of him. "India," he said. "It can take all your time."

He asked me what I did, and I kept it simple. Nonprofit writing, scaring up money for schools and health projects in the developing world. Living in New York. I didn't talk about writ-ing poems or restoring furniture. Nor did I mention Mark and Dad or the unwelcome knowledge that I had turned out to be someone who could cry in public. Anything could trigger the tears. Brass plaques with doctors' names screwed to buildings. The word "blueprint," the smell of sawdust if I was thinking of Mark. I wept on subways, in the gym, on rocks in the park. If I'd drawn the route of my grief, it would have covered signifi-cant territory. It would have been a chart, too, to madness, because deep grief leaves you crazed, possessed by its own nar-row logic, which notices only absence, irrevocability. I kept silent about Rose and her pages, too. She's almost as hard to discuss in casual conversation. Yet even with the bulk of my personal history suppressed, I enjoyed his company.

He offered to show me Varanasi, but even better, he trans-lated a poem for me. It's about the river and it is painted in tall letters on a wall near the main ghat. From Sanskrit through Hebrew into English, but accuracy doesn't seem to be the is-sue. He wrote it down for me on the back of the hotel receipt, which features twelve different lines for possible charges. Amenities. G. tax, L. tax—government and local getting a bite. On the back of this he wrote: "I come a fallen man to you, up-lifter of all. / I come undone by disease to you, the perfect physician. / I come, my heart dry with thirst, to you, ocean of sweet wine. / Do with me whatever you will."

I am feeling a little better. I'm adapting to my new clothes, which cover more of me yet keep me cooler than what I'd brought from home. I am sleeping. Mr. Dutt's mattresses are clean if thin. Lev is kind and interesting. "What a place," he said, passing me a handful of roasted chickpeas. "And I complain about Israel." He went entirely still for a moment after that. He glanced at me then, perhaps anticipating a response, a political dig, preparing one in retaliation. Both our homelands are easy targets. But I decided not to speak. I wasn't anxious to spar, to assume a posture. No one likes foreigners to step on the scars of your country, even when it follows policies you find disturbing. Like a mother. Only you are allowed to criticize your own. But something relaxed between us then. It was clear we weren't going to treat each other as if we each came in a box labeled Israeli or American, angular and sealed.

I listened. He's deep into yoga. He works most days with lepers or kids with a host of rough diseases. He studies his Sanskrit. I kept my ear tuned for notes that would suggest he was in over his head, a little nuts, a bit adrift, but I didn't hear any. He was just living, he said, testing out some new idea of living, new at least to him, and he seemed to be telling the truth. "Planning on staying for good?" I asked, wondering how far he was intending to go. The sadhus here travel the distance, twisted into poses that defy physiology. Some of them have vowed to stand on one leg for years at a time. And this is nothing compared to what other practitioners are up to. There are men who walk naked the length and breadth of India, rocks tied to their scrotums. I wondered how much Lev was willing to part with. "As long as she'll have me," he said, gesturing not at the city but at the river.

"How many more days for you?" he asked. When I said "Seven" and opened my guidebook, he said, "Slow down. New Yorkers are as bad as people from Tel Aviv. Nothing here happens fast. It can take you a week just to make a phone call, much less see all those temples on your list."

He makes me nervous for a couple of reasons. The first is

that he seems to have adopted Indian gestures of reverence and thought very casually. His radical personification of the city and the river, for example. The river is not just itself, but a goddess, and not just a goddess, but an emanation from Vishnu the Preserver's toe. Ganga Ma, he calls it, as Indians do, as Rose did. The Hooghly, one of the Ganges's tributaries, frays and spills into the Bay of Bengal near Calcutta. And even more, Ganga Ma hides the Sarasvati, a sacred, mythic river flowing below it. The whole city is about six universes superimposed upon one another, superstring theory gone holy, dusty, and loud. Benarsis appear to float from a temple born of a lingam that miraculously alighted a few eons back to the daily tasks of buying batteries and vegetables. I envy their smooth travel from the ethereal to the mundane, but I find myself bathing not in the Cosmic Sea of Milk said to be Varanasi's celestial suspension fluid but in my own harsh sweat.

Or do I want that? What do you want? I woke up asking this morning, and I could answer with clarity that I didn't know. The images that emerged could have been veiled in the cosmic sea, they were that confused. Mark keeps returning, and of course Dad. They are the other reason Lev makes me nervous. Mark arrived in my life as suddenly as Lev, and Lev has both Mark's and Dad's certainty that answers can be found through intense study of an anointed topic.

For Dad it was history even more than medicine. He loved maps and pinned the ones folded inside issues of *National Geographic* all over the house. Not quite decoration, not quite wallpaper, they hung in almost every room. A few watercolors, Concord scenes of gabled eaves, then wham! contours of big trouble: the European Theater, 1942. As you headed off to watch television, you were meant to get waylaid by the recognition that five countries bordered Hungary. Pretzels in your palm, you'd stop and count, salt tang in the corners of your mouth. Drifting on to the jittery picture on the ancient tube, the pink and green of Ukraine and Austria sliding into your mind as you watched the Sox flail away and usually lose. The maps meant history and struggle, but they also implied Dad had gotten out of that landlocked place in time and that he was around somewhere, to answer questions you might have.

That was the other side of his preoccupation: you were supposed to learn about the world at every turn. His low voice in his small body, his hands flipping through the gilt-edged pages of the encyclopedia to find out how many people lived in Rio and how tall Makalu was. Even when I was old enough to find the information myself, I used to ask him to help me, to have the chance to see him put on his glasses and look at me happily. The pursuit of knowledge, he was sure, would furnish us with wisdom, a comfort as palpable as a good meal or clean sheets. But those maps also suggested that nothing in the house was simply itself, as is true of objects in all places where people have lived a long time. Every faded rug, every threadbare arm on a sofa—someone had been responsible for it, someone had made it happen, and news could be pulled from it, were anyone to ask. We knew better than to turn to Rose with concerns like these. It was Dad who'd take the time, trace the flaw, relate every story but his wife's. It hardly mattered if it was about the rubber trade or the water stain on the kitchen ceiling.

Yet the maps were also important as statements of fact, stern announcements of boundaries and history, the tough old news that mountains and oceans existed and would have to be crossed if you were actually there. Everywhere in that house, geography. The broad fist of China. The lopsided martini glass of Vietnam. The triangle of India, with its patches of color, each swatch a different language, a quilt of words designed by some visionary of grammar. Dad, standing behind me as I looked at

Asia, asking, "North Korea?" to which I'd say, eyes rolling, "Pyongyang."

Mark's concerns were more rooted in what could be seen and built. He believed that architecture could defeat bad taste, poor engineering, and social inequity. Theory and good intention meet steel, cement, and city planners. His buildings were as sleek and handsome as the people who wanted them, even when they accommodated apartments for the homeless, a garden that the whole neighborhood, including drug addicts, could use. They were environments, not just dwellings. At first I'd appreciated the balance he was aiming for, his quotations from Louis Kahn: "A street is a room by agreement." But often the projects didn't function well. Rich people didn't actually want to live so close to poor people. The disparities were too glaring. Gardens and nursing homes were easier to integrate. Yet it always frustrated him when a plan didn't work out. He was trying to have it all, Mark. That's human, forgivable, but what I grew suspicious of was that you could smell him everywhere in his work. He couldn't not stamp his signature touch on everything from a sink to a wood floor.

When Lev talks about Sanskrit, he gets the same clouded zeal in his eyes: for him, the answers lie in Pali, the shape of the alphabet, all of it sacred, every serif, every swoop. Like Hebrew and Arabic, the letters themselves have their magical weight, their necessity, and are owed their devotion. Once mastered, the language becomes the key to mastering the civilization, an idea that presumes that a language can be wholly conquered, wholly grasped.

I admire the reverence for knowledge and the confidence these men have in their right to mold a landscape and interpret a text, but I'm not sure they can see the people crossing the mountains, living in the houses, or using the language quite as sharply as they should. The human factor has gone muddy, the messianic gleam grown a little pronounced, their own roles slightly amplified.

Lev is also eight years younger than I am. Worse, he's the first man I've met in more than a year whom I've wanted to touch. It doesn't matter that he's shorter or that he smokes. Through the loose fabric of his pants, his thighs are taut and full. All I could think about, after talking with him on the ghats for no more than a few minutes, was what my hands would feel like on his legs, though I didn't of course go near him.

The body is so dumb sometimes and so insistent. That's what pulled me first and most completely to my husband, falling entirely captive to what it told me it needed. It rarely spoke to me that way—that's perhaps what surprised me, made me act on impulse. When I first saw Mark, he was eyeing a broken chair that I liked, too, at the Saturday morning flea market on Sixth Avenue and Twenty-sixth Street. He was as tall as I was. Even when he stooped, I could see how much of him there was. In the pocket of his jacket was a tape measure, its metal tongue a short yellow flag. I asked him if he was serious about the chair. He said he was always serious about chairs. Too late I realized this was not a joke. Sadly, this didn't matter. He was lovely. Gray eyes, real gray all the way through, not stained with hazel. Hands that had worked with tools and wood. Polite. He's taken, taken, taken, I thought. I was right, but not so much with other women (though they were there) as with an idea about himself. He was ambitious. It's a marvel how bodies hold that quality. It can lurk in the eyes, ones that don't quite meet yours because they are too busy searching out the horizon. It's in the set of the shoulders, the walk, too. First the body cups it, then it travels to the mouth, to talk and conversation. He had it. He had big ideas and a gorgeous face. By the time I had let him claim the chair, I was his. Two minutes was all it took, and my old caution collapsed.

Rose and Dad had frightened as well as taught me. The committed attachment I saw them enacting wasn't something light. It wasn't to be confused with desire. It was a letter of intent, a contract. I had always been leery of getting caught in so much compromise. Marriage might begin with passion but end with heavy furniture and curtains. Rose and Dad had lost the heat; I wonder if they ever had it. They were people who'd known hardship and whose expectations of happiness were chastened by misfortune. Enough, they might have said to each other. It's odd what we have, we don't look right together, but it's enough to get on with the queer process of turning ourselves into Americans with a patch of lawn and pair of kids.

My childhood had fewer obstacles, and that ease allowed me to make of love something perfumed, a bower of a place. Then I went to college, got busy with work and life. Men were part of those years but not, I found to my regret, the most interesting part. I moved to New York and got woven into work and city living, men still there yet not the primary focus. Love of the kind I'd once imagined came to feel not like something extra, but something I just might not make space for. Then, thanks to that encounter with a crouched man at a flea market, I was conclusively in my body, on the ground, definitively human: brave and fragile all at once. Years of relative indifference, gone. Mistaking profound mutual attraction for fate, which for a brief moment I believed in.

I stayed up late with Mark when his critiques were due, made the coffee that kept us wired for days, wrote his proposals, visited lumberyards and building sites with him. I did well at my job; I made our small apartment beautiful. I wanted to be someone he admired. Because he'd arrived so fortuitously, because he seemed to love me back, I thought the answer was to tie him to me for always. Once I'd tasted that kind of attachment, that kind of pleasure, it seemed impossible to live without it. I did everything to secure it. So my real work was convincing him to marry me before he found out that I broke everything I touched. I've always had bouts of clumsiness, months where glasses shatter on me and lightbulbs pop to shards. I did cajole him into a wedding and then discovered what I should have known all along: that sort of breakage was nothing next to what people could do to each other. I do not have it in me to tell Lev, Look, I've got nothing left to give right now. There's nothing there, and even then, I could destroy you here in Siva's city.

It's the next morning, before dawn. I got distracted by Lev and men and didn't finish writing about Rose and her isolation and the concern her story set off. I've been feeling glum and guilty, as if I should have guessed more about her sad childhood. I couldn't sleep last night for thinking about my mother. I tried to turn the lights on, but the power was out. My flashlight's batteries are almost spent. It's finally bright enough to see. I recognize now that Rose's implacability was something earned. She armored herself early on, like a tortoise. No wonder. She had an ayah whose attention arrived in violent scrubbings and toy elephants. A father who would not talk about her mother or teach her to swim. No wonder she got so taciturn when he came to see her in the States. When Grandfather arrived on one of his rare visits, he stayed in Cambridge to be near the used-book stores in Harvard Square. We would drive in from Concord, and as Rose steadily grew more silent, I would chatter. "Why does the traffic slow down at the Arlington exit?" "It just does." "Why doesn't Grandfather like TV?" "He just doesn't."

She drove grimly ahead, sealing her worries from interference. Though he was forbidding, I admired my grandfather and could not see why Rose, so rough and competent, should fold so deeply in on herself when she was near him. They were so much alike — so tall. They shared the same design. I was always aware of their bones. But when we were with him, she tried to dim her energy and breadth. When I saw a piece of a meteorite at the Museum of Science, I was disappointed because its mild glitter was so hard to link with the brilliant shooting stars that we watched in Maine each August. But that was how Rose was around her father: dulled and far less impressive up close than at a distance.

I talked to her last night. She was instantly prickly and shy, guessing that now I knew about parts of her life that she had never discussed. "Staying healthy?" she asked. "Have the rains come?" Yes, I said, and no. But she didn't mention the pages she'd sent. Her pride wouldn't have allowed it. So I tried something personal but smallish. "What were the names of Ayah's girls?" I asked from a cramped booth scrawled with Hindi graffiti and pictures that crossed linguistic boundaries. A meter ticked away in rupees to my left. A fan whirred in the corner. A bundle of multicolored wires was casually hooked on a nail near the phone. An electric candle below a picture of Hanuman flickered next to that. God, technology, and commerce all looped together in a makeshift way, safety the furthest issue from anyone's mind. Salvation ahead of that, and money and communication even more prominent.

She paused. "Oh my," she said, the satellite stretching her voice. Another pause. "Sujata, Sita, Padmini, Puja, and Radha. Yes, that's right."

"Pretty," I said.

"Indian names always sound to me like the names of flowers," she added cautiously, seeming to wonder what was coming.

"I haven't read everything, Rose. I'm doing it slowly," I told her.

"Well," she said, then asked me if I was enjoying myself.

"Not quite the right word," I answered, meaning both her writing and India. "But yes, I am glad I came."

"This is costing you a fortune," she said, hustling us away from too much self-exposure. Invoking our own rules: Don't waste money. Don't be lavish with talk. Don't dwell on awkward subjects. There wasn't time to catch up about James, the dogs, the garden. I felt rushed off the line, but we didn't dare broach anything more intimate. Our wanting to know about each other hung there, though, as did the fact that we did not have the sort of relationship that could be slipped into words as simply as a letter slides into an envelope. "Rose," I said, "do you think you'd like to come back?" but she was already hanging up, and I was speaking into the air between her ear and the body of the phone, the receiver on its way back to the cradle.

I've been remembering Sam Ellis, too. He was tall and handsome in both short and long hair. Rose was wrong about his letting us win at Monopoly. James was mostly unbeatable, I was competitive, and Sam was distracted. He liked our family, he said once, because people did things. "Like what?" James asked, aligning his hotels more neatly along Boardwalk. "Build stuff," Sam said, pointing to the stone wall we'd rescued from crumbling and the bench that Rose and Dad had stripped and painted. We stared at him. Why were rocks and secondhand furniture unusual? We envied him his boarding school, the electricity in his house, and the mother who was always cooking him fancy meals and tousling his hair.

I'm sort of poised—not quite with Rose and Sam, and not quite with Varanasi—here on the balcony at the Most Welcome. Lev is coming over later. He wants to show me the Nepali temple. Slowly, he said. An entire afternoon for a single

building. Think you can handle it? The rains still aren't here.
The English-language papers are full of turmoil in Kashmir, ex-
plosions in trains, unrest in Tamil Nadu, much of it blamed on
the delayed monsoon.

I am also writing so I don't pounce on two new guests
who've joined me under the canopy. They are English boys, all
elbows and freckles, leaning toward a pair of tired, luscious
Spanish girls, who arrived yesterday. The guys are engaged in
a brand of flirtation that may be specific to subcontinental
travelers—comparing dangers encountered, scams avoided,
courtesies and traditions observed, all of it threaded with the
suggestion that it takes a certain cleverness to manage India.
Post-post-colonial inflections. We understand them, you know;
we used to be their oppressors, but we've given up all that.
We're awfully sorry, and we got out, after all. Now we're just
curious and that's okay, isn't it? Hinduism's so fascinating. No
easy answers here in India, are there? Dipped heads at the
mention of poverty, slums. And mixed with this, isn't the south
nicer than the north, how's your tum been, brilliant *dolsa* at this
spot near the big cinema, did you get cheated by Indian Railways on the train from Calcutta to Patna? There's a way round
the porters, you know. Is it your first time? You know, here?

I want to cluck at the boys and then hustle the girls off to
feed them something thoroughly cooked. They look too thin.
They look hassled. I know, too, that if I weren't ten or fifteen
years older than they, if I were a brash young man, I'd be saying
much the same sort of thing. I'd be thinking about the most direct route between me and those pretty girls. I'd want to be listening to the unsteady whir of the fan in their rooms and the
blare of horns as I kissed the soft angle of their collarbones. And
that the long hair slick with sweat and henna, the bad English,
and the sweet hips were what I'd remember most about India.

Or I would want to be the Spanish girls. Long in the leg and unacquainted with the fact that the skin at the back of the thighs will grow dimpled. To read Sartre and think that it must have been so thrilling to be Simone de Beauvoir. To be lineless around the eyes and have only mild experiences with heartbreak, to be the dealer of the heartbreak, not its recipient. To smoke and know that it was bad for me and even wake with a cough tickling my lungs and still feel that it was not quite me the doctors were talking about. To drive boys wild and be slightly disdainful of their lack of control.

I want to get up and write in my room, but I don't, a decision that's not entirely related to the torpor the heat brings on. I stay because I feel I should, as if there's a reason I'm supposed to be listening to the boys making their heavy-handed overtures. In India, nothing feels unconnected or simply itself. A newspaper, a cup of tea, the little boy pouring out more tea for all us. He is Mr. Dutt's son, twelve years old and very small compared to most American kids that age, but far more grown up, at least in the gestures he uses, which are cribbed from his father. I can't separate that boy from those British kids, those Spanish girls, the sounds of the city below us, the curve of the river, my own body curled here on the balcony. Borders here are both starkly apparent—NO FOREIGN WOMEN IN THE MOSQUE, MOST RESPECTFULLY REQUESTED—and amazingly fluid. At the post office, a clerk recommended a restaurant and a place to buy silk and later found me at the silk shop and helped me bargain for a length of turquoise fabric. I'm saying, I suppose, that I've got no idea what may be in store for me with my fellow guests, with that young boy, with the river. It's a surprise, a slightly unwanted twist, to sense that something will be.

It's late evening. I've just plugged in an antimosquito device that's horribly effective, probably pure DDT, which is still used everywhere here. The Knightie Knight is a pink plastic bulb into which you insert lozenges of pesticide. Then you stick the whole contraption into an outlet, and it releases its fumes. Mosquito netting is not a feature of the Most Welcome. The Knightie Knight's poison smells cloyingly sweet, like Indian candies or jellies, like the incense.

I toured several temples with Lev from dawn to dusk and am dizzy still with all the gods. There are deities for smallpox and war, others for the birth of sons and the health of crops. Lesser ones, greater ones, Siva arching over all of them. The whole city is a manifestation of his body, his powers, his history. Buildings and streets are his limbs and muscles; trees and stones mark where he came to earth and his power penetrated the land. And if Siva hasn't visited, some other god has. Every corner's had its brush with holiness. Divine entities of all shapes, sizes, intensities have left some dazzle behind that Benarsis remember with their offerings of fruit, candles, marigolds, and oil. What's strange is, even when religion seems a language you'll never speak, you can tell something's happened at these special sites. Cows and their stench, the dazed Germans, public death—these elements are a piece of what is real in this city, but something else is, too. Believers claim that Varanasi is rife with invisible springs and forests, and despite the scooters, dope dealers, and rangy boys traveling in packs, it's not such a leap of faith to acknowledge this version of geography. One hundred and sixty-six generations of people have lived here. Focusing just on the hands of passersby made it possible for me to visualize four- and eight-armed deities shared out over many bodies. Faith is spread in a wide, bright veil across the whole landscape. God hasn't pulled away to a hilltop monastery or secreted himself in a grotto. He's got room to settle here, get comfortable.

Visiting temples is still a tricky affair. Their entryways, often narrow openings or gates that look as if they lead to someone's home and not a brightly painted, garland-draped courtyard, bristle with soldiers. Lev explained that since a Tamil suicide bomber blew Rajiv Gandhi to pieces last year and the murderous rioting at Ayodhya, the military presence in and around Varanasi has become large and swaggering. No one likes it, Lev said, but they'll put up with anything to keep religious violence from igniting. That's the fear, he added. Once a riot starts, it will be impossible to stop, and in a flash, thousands will be dead. This may be a city where people come to die, but not beneath the feet of a raging crowd.

At Vishwanath, the great Siva temple at the heart of the city, a guard named Singh went through every item in my bag, flipping through this journal with particular care before he would let me in. He held my passport up to the sun and looked closely at the visa. "Traveling self, madam?" he asked, and I said yes, I was.

I stood there with Lev, who is used to this sort of thing from years in India and childhood and army service in Israel. Mostly he goes very quiet when he has to pass a checkpoint, scrupulously blank. At Vishwanath, he didn't even glance at me, but I knew he was smiling. Traveling self. We'd just been thrashing around a couple of problems with reincarnation. I'm a skeptic, but he's quite convinced, and he took the guard's comment as a scored point. We paid close attention to Officer Singh as he returned the key to my room, the journal, the passport, stomach pills, water bottle, pens, the goods that prop up my travel here.

Lev has done a lot of gentle explaining about how to get around, when the power cuts happen, which person at the money exchange to trust. He's done an even gentler job of not asking me too many questions. He's letting me absorb the city at my own pace. He's also right: it will take more than ten days to explore Varanasi. I have had to move more slowly. After we visited the temple, he took me to a store that sold large glass beads and bought me a dark purple one. He undid the barrel clasp on the necklace that Kamala had insisted I buy and slipped the bead on it. "Lucky color," he said. "According to whom?" I asked. "Me," he said. "According to me." The glass stays cool where it rests on my collarbone. "I had a good day," he said as he scraped cow shit from the bottom of his sandals onto the curb in front of my hotel. "I did too," I told him. He took my hand, held it for a moment; then a carful of women swerved close and nearly killed us. They swore at us like soldiers, Lev said. A gong sounded from somewhere deep in the center of a temple, and we waved good-bye to each other. A volatile completeness, lived with. A good day.

I'm writing now from a small shop where I've taken refuge to drink a sweet *lassi* from a green glass. This morning I walked alone through the gullies, which are Varanasi's back streets, following a cryptic map Mr. Dutt gave me. He's used to the questing ways of tourists, our oddball notions of what's worthwhile, and with a short sigh he drew me a picture of where to find a shrine devoted to Annapurna, goddess of harvests. It was complicated, the alleyways so old and narrow, the proportions not to scale. I gave up and forced myself to use my Hindi to ask where I was. This made people howl. Kids followed me everywhere, wanting candy, rupees, pens. I've just taken some acidophilus. My stomach's been fine, but India's primed me for sudden reversals of luck.

As I walked, I was struck by how it was hard to tell exactly what year or era I was in. Of course, radios were blaring and electric lights burned, but if you removed those indicators of modern times, you could believe that the scene in front of you dated from 1900 or 1400. The priests and sadhus guided streams of pilgrims through the streets as they had for centuries, starting the day as perhaps their ancestors had well before the birth of Christ, Buddha, or Allah. But I couldn't ignore for long the devotees' crackling plastic sacks of food, their bottled water and eyeglasses. It is hard to link all this religious industry, this industry of religion—ash-smeared ascetics and plump, bespectacled ladies—with blazing temples, God shoved up against man-made, very contemporary rage.

Signs like these are posted everywhere in English: NON-HINDUS FORBIDDEN IN INNER SANCTUM. From what I've glimpsed of the fires and the chanting Brahmins, I am not so sure that I would want to venture in anyway. On our temple tour yesterday Lev asked me what I'd been raised as, and I told him a bit about Rose and Dad. "Ashkenazi meets one of the viceroy's last subjects," he said. "You should have been a translator." He turned over my palm and said, "Strong head line. You'd need it, making your way through that."

When we were little and friends asked if we were Jewish, Catholic, or Protestant, Dad told us to say, *Homo sapiens*. We whined enough about Christmas, so that eventually Dad took that shift at the hospital and left Rose, James, and me with a small tree and the solid, unimaginative presents Rose gave us. Grandfather sent gifts like mounted butterflies or treatises on the North Sea, and a long letter in writing that was close to impossible to decipher. The holiday was treated more like Election Day, a secular obligation, than a seminal moment in the Christian calendar or an opportunity for enjoyment. I loved to go to friends' houses to hear carols, eat cookies, and read the jolly greetings in the cards displayed on mantels. We bypassed Easter altogether. Thanksgiving featured the awkward combination of Walter, Isabella, and Rose, with Dad talking too much as he ruined the carving, none of them born to American abundance. There was never a question of church or temple.

Sundays, they read the papers, listened to music, worked in the garden, walked the dogs. Our gods were local ones, lords of the lawn mower, potting soil, and furnace.

James once asked what happened in heaven, and Dad, always on the side of the underdog, said, not even lowering the newspaper, "The Sox win the Series against New York in four." A couple of years later I was teased at school for being an atheist, and I shouted back that I was not, though I wasn't sure what the word meant. Curious to know what it was the other kids had that I was missing out on—God as consumer product to which I jealously felt entitled—I put it to my father. Where was God, what was God, why didn't we do anything about it? "There is no God, Anna," he said firmly, and put his knife down. He explained that religion was not just the opiate of the people (I had to look that up later) but a grotesque flimflam centuries in the making, as believers in all traditions tried to justify terrible kinds of behavior for their own gain. It was best simply to admit, he said, that there was no God. Given the evidence, how could there be a divine presence? How was God possible, he said, pointing to the plague, Nazis, Republicans like Goldwater and Helms, not to mention Stalin, starvation, and Kissinger? He looked ready to spit as he said this. We make what we live, he insisted as Rose looked down at the tablecloth, not interrupting, not steering the conversation somewhere else. What happens is our responsibility, Dad said, and I never asked him again. Judaism for him was not a practice but a ripped heritage, a way to keep himself from accepting false security, spongy thinking, supposedly safe offers of passage. Chronically alert and earthbound.

I don't think James or I ever dared ask Rose if she believed in God. I can imagine her snorting and saying, "Be reasonable." Yet she came close to being a deity in her own sharp, northern way, her refusal to explain herself. Her mood, if not her looks, reminds me of these vivid, imperious Hindu deities, given to fits of activity and abrupt changes of temper. She devoted herself to scrupulous observation, lack of self-pity, and terrific self-control. It was not exactly confidence as much as it was a learned, protective gruffness. But it must have confused her to find that once she'd acquired this mettle, she couldn't peel it off. It stuck fast.

I've decided, too, that I am going to call her again and ask her to come to India while I'm here, to see even if I can persuade James as well. He had looked so curious when I showed him my itinerary and my books. He's never been here, but he informed me, instantly, what India's bond rating was. Not his field, but he'd kept up. A personal interest. Rose will be harder to convince. She's steeled herself for so long against a return. But she gave me the pages; after all these years, she's admitted something. She's invited a response.

Back on the Most Welcome's balcony, I'm watching the sun go down. Below me, on Assi Ghat, a goat bleats, and a pair of boys spread a towel and on it the cigarettes and packets of gum they are trying to hawk. No one's interested. A temple bell rings. A breeze skims the river, and the heat eases down a degree or two. It moves in barely visible clouds, curving ripples of air, spreading across the water to the far side. Pure buoyed energy. You could spend all afternoon just watching it shimmer and disperse. I haven't noticed something like this in years. The English boys and the Spanish girls are sitting at the other end of the open space and are ordering tea from Ram, Mr. Dutt's son.

Lev is away for the day, a short period of time, but it does not surprise me to find that I miss him. We've been trading more stories. I've told him some about Concord, New York, my work, and even about the poems. He knows now that Dad has died and that my marriage has ended. Neither seemed to frighten him off. India and Israel have created tolerance for breakage perhaps. I've learned that his father is in the intelligence service and his mother is a nurse. They were born in Greece during the war, where they spent their first years in hiding—seeing the sun made square, as Lev says, framed and halved by windows. He has two sisters, one a student and one already married to a rabbi. "Israelis for the duration," he says. Not even interested in coming here, except maybe his younger sister. But his parents have already had one child swallowed by India; they don't want to risk losing another.

He's doing some work at a clinic, a vaccination campaign he promised a doctor friend he'd help with. I asked him what his medical training was, and he shrugged. "Nothing official," he said, and at once I regretted the question, born from being a doctor's daughter. He had probably bound wounds not just here but in Gaza, where he'd been posted. He's told me that much but no more, and I haven't insisted. I should have guessed that he'd have seen friends or children bleeding. He would have learned what he could, using the tools at hand. A license saying he could stabilize a broken arm or give a shot hardly mattered. Even young Israelis feel old, and I realize I could listen to him for hours.

It's a good distraction, then, to eavesdrop on the young Europeans. The boys are telling the girls that they've just come from Leh, and before that, they'd been in Srinagar. It is curious to me that these British kids managed to get to such a strife-ridden city, and even more curious that they got out. They're the wild-eyed sort, with round glasses and hair of light brown tangles. They look hapless, improvised, the sort to misplace passports and get cheated. The kind of tourist unscrupulous Indians would prey on with one eye closed it would be so simple.

"Oh yeah, it was a mess," the curlier one says, and smiles, which he shouldn't do given the condition of his teeth. They smoke cigarettes they roll themselves and wear cotton scarves around their necks as I guess they wore the woolen versions from their schools just a few years ago. They badly want these girls to like them. They want their bravery in the face of Kashmiri independence struggles—not war, no one uses that word to describe what's going on in the far north, the province caught between Pakistan and India, claimed as territory by both—to impress the women enough to let them touch them. As if seeing a grenade explode were a badge of manhood, an irresistible lure. Closeness to serious trouble is proof of their bravado, though the thought of one of them with a weapon is laughable.

Violence to me is not an abstraction, but in its most vicious, widespread forms it's not familiar. The wretched conditions and terrible stories I read about for work cause me deep worry, but I'm acutely aware that that is not the same thing as actually living in a place where bombs go off in market squares and kill your mother. I'm guessing that the worst any of the guests here at the Most Welcome have known is cuffed ears, a mugging, a bully at school. We all know about drugs, AIDS, and poverty, but what we probably know most intimately is this—the general whir of mayhem seen in athletic contests, advertising, films, the broth of culture we all live in, where the staged rivalries and destruction enact the old hungers for blood.

War for Harry and Victor (they've gotten to the point with the girls where they've traded names) is not unlike sport. This is partly because of their age, partly because of their nationality. They aren't Irish, after all; they're from Brighton. They've grown used to the relatively stable peacetime their grandparents or parents earned for them. And all that prosperity bores them. For trouble and maturity, they've sought out India. For color and danger, they've traveled across oceans and gotten sick and been cheated. Earning their stripes as thousands of people with brown skin and brown eyes look on.

I wonder if the Spanish girls, called Marisol and Luz, hear the relief in these boys' voices: they are very glad to be speaking about Kashmir in the past tense. At some level they know they've been stupid and been lucky. They don't have to travel there again. The adventure's safely finished. They'll be home, they're sure, in a couple of weeks.

The Spanish girls are smoking cigarette after cigarette and jiggling the last centimeters of their tea in the short glasses. Luz is a bit green and gaunt; the short ribs visible at the top of her T-shirt press against her skin. A rancid plate of rice somewhere, a bad glass of water, with the usual consequences. India has shaken up their gold-and-auburn prettiness. They look too tender for its rigors, its brassy noise. I'm guessing that they are Catholic girls just out of university, trying to break loose from an umbrella of parents, siblings, and family back home in Madrid. The trip to India is the bravest thing they've ever done.

But I know I'm in much the same position as they, which accounts for my scorn. I'm embarrassed about my own unearned privilege. Rose talked about that as well: the weight of good luck. The wars I've been alive for were in jungles and deserts thousands of miles from my home, and they did not disrupt the availability of my milk, power, newspapers, or fruit.

My father stumbled on this problem often. Wrapping up ankles sprained on country-club golf courses felt insufficient. He led immunization drives, spent time at a South End clinic. The patients loved him. He didn't sound like a doctor, talking to his patients as if they were machines that had the audacity to malfunction. He liked finding the right words to describe someone's illness or injury. Being precise with language gave him a refuge from the bad choices and even worse luck that brought people to his office.

But none of this good work assuaged his sense that he could be doing more. A few years ago he'd wanted to volunteer for Doctors Without Borders, but Rose halted that drive. She knew, I think, that they must not steep themselves in suffering. They should be conscious of those worse off, perhaps, but not wallow in shame about their own good fortune. They'd both seen and experienced their share of misery. But how do you live once you know just how bad it can be in the world? Where do your obligations start and stop? Even helping didn't always help. I know from my own work that it is still possible to be overwhelmed with the magnitude of need, the faces of the children you haven't protected. Staying late, writing proposals, trying to dredge up more dollars—I'd devoted more time to those projects than I had to poems, family, or marriage.

Rose had never fully approved of what I did. It was arrogant, she felt, to believe you could make a difference for people in countries whose languages you couldn't ever hope to speak. Righteousness could puff you up into self-delusion if you weren't careful. The answer for her was more to keep suffering from creeping in toward you and the life you'd managed to salvage. Don't go in for a lot of hand-wringing; just pay careful attention to what you've been allowed to cultivate yourself. Don't question why you survived, but survive with some dignity. Don't try to be better than others; just try to be. That is hard enough. Paint the clapboards and the shutters. Change the sheets. Turn on the news, but not too loud, and certainly don't moon about the past.

But she did moon about the past, and what she learned and saw in India did change and stay with her. There's an element of fear in her calm, a tremor in it, even as she hoped that steady action and sensible living would keep the dark eye of bad luck from finding her. That of course is also mythic thinking. Bad luck found her anyway. No one understood Dad's accident. Witnesses said it was incredibly strange. It wasn't as if he'd steered toward the tree. One woman said it seemed that the tree had reached out to him, but that's crazy, she added, in her official testimony. That couldn't possibly have happened.

My brother believes in his tables and forecasts and cool appraisals, the building of financial systems and chemical plants. My own work's a little more impassioned, but it's not as if I drink the bad water in the countries where the projects I write up are taking place. Poems, in their way, are attempts to make small things exact, but they're poems, not the redistribution of wealth. In finding Mark, I tried to turn marriage and family into a challenge to the world's grim news. These were compromises, all of them, between Dad's desire to soothe and Rose's view that this was condescension. I want to talk to Lev about all this, especially about the Indian interpretations of obligation and suffering. The Upanishads, typically earnest, say that purity of heart is the guide to trust. I can't even begin to describe this state much less feel it. Openness to all sensation and thought, blended with stamina, Tagore suggests: "I have suffered and despaired and known death and I am glad that I am in this great world."

The goat down below the balcony bleats again, a loud sound for such a small animal. The boys are still trying to sell cigarettes from their towel, and I tune in again to the conversation between the young travelers. "Bombs, man," says Harry, the one with the curlier hair, his hand tracing a trajectory through the air. "Exploding all over the place. We were in this houseboat drinking tea, and it started in the market." The houseboat, he says, started to shake and kick up waves. The whole bloody lake, he says, was jiggling.

"Yeah," says Victor, laughing. "Then this fire started on

shore, in a tea shack, and all these Kashmiris started racing out of the houseboats, screaming." Did he find it funny, the propensity of Kashmiris to scream when a bomb went off and a fire started? I think I understand his laughter: not callousness merely or a desire to impress the girls with his English cool, because his hands have started trembling a little and he is looking, for the first time it seems to me, at the river. His glance has pulled away, and his words don't match what he is feeling. The humor has gone hollow because there is no way to make a jiggling lake be funny.

The Spanish girls respond as they can, which is literally. They only have this language to communicate. "You were laughing?" Marisol says, putting down her glass with a tap on the table where they had crowded their tea and ashtray and lighters. "Their houses they are burning, and you are laughing? Maybe children are hurt." Luz makes a comment to her in Spanish, the Castilian *c*'s in her words dragging into lisps, which makes it hard for me, used to Mexican and Puerto Rican accents, to understand. But her tone is clear. They might like the boys around to protect them as they walk down the street or change money, but they don't like this.

"No," protests Harry, "that's not it. It was just, like, so weird." He's at sea, not so much in his native tongue, but with the power of words to capture strangeness. I sympathize. Most language feels pretty useless when trying to describe what I've seen so far of India.

Luz sighs and whispers to her friend, then tells the boys she is going to her room to rest. Once she has left, I can feel the shape of the conversation wanting to include another person. They are thinking about bringing me into it, but I decide to bury myself in my notebook. I watch Mr. Dutt's son as he leans against the balcony, occasionally sending a perfect gob of spit to the street or calling loudly to a pack of boys. I haven't seen his mother. Women bustle about the kitchen in the back of the hotel, but they don't come out to deal with customers. It's the boys and men who handle the tricky interactions with us. He pours me more tea. In the growing darkness I can just make out the boys on the ghat folding up their goods in the towel they've used for display. Harry, Victor, and Marisol are silent. Smoke wreathes the air above their heads. I miss Lev more sharply than I'd like to. The heat goes down slightly. Tagore, again, helps me to see what's in front of me, that clarification enough for now: "The evening sky to me is like a window, and a lighted lamp, and a waiting behind it." The goat bleats again, but it is too dark to see it now.

I sent a fax to James, because Rose, of course, doesn't have one. "Please, James, come here with Rose. Both of you. Check into flights to Calcutta. I'll write in the next couple of days." When you are from a family where people don't talk a lot, it is possible to dispense with ornament. I didn't have to waste sentiment on James. He would know I meant it. He'd respect that I wouldn't ask casually. The young guy who manned the fax read the message with interest. No pretense at privacy, which I appreciated. "Your husband?" he asked. "My brother," I explained. "No husband?" he asked, and I said, "Just a disappointing one."

"Quite common, the disappointment," he said. Reduced charge for the fax, he added. I missed Dad badly then; he would have enjoyed the exchange and the unexpected generosity, the way a transaction can be both intimate and polite at once. A dozen people might have to brush their teeth at a pump in the street, but they manage to do so without looking at anyone else, as if they were all in their own separate bathrooms instead of leaning away from a rickshaw driving so close it mottles their fresh clothes with dust. Despite all the gods, Dad

would have loved it here in general—though love is a complicated word in relation to this country. I wonder if he ever
wanted to come. Would Rose have forbidden it? I am guessing
that he would have looked at India as well as any outsider
can—with a heady blend of admiration, pleasure, horror, and
sheer awe. It works! I can imagine him saying, wedging into a
bus, refusing to take a seat, holding a mother's child while she
got herself settled. It was his great talent: stepping close to people's lives, never denying their pain or difficulty, and trying as
hard as he could to let them know he was paying attention. Lev
reminds me of him, with his careful hands and his attentive way
of dealing with things that have cracked. It occurs to me that
that's what Dad might have thought he was getting into with
Rose. He was probably surprised and chastened to find out
how guarded her broken pieces were, how she wouldn't allow
any of us near them.

This morning, instead of walking, I went for a boat ride past
the cremation ghats at dawn. The tendons of my boatman's
wrists pressed against his taut skin. A red holy mark was
smudged between his eyes. The powder is hard to wash off: it
threads along the palms, the folds in the neck. I bought some in
the gullies the other day and pressed a few small dots between
my eyebrows; the colors are still staining my hands. I hadn't
meant to get it elsewhere, but streaks traveled all over me.
Meteor trails of purple and green.

As the mist spread along the water, I realized how still it
was on the river. We were far enough from shore not to hear
the temple bells as anything more than a muffled tinkling. Sadhus' robes hung like orange flags on porches. I watched the
action on Dashashvamedha, the main ghat. The stairs were
fringed with palm-thatched tea stalls and makeshift shelters for
the yogis. Old women squatted to dunk brass pots into the

Ganges. Young foreigners sat blinking in the sun, taking cautious sips of tea.

We passed Manikarnika, the main burning ghat. Firewood was piled in neat stacks to the edge of the water. When I'd walked past them earlier, funerals had just ended, but Lev, walking with me, had quoted more poetry. " 'This is Manikarnika, where death is auspicious, / where life is fruitful, / where one grazes the pastures of heaven.' " He'd been silent as we looked at the piles of ashes and the gray-dusted men who poke the flames and attend to the pyres. Today, however, there were bodies wrapped in gold foil. The rib cage of a white cow sank into the river near its edge. Around it floated garlands of marigolds, and past that swam men in loincloths. Next to the corpses were washermen smacking dirt from wet saris and sheets on the rocks that fringe the banks. Dead men next to swimmers next to cows next to laundry. The pink of a sari dried in crisp pleats of silk along the steps. The wood popped with the heat, the gold foil melted. A widow, a tiny woman in white, the color she would wear for the rest of her life, put her face in her hands.

I thought, of course, of Dad. After learning that he had died, I couldn't take a full breath. Most mornings I still woke up with the sensation of not having air in my lungs. James had phoned me, and I knew from one word, "Annie?" that one of them was gone. My brother hadn't called me that in years. The grief about Dad will be slow to fade, stubborn as a bad stain and fiercer than that. It alters you, rearranges your organs, complicates your cells. Memory could finger me at any time— Dad in running shorts as he drank a glass of lemonade; padding out to get the Sunday paper; mincing garlic on the ancient cutting board—bits of our experience come flying back without being bidden, without the possibility of living them again. What was once casually duplicable, so common it was hardly worth remarking on, was lost.

I would not be at Mark's side when he died. That, too, took the air from me, but then the sensation left. What stayed was unexpected: I badly wanted someone in my life—not to prop myself up against, not to tie myself to, but to enjoy, to know with such sympathy that I would have to expand myself to accommodate the extra generosity. I had grabbed at Mark. He felt pecked at, stolen from. I had loved him with insufficient patience, tact, or hope. I had helped diminish him when I thought I was showing him how much I loved him. It was time to apologize for that. He might have done the leaving, but the way I'd translated love had helped him get there. My heart ran in a rhythm that couldn't possibly be normal. The foil fell away. The bodies smoked. I glanced at the boatman to see if he was looking at me, but he was focused on a spot onshore toward which he was steering.

He pulled up at the bank, and a small girl hopped on. "Mine," he said, pointing to his daughter with a curved nail. He smiled. Her name was Guriya. She carried a cloth bag through which I saw the arched spine of a fish. I wondered how often she caught a ride with her father. The sun was high. I offered Guriya some Marie biscuits, which she ate while looking at me. She wore her hair in two braids whose ends were anchored with a bobby pin to her scalp, so that loops like empty paisleys bobbed by her ears. None of us spoke. I wondered if James had answered the fax. I gave the boatman and Guriya more biscuits. I noticed what I thought was a bruise on my hand, but it was only another remnant of the purple powder I'd bought in the market. Below the color lay some flakes of mica that Indians mix in to make the holy stuff stick, to make it shine.

James had scribbled, "Am working on it. Will let you know in a couple of days." I had no idea how happy the possibility of their coming here would make me. Classically terse, but if there was no chance, he would have told me. The fax man gleefully waved the sheet in the air when he caught sight of me; that's how I first knew the news wasn't bad. I wrote back, "Thank you, James."

I met Lev for tea and told him about the boat ride. Not about how stingily I had loved my husband, but about the cremation. He explained about the hierarchy of death, that it cost fifty rupees for a cheapie in the crematorium, but upwards of ten thousand for an authentic one with wood and incense and incantation. He also loaned me his copy of *Lonesome Dove* to supplement my reading. He'd groaned when I showed him my fresh copies of Tagore and the Hindu scriptures as well as my new books about Siva. "Lighten up, Anna," Lev said. "This place is too hard to take when you don't have a good read."

"A western?" I asked. Former soldier, yoga student, inoculator of small children, speaker of Hindi, reader of McMurtry.

"Great stuff," Lev insisted. When it got too crowded in Varanasi, he turned, he said, to the plains. He'd found a place in Calcutta where you could buy everything from Zane Gray to Louis L'Amour. I was impressed. I'd seen the Eliot and the Kipling in their bookshops, but Lev had turned up a stash of pulp fiction.

We sat in a restaurant a few blocks inland from the river and looked at cows lolling their way through the traffic. "Tell me more about your work," he said. "I like the people there," I said, and thought about my kind boss who'd given me stacks of material on India before I left, as well as a week more leave than what I'd asked for. "Stay safe," she had said. "Come back with stories." I thought about Mira and her command of five languages, and all the other busy, hardworking colleagues who wanted badly for things to go better for people who lived in harsh conditions. The bustle and thrum of the office, the deadlines and the pleasure of getting the nod from a big foundation. I was proud of what I did, but I also wanted to admit that I was tired of my job being the only part of my life that functioned well. There were other pieces I wanted to have flourish. Lev waited. I was conscious of his strong arms and wanting to say something that would make him put them around me. I wanted even more to say something that was as true as I could make it. "It bothers me that it's just about the only thing that's left."

"Stay here awhile," Lev said, and ordered more tea, purposely not meeting my eyes, reaching for a casual note and missing it. Young enough not to be able to mask tone and feeling entirely. "Teach. Learn some Hindi."

"Like this," I said, reciting from my Hindi phrase book, which offered translations for "Let's go ice-skating!" and "Doctor, is this an abscess?"

"Yes, exactly. You're good at it. You're getting better. You get the accent."

"No," I said, not daring to look at him either. "No more words, not right now." It wasn't that words didn't fit here, I said, though they didn't. It was more that the whole country was itself the most concrete metaphor I'd ever run across. Especially this city. A street corner with a candy kiosk turns out to be one of Siva's eyebrows. And once you know one layer, there's always another to peel away. I told him about sitting on the ghats one morning, getting used to the sun, when I sensed that someone had sat down next to me. I turned and saw a rishi, a seer, in white robes, with long hair and eyes partially opened in meditation. But it was his fingernails, all ten of them grown to talons far longer than an eagle's, that really got me. I told Lev I knew we were not looking at the same Ganges.

"Of course not," he said. "You never are; you never will be."

I shook my head and said, "That's what's hard. Feeling that I never know what I'm seeing."

"It's not easy for Indians, either," he answered. "You're avoiding the point. That's Kant, twelve years and a Ph.D. later, and no solutions even after that. How do we know what we know? Yes, ask it, think about it, but do something at the same time." A cow walked past us, swaying its grand, cavernous hindquarters. Scaffolding hung with skin. Architecture as sophisticated in its homely way as the Sydney Opera House, yet shit-smeared and someone's source of milk, too. Beaten, even, but never killed.

"Do they really want us here? Not Americans certainly." I didn't mention the general response to Israelis; over and over, I'd heard bleak mutterings about them. Many of them came and bought motorcycles, restless after army service, and they could be a rough crowd. "They kicked the Peace Corps out years ago."

He paused. Flies hummed in stereo around our faces. "Depends on what you mean by 'want,' " he said. "The government might not, and the antidevelopment squad is loud, but that kid on the street"—he pointed to a boy on a bicycle—"might like nothing more than to learn enough English to get into a decent school." He swished the flies away with his long hands. "Besides," he said, "why is it so scary doing something that you want? What if you used your luck, being here, to do something you like?"

I leaned over and poured him more tea. "The only thing I know I like for sure is sitting here, pouring tea for you, watching you want to kill the flies and not doing it," I said. I could also easily have added that I was watching the way the sun glinted on his arm and the way he nodded at people he recognized in the street. Even a fraction of time made for everyone he knew. He was giving me time, too, time he was hoping to expand, and he'd been brave and kind enough to say it. Only twenty-seven and already so courageous. We looked at each other then, not smiling exactly.

Eleven o'clock the next morning, and I am sick, still under the sheet in my room, the fan at full blast overhead. I unplugged the Knightie Knight. Maybe its poison is what has made me feel so ill. Lev stopped by to say hello, discovered I wasn't well, and went to make sure that Mr. Dutt would check on me. He also asked a series of pointed questions to see if I had dysentery, and it startled me that I did not mind describing my symptoms. He was concerned, but he didn't think it was anything more than the usual Indian trouble, and he told me the best thing was to drink weak tea and eat rice. He also loaned me a Dick Francis. More horses? It's not the horses so much, he said. "It's another antidote to India. It's all plot: so predictable. You know exactly who's bad and who's good and that the hero gets to sleep with the girl." But that piece of the speech had gotten the better of him, and he turned his back to me so he could adjust the angle of the slats of the shutter. "You have twenty-four hours to get better. I haven't read it yet," Lev told me. I am relieved that someone knows where I am and that I am not, just now, traveling quite solo.

It could have been the *lassi* or opening my mouth during a shower. Or perhaps it is that Lev likes me enough to disagree with me and to look at me with understanding and to be tactful about what he asks. In other words, as much as I like him. But this is also terrifying, and thoughts of Mark return in sharp detail. Memory after memory, over and over, and instead of wearing themselves down, they get stronger and stronger, as heavy as an inherited, unloved house.

"We're done," Mark said when he left. "Keep the plants."

Keep the plants? Keep the fucking plants? "I don't want the plants!" I yelled. I want us, you, in the bed, Saturday mornings over coffee, solving the crossword, our brains and voices scratchy from a party the night before. Scrambling for the atlas to find the name of the largest island in the Philippines. Shrieking, "Luzon! How stupid!" Visiting my parents and inventing suburban personas. Dick and Lydia Fitch, golfers, sippers of gin, wearers of plaid. What's going to happen to Dick and Lydia? Mark telling me about slate from Turin so expensive that only kings and drug lords could afford it for the roofs of their love nests, something in it able to drown out sound even in thin layers. Making love. We always did that well. But that wasn't a skill he limited to me. Her name was Nicole. She was young, she was deep into theory since she hadn't been alive long enough to acquire many actual experiences. He lied for a long time about why he wasn't home when he was supposed to be. Hours of silence would pass with no reassuring message, and then he'd be astonished that I should have allowed grim pictures to enter my head. "And you want children?" he would ask. "You'd be ruined with anxiety."

Mark was thirty-five when he left, and we had been married for five years, but he had not wanted animals, much less kids. "You knew that about him," my father had scolded. "You knew that." I thought he would change, I told Dad, and at first I wasn't even entirely sure that I wanted children, either. But then friends started having or adopting babies, and I got to hold them, and longing exploded like a slow comet: to crook my body over something that small and warm, to rock in my arms such a delicate piece of the world. It wasn't explicable, the desire to make a baby. There was no justifying it through hormones, the pressure of culture, or deepening self-knowledge. It wasn't what we quarreled over at the end, but that was where it started. When I didn't want to let a friend's baby go. When I kept kissing her pliant head.

But what about the ozone layer and world population? Mark asked. The selfishness of reproduction. Someone with my politics, he implied, should worry more.

I know, I know, I told him. It embarrasses me to be so human and ordinary, to sound so much like Lydia Fitch. I just want a baby, a little person to take care of. I promise, no plaid, no field hockey. "In New York?" he said, appalled. "You'd bring kids into this?" his arm sweeping around to include my messy desk, the ringing phone, salsa music rolling in through the window. New York in all its unstoppableness. When I'd answered that yes, I would—I would even introduce it to the bad-mannered landlord and take it to Katz's Deli—he said, "You are so selfish." What he had not said was that he had stopped loving me.

Varanasi honks away; the fan beats the air to a breeze; my stomach aches. I lie here reading about improbably tall jockeys, steeplechasing, and then stop to write, to remember Mark and Dad. I wish I could unclip myself from all those troubling scenes from the past. Rose and I have this in common, this carting around of burdensome stories. But telling them doesn't always make them easier to bear.

Mr. Dutt's son Ram has just come by to get me another pot of tea. We never speak much, but we seem to like each other's company. He borrows my pens, and he's very careful with them. I have given him a piece of paper, and he is sitting on the chair in my room drawing while I watch him and write. It's the best I've felt all day. He's paying very close attention to what he is making. He's lost in it. All I want to do now is drink the cooling tea and watch how hard he concentrates on drawing fighter jets. I know that's what he's making. He's given me three of his earlier pictures.

But I was wrong. Ram's picture was of a foreigner on a bicycle, tall and thin as a Swede, his Indian pants billowing out so far that they'd become sails. His glasses were flying off his face. He was about to fall, and he looked both frightened and a little gleeful.

I finished the Dick Francis, and as soon as I was done, I realized I felt well enough to go out. I spent the rest of the day exploring, and found Harry and Victor in a café near our hotel as they described an encounter with a leper colony on pilgrimage. "Stubs," was all Harry could say. "Putrid," Victor added. I'd seen the lepers, too, and it was daunting. No noses, pigment worn from their faces, hands like clubs, several hundred of them from Orissa, come for the cleansing of their illness or their sins, or both. Or to die. Some of them looked ready for that.

There's no tranquil passing through this country. I think of Lev's questions again, why not stay and lend a hand, learn something in return. An exchange of gifts? I hear Mark say. And what skills do you have? Repairing hyphenation? Writing keynote speeches?

How much influence do you get to have in a life? I think about Rose and her cautious solutions after a difficult start. We should be more careful about whom we love and know. It all accumulates. Rose said we were more responsible than we felt, the great tally of actions affecting who we are and who we're likely to become.

For the devout Hindu, moving out of life in the City of Light means that you get flung somewhere past the grim cycle of the soul trudging through the same old horror. If you're lucky enough to die in Varanasi, you skid out of all of that, and you're not even you at this point, but a piece of overarching consciousness, a quiver of air or spirit that's curvy with intelligence or love. Something that is not, as the Sanskrit perplexingly has it. Something the earthbound can't grasp. Heaven not as a destination but as a form of total knowledge blown past the confines of a body. It sounds as if it's past everything. Something so big that even concepts as large as "all" or "knowledge" or "total" or "universe" can't contain it. Something not pinned down by so flimsy and indeterminate a thing as language or letters, even the feathery strokes of Pali.

I was sitting on the ghat thinking about this and about the lepers, when I felt a warm tap on my shoulder. A woman in a blue sari had seated herself next to me. She was ripply with fat and began talking to me in Hindi as if I could understand, and when I said, "Please slow down," she only spoke louder, the way people do when someone is hard of hearing. She reached into her purse and gave me a cardboard rectangle the size of the baseball cards James and I used to collect. It was a picture of Jesus, with a halo around his curly golden tresses and those large, warm, kitten-y eyes that Indians give all gods. I had to laugh. I pressed him to my forehead the way people here do with the picture of everyone who's holy. She said, *"Bahut accha"* when I sat up straight. Very good. And I did feel better, my head aching with the sun, Jesus in my palm, the Indian missionary patting my back, the spiced smell of her hair flowing out around us. She stood, gave me her hand to hoist me up, and then, thwapping at the dust on my pants, she said, in English, "Pray, you tall girl."

James has sent another fax. "News not so good, madam," the fax man said this time as he saw me coming into the shop. He gave me the curled paper. "Rose being stubborn. Still working on it." Abu is slim and wears a large, drooping mustache. He loves managing all this correspondence abroad, except to Israel. Circuits are always jammed there, and the Israelis are not

patient, he says. He speaks some French and Spanish. Maybe
the Israelis are less favored as customers because the Hebrew
alphabet defeats him and his access to their news. I asked him
why he ran the shop. "Good money," he said, shrugging, and he
couldn't afford to go to university. Four sisters, father dead a
couple of years ago. "I play tabla," he told me shyly. "I am
studying with a master." I noticed the pads of callus on his fin-
gertips. It looked like he practiced very hard. He told me that
to play the trilling notes well, first you had to sing them. To
hear them purr in your throat. He asked then, "Who is Rose?
Another sibling?"

"No," I told him. "Our mother."

"And you are calling her by a given name?" he asked, scan-
dalized.

"You'd have to know her," I told him, but he might be right.
Perhaps it's time to reconsider this. It's been so long since I've
called her anything else. Mom or Mum or Mother all sound
ridiculous, far too cozy and lacking in respect. Rose still feels
better. "It's hard to explain," I told him. "Americans are a little
crazy."

"That is the absolute truth, madam," Abu said, nodding as
he took my reply to James: "Work with it, James. You both
need to get here. I'm leaving for Calcutta in three days."

"Only three?" Abu said as the machine sang its off-key
scales. "You must be watching out for those Bengalis. Real
tricksters."

"And Benarsis?" I asked him, forking over money. His rates
had doubled in a week. Rising telephone costs, he explained.

"Lord Siva's chosen people, madam."

Lev and I sat on Raj Ghat to watch the pujas for the full moon,
which seemed to be enacting its own purification as it rose

through layers of pollution, moving from deep orange to apricot, golden yellow to canary, cream to eggshell, and, finally, high above us, chalk white. We listened to the chanting, stared at the flickering candles, made way for pilgrims, drank tea. Lev was talking about the lepers' clinic. Wrapping wounds, pulling out maggots. He explained how the disease shuts down nerves, so people don't know they've cut themselves or got a festering sore. It runs in families, but it's not genetic. The disease is bacterial, and it takes familial closeness to spread it. Months and months of sleeping next to the same person. Unless you see poverty as part of the genetic code, he added—something incredibly hard not to live out if it's been your way for generations. Poor immune systems, inadequate diets, bad health care, and bad water made people prone to it, so whole villages could still suffer. Less of it now, of course. India had the world's biggest middle class. But it was still a problem.

There was only one leper colony in existence in the States, I said. In Louisiana, and they didn't call it leprosy anymore, they called it Hansen's disease, as if that tidied it up.

"Tidy up," he said, testing the phrase. "You sound British sometimes."

"It's funny," I said. "It works into your language, and you don't mean it to happen. It's just part of you. I hear words here, and I think of my mother. Petrol and windscreen." I'd told him about trying to get Rose to come to India, though I still hadn't mentioned what she'd written about her childhood. I didn't want to talk about why I didn't want to read it. The story was private, written in the fog, given to me not quite confidentially, but quietly. Not information to be bandied about.

"You miss her," Lev said. I did, I admitted. She was spiny, but she was what I had.

"I don't miss mine," he said. "My sisters, yes, but not my parents. Not yet."

"But you haven't been back in five years. You really don't want to see them? What if something happens to them, or you?" Even more, I was curious about why the gulf had to be so complete. What was he running from? Had he been jilted? Was he a bad soldier? A poet in a country where poets have to bear arms? A recovering addict? A God junkie? What was I missing?

He looked at me and said, "No, and nothing went wrong. I just like it here. Being with little kids and sick people in a place where it all, all of life, happens right in front of you." I could have asked if that wasn't true in Israel, but I knew what he meant. What was allowed to happen in public in India was breathtaking, as was the intensity with which beauty and horror smacked into each other.

He lit another cigarette and looked at the black river tinged with silver. It was getting late. "I don't know what's going to happen." He made this seem eminently sane, though I doubted it was that simple. God was definitely involved. He'd mentioned his mother's fervent beliefs, his father's relative skepticism, a split enacted by his sisters as well. It wasn't over, whatever struggle there was between him and religion. He had layers of stories to relate. He hadn't finished telling them, even to himself, and that was one reason he listened well. He was still curious.

A man holding a trident passed us. We made sure he could get down to the water. After only a few days here, this is no longer a strange sight. I mentioned this to Lev, and he said that these days it was Western children or a new motorcycle that looked odd to him. "Things without dents," I said, and the bells started to clang in the temple behind us. He wanted to touch my hand or knee, but it is wrong to show open affection between men and women in India. Boys can drape themselves on one another, girls cling to each other's hands, but men and women keep themselves yards apart. That he did not reach for

me was oddly delicate and all the more arousing, his reticence a
sign of his respect for where we were and his willingness to live
within its strictures. We walked back to my hotel, and I
thought he was going to wish me good night in the courtyard
and go, but he took my hand and pressed it against his own,
making a lumpy star of double thickness. Palm to palm, and I
could feel through the tip of my ring finger the strong beat of
his pulse.

"You look like my sister," he said. "That long hair. It is so
pretty when she lets it out of the braid."

"It wouldn't be now," I said, but I didn't withdraw my hand.
A shower technique that involved buckets of cold water had
left my hair thick and still quite dirty. I didn't want to lie to this
kind man shining in the moonlight, looking hungry and shy at
once. He didn't do this much, I suspected.

I was glad that India forced us to modesty and slowness. It
gave me time to realize that I wanted to show him before he
touched me how the skin puckers inside my elbow. The star of
burst capillaries on my calf—not even to make an image out of
the flaw, but to reveal to him, this is a body on its way toward
forty. This is what happens. I'm a record of my years, and
there's no denying them. "My hair needs washing, Lev, and
there's gray in it, too, and look," I said, turning my head
to catch the moon, "wrinkles," a web of them by my eye. I
wouldn't, I knew, have been bold enough to do that in the mer-
ciless Indian sun.

It was, for once, quiet in the courtyard. The stairs that led to
the hotel were dark, as was the lobby. The other guests were either in bed or still out. Mr. Dutt and his family were probably
asleep. The alleyway, which I could glimpse because the moon
was so bright, was empty, not even a cow ambling there, flies
miraculously absent, though of course it smelled still of hay and
shit.

"I see all that, Annaji," Lev said, pulling me closer. "I see you're too thin and that you bite your nails, which is a bad idea in India." I smelled his heat and tobacco and something Indian, like old incense. It felt easy to wrap my arms around his waist and to breathe his smokiness. "And you are half dead because you're sad, and you don't trust me, because I am young and I live here. You're worried I'm a little crazy. You're worried about AIDS. You're worried you might want to stay here with me, and then I'll leave because eight years' difference in our ages is a lifetime, and how could I know what I want."

"Well," I said, my finger tracing his cheekbone, moving along the line of stubble. "That's about right." We managed to get ourselves seated on the stairs without knocking over the plants on each step. We leaned our foreheads together. A sudden swarm of gnats whirred near our faces. Pilgrims chanted somewhere by the river, and the sound floated toward us. But no one entered the courtyard, and the only noise in the alleyway came from an unsteady cyclist steering his way home.

Lev reached then to pull the loose fabric of my tunic off my shoulder. He nudged down the bra strap and exposed a triangle of skin. I'd been expecting kisses, but he reached over to move his fingers in a fluttering pattern near my collarbone. "Guess," he said, and I realized he was spelling, moving from my throat toward the wedge of my armpit, sketching a word with light quick strokes in an alphabet I didn't know. Not Pali, because he moved from right to left.

"It's Hebrew," I said, then added, because he'd written with both hesitation and pleasure, "House."

"Orchard," he told me. "There's a peach orchard my father helps take care of, and you will love those trees."

"Another," I said, and he spelled again, more roughly this time. "Smoke," I told him.

"Close," he said. "War," and he cupped my shoulder with his hand and leaned his head there. That was why he left. He's not a bad soldier; he'd been too good. He's telling me about the people that he killed. I rocked him, my lips on his short hair.

"My turn," I said into his ear, and took his right arm, pulling back his shirt to reveal the cords of his tendons, the ones that must have tightened when he pulled a trigger. I smoothed his skin as if clearing a slate, and spelled in Spanish *mi amor*. My love. Darling. Cherished person. "Strength," he said, his head still pressed on my shoulder.

"Exactly," I answered, and kissed his wrist.

"There's nowhere to go," he said, sounding miserable, and I knew he meant more than Varanasi. I imagined us making love above the rough music of the falling ladles or in the thin bed behind Mr. Dutt's thin door. The problem didn't stop there, and would have been easy to handle if it had been confined to mattresses. It was hard to say what sort of place would open itself to us, what kind of language or city. A light went on above us. Mr. Dutt or one of his sons, perhaps. We unwove our arms and bodies. "One more," Lev said as he pulled my clothing straight. "On your hand."

Confident, deep strokes now. "Patience," I said.

"You're not brave enough," Lev chided. "Promise." A small burst of Hindi came from the lobby. We stood up slowly. Mr. Dutt probably didn't know we were even there, but it wouldn't do to have him discover us. He was punctilious about his rules, and who was I to blame him. It was his country. We smoothed ourselves down.

"Sleep well," I told Lev. "I'm going to read more *Lonesome Dove* tonight."

He nodded. "The open range. Maybe that's what's next."

"Maybe," I said, his last word still sitting on my palm.

"Don't let the bedbugs bite," he said, and we laughed in the moonlight because as usual in India, that was nothing we had control over. It seemed a small miracle that desire could overcome the certainty that our bodies would be covered in angry red spots, that in spite of the bumps and the scratches, we'd told each other, Yes, I know about those, but they won't stop me wanting you. Orchard. War. Strength. Promise.

The pollution is heavy today, and my mood not much better. Lev has pulled back, claiming a need to spend more time at the clinic. I should have known, I've been saying to myself. I should have remembered nothing but his youth. I'm here at the Most Welcome because Mr. Dutt has advised me not to go out. A bad wind, he said, and he gave me a surgical mask. It happens sometimes before monsoon. A good sign, in its way. Harry and Victor didn't listen, and neither did Luz or Marisol. Brash in the face of warnings, which I am not. There are many I've not taken seriously enough. People in the street were also protecting themselves. Women in saris clutched the white ovals to their mouths as if they were about to head into an operating theater. Others chose handkerchiefs, which made even the businessmen—the babus with their serious glasses and ties and short-sleeved shirts—look like bandits. The word for gangster, I've learned, is *goonda*. Maybe a better translation is brigand or even thug, a word that's Indian in origin, for robbers who committed crimes in honor of Kali. *Goonda* is performing one of those lexical tricks: once you learn a word, you see it everywhere, as well as its actual reference. There they were on Assi Ghat, spitting *paan*. A band of men with oiled, curled hair, the local pack of *goondas*. I wondered if they were armed. The crimes described in the paper usually involve knives, rope, or lengths of pipe, like the thuggees of the nineteenth century.

There have been headlines the last two days about caches of AK-47s found in Kashmir, submachine guns piled in heaps like jagged logs ready for a bonfire. I don't know if it was just the weather making me think this, but I have been more conscious of the soldiers everywhere, the casual swing of their weapons against their often bony flanks. Policemen go barefoot sometimes in this country, but they are almost always armed, even if only with billy clubs. I wondered if Mr. Dutt had a gun. He was very careful about whom he let into his hotel.

I've been remembering Dad's face when he came back one night from the hospital after trying to treat a girl who'd been shot by her brother with their father's pistol. She had died in surgery. He got quietly and thoroughly drunk, and Rose sat there with him, making him take a cup of tea for every glass of whiskey. I surprised the two of them at the kitchen table. They weren't holding hands or touching each other, but were bound in a kind of closeness that made my breath catch. What was possible between adults was thicker than the ties they had with either of their children. Rose and Dad faced the terrible evening with tea and whiskey and were that much more grateful for each other and the grief that had brought them there.

Eight hours later—a bad span that seems a continuation of the bad air that's invaded the city. I'm writing from the hospital at Benares Hindu University. In the smog yesterday, Harry was killed by a small truck. His head was crushed, the roundest part of the skull flattened and shattered. I know because I saw his skull fragmented into flakes like shale. There was hair attached to the pieces. He was the curlier one.

I had been in my room, drinking tea, reading, thinking of getting up for food or a walk, to shake off the bleak feeling of the day. I was reaching for my surgical mask when I heard pounding footsteps. It was Mr. Dutt, crying, "Terrible accident, madam, please to be coming now." Marisol and Luz had found him by chance at the market, where they'd been with Harry and Victor, bargaining for a sitar. Harry stepped out into the street, holding the big instrument, looking for a rickshaw, and he'd been struck. Mr. Dutt explained these details to me when his motor scooter had to slow down to avoid a person, a car, a cow. We were not wearing helmets. I didn't think about refusing to go, but I didn't know that Harry was dead until I got to the hospital and saw Marisol and Luz. No hope left in them. Their minds already back in Madrid, in their mothers' arms, in their soft beds. They were done.

It's about 1 a.m., but it could just as well be midmorning. The streams of people coming through the doors and settling on the floor make the building feel less like a hospital and more like a bus station. Harry hadn't been brought in an ambulance. Another truck, one right behind the one that hit him, had apparently slammed on the brakes and stopped. Its driver had scooped up Harry and torn off. Probably leaving pieces of his brain on the street and probably staining his own clothes with them, too. The sitar was nowhere in sight. The driver who'd brought Harry in was gone by the time I got to the hospital. The girls couldn't have identified him, the same way they wouldn't have been able to say what the man who struck Harry looked like. The killer bolted while the crowd looked glumly on. At least that's what I'd gathered from Marisol, who was smoking and frightened and shaking, all of which further derailed her English. I could be making this up.

Right now the girls are dozing near me. They are wrapped around each other, their jackets thrown over their heads, sighing in their light sleep. They will be as exhausted when they wake as they were a few hours ago. Victor is off trying to find a bathroom, and when he gets back, I will try to talk with the hospital administrator about processing Harry's papers. The parents haven't been called yet. The number is back at the hotel.

Mr. Dutt has returned to his hotel, too. I've become the elder statesman of the group, the grown-up in charge of the young foreigners. I'm the one who will have to explain it all. What Mr. Dutt did not know is that I've got experience in this realm. I lost my father just this way, in an accident out of the blue. I wonder if he sensed it.

In the last day, time has suddenly appeared to have sped up, to move at a radically different pace. The ride to the hospital, our arrival here, seeing Victor vomit in a corner near the single plant—a palm tree that was barely alive. Marisol and Luz were all tangled hair and lisped *c*'s, not even bothering with English. "Cut it out," I told them. "Give me a handkerchief," which one of them did. I wet it with water from my bottle and went to Victor to help him mop himself clean.

"I should have stopped him," he kept sobbing. He'd reached out to grab his friend, but he'd missed. Now his arms were wrapped around his own body. I settled him with the girls, gave them my biscuits and water, and told them, fiercely, not to move. The Indian patients and their families watched with cautious detachment. I noticed, as I went in search of a doctor, how illness here was a family affair. Patients were surrounded by children, blankets, bags of food and clothing. Encampments. And the illnesses were advanced: goiters swallowed necks, tumors ballooned on faces. No doubt it took a great deal of time and money even to get here, and the trouble, in the meantime, would have had room to grow.

Eventually a tall man named Dr. Desai said, "You want the British chap?" and he showed me to a room full of stretchers lit with uncertain fluorescent tubes. He pulled the sheet down from Harry's face. I remembered that I had not seen Dad after his accident, that we were told we would not recognize him. Rose went in, but James and I decided not to, shielding ourselves from pictures we did not want to hold on to. I wished then, watching Harry's still, blue face, that I had made the effort, just to know for sure that he had really died. It is so clear, seeing a dead body, that the animating force has left. Death is obvious, not even in the stillness or the chill of the skin, but in the sheer nakedness of the face, the set of the expression. The lack of awareness of another person watching.

"Not a chance, the poor blighter," said Dr. Desai. His English was English English. "Smashed like a watermelon." The bleeding had stopped, but the wound was open. "He just got here. His papers are still to be processed. We'll keep him in the morgue a day or so, but it's a good idea to get him shipped home. The heat and all," he said, being medical, being not at all pleased to have a dead British boy here.

I didn't want anyone talking like that about Harry. He was someone's son. Then I saw the doctor crouching down to pick up a girl who'd run into the room, scooting past a brother who had chased her. I saw the man crook her into his body and speak gently. Why waste time on the dead? There are children to look after.

I touched Harry's hand and saw how slender his fingers were. He was wearing a cheap Indian cotton shirt, fanned with blood. I wondered if he'd ever gotten to kiss one of the girls. I doubted it. I doubted he'd kissed many at all. Then the lights went out. It was black for a few seconds, totally so, and I kept touching Harry's hand. Then came the thin beams of flashlights—torches, as the Indians still call them—bouncing through the air, and the chatter of Hindi as people made sure their families were still together, as they accounted for one another. I pulled the sheet back over Harry. He'd seemed small when he was alive, but that sheet in the dimness was long and wide.

Marisol and Luz have left Varanasi. They gave Mr. Dutt a note for me on the back of a postcard of Siva at his bluest and most benign. "Thank you, Anna, from Marisol y Luz. We return now home with great sadness about everything. Kisses from us both." I've pasted it in my journal, next to Jesus.

I'd gone back to the hospital the next day with Lev, as Victor was too distraught to leave the hotel and the Spanish girls were fluttering from one travel agent to the next in their anxiety to get out. Harry had been moved. When I found him, I realized he was starting to smell. A marigold garland was draped on his chest, acrid yellow on his white sheet. They'd given him flowers, but someone had stolen his sneakers.

I got to work. Trying to locate a casket in a country that burns its dead is not easy, but Lev finally discovered a Muslim coffin dealer. I phoned the British embassy in Delhi to talk about protocol. Fantastically polite, the man on the line asked if I wanted him to call the parents. "Would that be best?" he asked. But, still polite, "No, we're not responsible for the body or for getting it back." Better to have him buried here, perhaps? I said it was up to the parents, and no, I wanted to call myself. "Best of luck," the voice said. Sticky situation.

I had promised Victor I would tell Harry's family. He was in no shape to do it, still a sobbing wreck. He was going to have to be manhandled onto the plane to London. There was no time to see if James had answered the fax. My head ached with conversations repeated three to four times on sputtering phones with sputtering clerks and minor diplomats. If it hadn't concerned a poor dead boy, some of the exchanges might have been funny. "How long will it take to get a coffin to the hospital?" A long pause ensued, followed by staticky conversation in a language that was not Hindi. Lev was listening in. I asked what they were speaking. Bengali, he said. Many Muslims here came from Bangladesh. Finally, "Two days, madam." "From across the city? Two days?" I yelled. Another pause. I felt him corralling the right words. "It is a funereal time in the Muslim community, madam. And no, it will only take two days." This shouted, very loudly. "So it will take two days," I screeched back. Then, patiently, as if to a dull or tired child, "No, no, no, madam, it will take *two* days."

All of this was easier than talking to Harry's parents. I don't know how Rose managed to tell James and then how he managed to tell me. The abrupt end to someone's life shouldn't be announced in a disembodied way. It's a double violation: a death at the wrong time, transmitted just by voice, and a voice not anchored in a person who could hold you. The woman who answered, so quiet and suspicious and English, was Harry's mother. I was in the same telephone exchange where I'd spoken to Rose, the place Indians and foreigners go to place important calls. The tourists say things like "Mum? Need more money." The Indians go, it seems, to arrange for people to pick them up at train stations and to plot family get-togethers. "Seeing you twenty-fourth. *Accha.*" The stalls offer the barest sort of privacy along with a smattering of God and graffiti. The cartoons were graphic, and some featured English. VIJAY LOVES GITA 4EVER. This one held a small shrine to Ganesh, filled with rose petals. Something was scuffling around there, I realized as I dialed the unfamiliar range of numbers. A mouse. The ringing started, and I knew I must have adjusted somewhat to India, because the mouse didn't trouble me. A rat would have. A mouse I could live with. Rose petals drifted to the floor.

The woman knew, I swear she knew even before I said a

word. I grasped that one of my parents had died as soon as
James said "Annie?" but this woman knew before I had spoken, from the series of hums and clicks that signaled a complicated overseas call. She was screaming before I finished saying
my name. "Harry! Harry! Harry!" and then the phone fell with
a smack to a wooden floor, and I could hear a man shouting to
her to calm down. I heard his voice next, only slightly more
composed. "What have you done to upset my wife?" he demanded, and I sensed exactly what Harry was escaping from.
It wasn't war, it wasn't violence on a grand scale, just a home
filled with people who were sour, cramped, chronically suspicious. People who expected the worst. People who bellowed.

I told him who I was. I told him what had happened. I said
Victor was coming home that day. I told him about the arrangements for the body, the name of the man at the consulate he
could talk to. I waited for him to ask questions, to interrupt, to
demand details. But there was nothing. I listened to his harsh
breathing. I could hear the wife's sobs. Then came the most
breathtaking streak of foul language I've ever heard. Fucking
India, fucking country, fucking Pakkies, fucking idiot drivers,
who the fuck was I to be calling and wishing him condolences
about his son? Oh God, I kept thinking, poor Harry. I hadn't
given him enough credit. I hadn't imagined widely enough. I
hadn't read the slump in his shoulders correctly. I hadn't seen
the lack of confidence and the mooniness in the right way. No
wonder he'd sniggered in the face of jiggling lakes and tea
shacks on fire. He was running from a father like mustard gas.
The meter sang away. The call was going to be almost as expensive as my hotel bill for the entire ten days.

I let him rage. The meter kept clicking. I kept saying, "I am
so sorry, Mr. Edwards. I am so sorry." The profanity clipped
along, sweeping the subcontinent away like a typhoon. We
should have stayed there, fucking drivers, taught them how to

fucking drive. He paused for breath. I heard him panting. And then he said, his voice cracking into separate pieces. "He was my boy. He was my only child."

Finally I heard Harry's mother ushering her husband off the phone. "Darling, darling, let me talk to her, let me," clucking at him, all of this amplified by satellite. She returned to the conversation, her own voice breaking but able now to hear the details about the flight, the body, the consulate. "Thank you," she said when we were done.

Groping for a way to say good-bye, I told her that my father had died recently, and I had some idea what it was like to lose someone.

"No you don't," she said, cold but raging suddenly. "I've lost my dad, I've lost my mum, but this is nothing like that," and she slammed the phone down. It took me a second to do the same, though more gingerly. Unbidden, the image of the two of them in their small Brighton house came to my mind—the pale English sun, the gulls, the tidy plot of lawn studded with gnomes. I saw them with Harry's curly hair and round face, more like brother and sister in my head than husband and wife. Mild blue eyes. Worried mouths. At least before the news. Now they weren't touching each other. They were standing apart, her hands over her face as he smashed whatever he could get his small, damp fingers on. The mouse scuffled, burrowing into its nest. More petals fell.

Harry, mock embarrassed, had shown me a picture of the cottage a couple of nights before he died. It was called something awful like High Tides or Fair Breeze, the name painted in blue italic letters on a narrow wooden sign. "Home," he said with a bent smile, flapping the rectangle. The picture did not include the parents, just the house sitting in the sun. He'd been told Indians liked seeing pictures of people's houses, so he'd brought it along to make friends. But he added to us on the balcony, "They just keep asking, 'What about your family?' And I keep saying, 'Didn't bring a snap of them.' " It seemed just then he wanted both never to go back and to be there, blinking in the seaside light, watching as his parents watered the grass, divvied up the fish and chips for tea, and argued about what television show to watch that night. Knowing—as he never would in India or anywhere else perhaps—exactly what the next moment would hold.

I headed to the fax shop afterward, grateful to have an errand to run, anything to focus my mind after that conversation. Abu spotted me down the block and came out waving a sheet of paper. "This came yesterday. Where have you been? She says she'll come!" he cried. The fax read, "We'll be there. July 3, 3:19 am. Dum Dum Airport, Calcutta, British Air Flight 459. I've got reservations at the Oberoi. Can stay ten days." A new line: "Looking forward to seeing you—James." "Such good luck," Abu said. "Your family. And the Oberoi. Very top of the line." When I had to sit down, he fetched me tea spiced with ginger and lemon. "Overcoming news," he said sympathetically. "More sugar?"

I found Lev later that afternoon, showed him the fax, and told him about Harry's parents. We drank one awful Kingfisher beer together and toasted the arrival of James and Rose. But we were still thinking about Harry's hateful father and the fact that I'd be leaving. He'd convinced me to fly to Calcutta, not to waste a day on the train. Now my family was coming: I couldn't postpone my departure from Varanasi, and I'd have to arrange for even more time away from work to travel with Rose and James. We went to our perch on Assi Ghat to watch the sunset, our knees nearly touching, and watched the graceful play of water on people's necks. Since the accident we'd barely touched, but he put his hand on my wrist and pulled me toward the water. "Take off your shoes," he said. "It won't kill you." We both knew he was wrong—fecal coliform counts in the Ganges run 250 times higher than the WHO recommends—but even so, I rolled up my pants, slipped off my sandals, and let the water slosh through my toes and up to my ankles. I wasn't, after all, drinking any. Lev stood next to me. Men and women stepped around us, next to us, filling pots and vases. The river was cool. Our feet were pale and blurred. Mine were the same size as his. "Feel different?" he asked, and I said I didn't think I'd be taking up life as a naked mendicant anytime soon. But yes, I told him, I feel different. "I can tell," he said as we sat back on the steps. "It shows." He pulled two clean handkerchiefs from his bag so I could wipe off every dangerous, sacred drop.

We spent my last day walking the ghats and talking, having agreed that he wouldn't come out to the airport. It was a long trip there, expensive, and too lonely when you had to come back by yourself. It was better, we'd decided, to say good-bye in the city itself. After dinner he walked me back to the courtyard of the Most Welcome. We sat on the stairs in the hot evening. I tried to return *Lonesome Dove*, but he wouldn't take it. "You're not done. Send it to me when you're through." I gave him a *mala*, a rosary made from lotus seeds, a beautiful old piece I'd found in a shop in the gullies, and also a lungi, the wrap men wear here, with a label that told us it was a Superman Action brand. The hero on the picture wore a lungi in addition to his red cape, his fist lifted defiantly. I also gave Lev a calendar, bought in a student bookshop. Almost every square was taken up with some event, eclipses or bank holidays, school closings or regional celebrations. I knew he would find the date I'd signaled in green, the day I was now supposed to return to New York, with my address and number and "Promise you'll write." It was also marked with a half-moon and a note that it was a day sacred to Zoroastrians.

He smiled and said, "Thank you, Annaji." He gave me the name and address of a friend in Calcutta he said I would like. A guy named Kartik who'd gone to Berkeley, a sculptor who'd come back home. "It's always good to have one person to see in a big city. And remember, Hurry Burry Spoils the Curry." I quoted back at him our other favorite: "Death and Speed: Both Have Five Letters." We liked trading the slogans painted on walls to warn drivers not to go too fast.

Then he said, and I could tell he hadn't quite meant to say it, "I wish you would stay here. Every day I would tell you how I like that English nose." He kicked a pebble on the stairs. "You are making my heart feel old and empty," he told me, an idiom gone wrong somewhere, but I knew exactly what he meant.

I could have said then, You are a Dick Francis–reading angel. You are an Israeli to cherish 4Ever. I could have said, Yes, I'll be back. But it wasn't fair to offer words that guaranteed a next time, a next step. It didn't mean I also wasn't feeling old and empty. Instead, I took his hand and traced his name, then mine, on his open palm and closed his fingers in a fist around it.

He held me for a long time, kissed me once, then stood, pressed his hands together, and held them to his chest. He'd added a good-bye the way Indians did, using their habits to pull himself together again. *"Ciao, bella,"* he said, and turned to leave, on the brink of being nimble the way Benarsis are. He was learning to move like the people he admired. I stared at him as he went out of the courtyard, but he did not look back, though he walked slowly, as if he might stop at any time.

I went upstairs to settle the bill with Mr. Dutt and engaged in a longish and respectful haggling over it. He gave me a key chain attached to a clamshell on which someone had painted the name of the hotel. "A keepsake for you from Varanasi," he said. A clamshell. Where had he gotten it? I asked. From a tourist who'd brought them up from the coast. He himself had never seen the ocean. Another story dismissed. Why clamshells? Why bring them up to Varanasi? Who was the tourist? There were other questions I wanted answers to: the origins not just of Mr. Dutt's shells, but of Dr. Desai's London English and Lev's affection for westerns. Mr. Dutt tided up the piles of rupees I'd given him and tucked them in his pocket. He was glad, I sensed, to have me gone, and he ordered a servant to sweep the hall, though it was already spotless.

I went to the balcony and sat down to look at the ghat where I'd washed my feet in the holy river. I thought about Rose and James. I'd promised myself to read the last part of my mother's story on the plane trip. It was the least I could do to thank her for coming all this way. Ram came to say good night. I went to my room and got the boy the pens he liked best and one of my spare notebooks. I took a picture of him on the balcony, sitting next to the geraniums one of the unseen women in the back had planted in an old tin. Ram smiled and smiled, used to this sort of parting gesture. He probably had dozens of these photos. This guy's from France. This one my dad kicked out because he brought girls to the room. These were missionaries from Poland. I wondered what he would draw with the pens I'd given him: more foreigners or more jets. Sometime soon, girls and starlets, famous actors. "Hey," I said, "I'll send you the snapshot if you draw me a picture of the full moon over the river." He looked confused, my English too fast or too complicated. Then a pebble flew up from the road and clanked on the cool tile. It was Lev, down below, serenading me with stones. "Hi there," I called. "Mr. Dutt would shoot you if he knew you were throwing rocks up here. I need help."

"What else is new?" he said. He was smiling in the dark, his teeth white in his brown face. I told him what I wanted Ram to do and asked him to translate. Lev cupped his hands around his mouth and shouted my request in Hindi. Ram nodded seriously. He called down a question. Lev laughed and said, "He wants to know if he's supposed to put in the dead bodies." "Yes," I told Ram as I saw Lev lift his arm in a last wave, then turn to walk down toward the river. "Put in everything you see."

Rose

June–July 1969 ❖❖❖ Port Clyde, Maine

Sam had promised to come and help walk the dogs this morn-ing, but he didn't drop by, so I took the two out myself and sat on the beach as they nosed about the kelp. Their coats are stiff with salt. Driftwood was scattered everywhere, mostly old pine boughs worn grey, looking more like antlers than wood. No re-cent storm, just a shift in the tide and wind that washed them in. It looks as if a herd of deer came to shed their horns and then swam back out to the ocean. I took a piece home and set it on a shelf in the kitchen where it will throw interesting shad-ows once the sun comes back out. It makes me think of the pieces of glass and shell I used to see on shrines, gifts to gods found on the way to the market. Offerings made with what one had, as a matter of course.

Cold fog has filled the reach, and I've had to light a lantern. It resembles the ones my father used on his expeditions, though this is weather unthinkable in India, except in the high moun-tains. He kept his gear in a closet, more like a small room, near his study, an exciting place full of rope and matches and folded tents that smelt of mildew and the jungle. It was where Ayah got the rope to tie together the sacks of rice she took to the starving people. I never rummaged about in there, probably the only rule of his I never broke. After he punished Ayah, I grew more compliant for a time. I knew he felt under terrible pressure. He spoke snappishly to all of us, and we all did his bidding, except Ayah.

So it was a great surprise when he told me in the early spring of 1942 that I would be coming with him to the mangroves. Now, with Quit India demonstrations gaining in ferocity, troops moving through the city day and night, the partition of India and the new country of Pakistan predicted, he invited me along. I should see what he'd been up to there all these years, he said, holding a sheaf of letters in one hand, the opener honed and deadly in the other. He sliced the paper, always limp from the heat, and despite the tool's sharpness, the envelope tore damply. He glanced at the pages but kept talking. Finally old enough, he said, though I knew the guides who helped him were often twelve- and thirteen-year-olds adept at steering heavy boats through difficult waters. I'd just come in from playing tennis. I remember standing in his study, breathing heavily, and wondering if I was imagining the invitation.

But I also knew he had no one he trusted to watch over me. And I do think he was glad to have me see the swamps. Though he pretended otherwise, we both understood it was to be his last time there. The project was being closed down; only his force of will and long missives to museum directors had kept it running this long. And he had, to his great displeasure, been ordered to give briefings about villages and waterways to intelligence officers. Now the Japanese were making their presence known in the area. British naval forces had stepped up patrols. He was going to do some small chores of gathering data, he told me. A replanting project after the last year's monsoon was his particular interest. Ayah said, "Sentimental fool. He's going to say good-bye. As if those old roots cared."

Yet she was also alarmed at his willingness to risk my well-being. After he had punished her, she was more open with me about how she saw him. "He keeps you here all these years, ruins your skin, and then whisks you off to the swamps." I saw her point, but I was not going to be denied an adventure. However ambivalent he was about my going there with him, I did not intend to lose this chance. I had so few opportunities for travel. The yearly excursions to Darjeeling, the trips we made to the south and to Delhi remained fresh in my memory. For years I had heard the stories about the mangroves and seen the sketches and photographs. In my mind I had an impeccable image of what it was like. Dense greenery, stalking tigers, and flocks of snowy egrets and flamingoes, a sea of white and pink birds.

I showed my father what I planned to bring, and he dispensed with half of my gear, especially the books. "You will be too tired to read," he said. We would be gone for five weeks. I couldn't imagine leaving without at least seven books.

"What will we be doing?" I asked.

"Taking water samples and measuring root growth. Mostly, staying out of the heat and making sure we don't get bitten by snakes," he said, for a moment looking doubtful about the project and my presence. Apart from the research, none of this sounded radically different from Calcutta, so I ferreted away some more novels. But he was right. I was too exhausted at the end of the day to do more than move my shoes off the floor and ensure the mosquito netting was in place.

Ayah refused to come out to the steps to wave us off. She muttered that the time for a trip was not auspicious and that she smelled ugly weather. "Go find out what sort of bad luck's coming your way," she said when I went to say good-bye. Though it pained me to have her sulking, I could not wait until the rickety jeep started us on our journey.

The trunk road south was crowded with soldiers, trucks,

oxcarts, men on bicycles. Calcutta thinned out slowly, and while we were still in heavily populated areas, our rather size-able caravan attracted little notice. My father, his assistant Deepak Pandit, and I travelled in the jeep while the other helpers, the ones in charge of the gear and provisions, came be-hind in a lorry that had cost my father the earth to rent. Most large vehicles were consecrated to the war effort. After a few hours we manoeuvred our way onto the smaller highways and found ourselves in the countryside, travelling through villages of thatched huts, where we attracted considerably more atten-tion. Men came out to stare, and women peered from the edges of doors or from behind clusters of palm trees. Children danced along the road, shouting and singing. After years of these visits, my father was known along the way. He did not have to tell me that the men with whom he exchanged long, ceremonious greetings were the people who gave him information on every-thing from where he might encounter dacoits to the best place to secure more kerosene.

I rather liked being introduced as his daughter and liked, too, the chance to visit a few Bengali villages. It was rare to find telegraph poles or hear the squawk of a wireless. Some-times we spied an electric light, which was usually a single bulb suspended from the centre of a low room. We saw very few English people, and it was hard, apart from road signs, the sight of a municipal building, or a portrait of the King in a candy shop, to believe that the English had much to do with making this part of the country function. In truth, they proba-bly didn't. The district judges and officials with whom my fa-ther visited were all Indian. I overheard them talking about food shortages. One night a fight broke out when Deepak Pan-dit discovered a man trying to pry open the trunk that held the tea. There might not be many of the English around, but it was clear we were still held responsible for the growing hunger, the high prices. When people came out to look at us in the villages, it was not with welcome. Only the children were truly glad for the distraction we offered.

My father did not talk about the edge of resentment the villagers expressed, but I know he was aware of it. He gave away far more of our rice and oil than Deepak Pandit approved of, and he paid top prices for supplies he didn't quite need. He seemed entirely at ease only when walking purposefully along the road to inspect the garages that cropped up on the shoulders. Calling them garages was generous: mostly these shops consisted of a piece of corrugated tin propped on tree trunks whose bark had not been stripped, under which a man had spread greasy engine parts on a sheet. My father knew what he was likely to need and would stock up on extra bolts and bits of gearboxes if he could find them. When, on the third day, the lorry did break down, he went through his entire oily collection to no avail. Luckily, one of these mechanic-wallahs came out with the very part we needed. I suspected that even if he hadn't had the piece required, he could have improvised a solution with a few scraps of wire and a pair of pliers.

After another day of jolting along unpaved roads, we came to what my father called the edge of the jungle, and I was terribly disappointed. I'd imagined the jungle as a sudden wall of greenery, bright with parrots and looping with vines. Instead, it was just like the towns we'd passed through, a landscape of dusty paths, palm trees, and mean huts. Not really green at all, especially since monsoon had not yet come this year. What surprised me was how many people there still were; the area was just as settled, although the roads running through it were more like ruts and impassable by motorcar or lorry.

Still, it was time to abandon the jeep and get on horseback, our gear and helpers coming along behind us in a ragged assortment of wagons and even wheelbarrows. I was beginning to understand the hard work it took my father to come here and why he might not have wanted me along on earlier expeditions. The horses were small, and my father's and my legs dropped nearly to their hocks. Sensitive to the ridiculous as all adolescents are, I wanted badly to walk, but my father insisted. Scientists arrived and left on horses. We would not be respected, nor would the aims of our search, if we walked. In India, station, high and low, is often literally understood. If you can afford it, you rarely touch the ground.

We had to ride for two days before we got to the edge of the swamp, my father explained, where we'd set up a more permanent camp. I hoped the landscape would be wilder there, but I doubted it. As we made our way towards the mouths of the Ganges, I saw the torches and smelled cooking from nearby settlements. Children would come stare at us; they particularly wanted our bars of soap. My father and I were the only ones of the group who drank quinine and slathered ourselves with repellent, a lethal mix of chemicals that made insects crumple in midair. Deepak Pandit and his men just slapped away at the bugs and made smoky fires of green twigs to keep them at bay. We all smelled of ash.

It was during this part of the journey that one could first begin to see tigers or, at the very least, begin to hear the tales about them. When we got to the spot where my father liked to set up his research, I met several women from a nearby hamlet who had been widowed by the animals. They took me to inspect a large shrine to the tiger god, Daksin Ray. He was a fearsome creature carved in wood, his teeth painted a glossy white. He wore a marigold garland and had offerings of fruit and bottled drinks between his paws.

Our tents and cooking area were a quarter of a mile from this settlement, in a relatively open clearing that was only another quarter of a mile from the water. As the helpers unpacked gear and Deepak Pandit tethered and fed the horses, my father and I sat down to drink tea and listen to the stories of the latest troubles with the tigers. The people in the area were honey gatherers, small and strong, who frequently dealt with the animals on their trips to search for the bees. That year, the headman said, tigers were taking men. Last year they'd gone after water buffalo, but it was rare for them to attack women and children. The animal that worried them most this spring had a wily way in the water, travelling almost below the surface, like a crocodile, before pouncing into a boat.

So if the jungle wasn't as undiscovered as I'd hoped, it was certainly as dangerous. My father grew more silent. The assistants and Deepak Pandit shared his concern, and all of them were assiduous in keeping fires lit and watches posted. The force of helpers grew larger, with local men arriving to help the cook or perform errands for my father. There was a man whose only job was to make tea. Another who was only supposed to fetch water for my father's assistants, another to inspect the boat each day for leaks. All the tasks were split into fractions, so one person would be responsible for the biscuits, another for washing the cutlery. There had to be translators: a man who spoke Bengali and the local tongue. As in the city, everyone was called by his appropriate family title—second-youngest brother, first or third uncle. Birth order was destiny, and people were unafraid to acknowledge that. Their lives were shaped by circumstances outside their will. These people knew and were vulnerable to weather, armies, the capricious ways of rulers. They were people around whom it was hard to have light conversation. They were too alert to sudden change for anything so flimsy.

My father and I weren't much better at chat than the local people in any case. Even as he listened to the stories of the tigers and supervised the goings-on of the camp, I knew he longed simply to be out on the water looking at the animals and the mangroves. I did as well, but once we were out there, I realised once again that my imagination had proved too fanciful: my vision of silvery water was inaccurate. The delta streams were as brown as milk tea because of all the silt the water had carried from the riverbanks. The air was also fantastically hot. The banks where the mangroves grew were steep, dark, and slimy. Over the next week, conversation grew even more cramped, and involved only the observations my father and his assistants made and other practical matters such as food and shelter. We continued to be careful about the animals. Sea snakes in particular were everywhere.

In time I grew to know the men who helped my father, though to show their respect for him, they barely acknowledged my presence. I had to put down my cups and plates before they would take them off to be washed. I dressed in loose trousers and long-sleeved shirts, an impractical costume for sampling lagoons, measuring the depth of silt, cataloguing shorebirds. On the water, we often saw smoke from steamers and warships in the distance. We never spoke of this and instead focussed that much more intently on the numbers of gallinules feeding on newly hatched minnows. A man stood behind me in the bow of the boat with an umbrella over my head. My father jotted down notations that were supposed to be the basis for articles we both knew would not be written. We ate rice, lentils, fish, and tea that tasted brackish, though the water was boiled, filtered, and strained. I did not like to admit this, but I missed Ayah. The people spoke a rough Bengali I could barely understand. The other women I saw were the wives of honey gatherers or fishermen, and we were all very shy in front of each other.

We were in a part of the mangroves where my father said the crocodiles were especially large. They were terrifying, with

their oily yellow eyes, very much the leftovers from an older ge-
ologic era. The coldness to their look signalled a willingness to
attack if given the chance. One day, a week into our stay, we
saw them in rather large concentrations around the spot where
my father hoped to measure the growth of a mangrove plantation that had managed to survive a bad storm the year before.
Even worse, one of the boatmen thought he spotted a tiger
swimming towards us. Once the crew got jittery, my father
knew the day's work was done, and we returned early to camp.

That was when I met Krishna Banerjee. He was sitting on
the stump of a sal tree, out of the sun. He was sipping water
from a battered canteen. He introduced himself to my father as
a student of botany at a Calcutta scientific institute and added
that he had also spent time at Tagore's Shanti Niketan, a study
centre that my father had several times spoken about with
some admiration. My father had never heard of him, and made
him stand there in his immaculate kurta and recite his education and background. He could have been one of Subhas Chan-
dra Bose's supporters sent to disrupt the study. Why hadn't he
volunteered for the war, my father asked, to which Krishna
replied that there were many family responsibilities and that he
was the eldest son, expected to take care of his parents. He
might have done well to ask my father the same question. It
was 1942. Everyone was supposed to be serving the effort to
stop the Nazis, and both of them, able-bodied and skilled, were
there in the swamps looking at roots.

I was not presented, even when it became apparent that the
young man was serious about science. Krishna's father was
a landowner in the area. Krishna himself had gone to St.
Xavier's, a Jesuit school outside Calcutta, and had earned high
marks on his placement exams. My father began speaking to
him in Bengali, but Krishna answered in English while still
looking at the ground. A daring move. He was tall but rather

slender, so next to my father's broad back, he seemed quite
small. His hair was thick and black and lay in a bright sheaf
over his left eye. He did not even look at me, another sign of his
good manners. It was not as if he hadn't seen me.

He wanted to be part of the research. He could supply letters of recommendation from his professors if my father was interested in seeing them. He patted a cloth satchel he had over
one shoulder. My father called for tea. It was going to be a bit
of a procedure. It didn't register for me then, because almost
everything in India took time and involved the lengthy smooth-
ings of pages, pulling out of spectacles, and cup after cup
of tea. Finally, my father called me over and said, "This is my
daughter, Miss Rose Talcott." Krishna bowed in my direction.
"Greetings, miss," he said, and he waited to sit until both my father and I had. He had slim fingers with clipped nails. His feet
were in the rope sandals the locals wore, but I sensed that he
wore them out of habit, not the inability to pay for sturdier
shoes. My father and I wore boots that cooked our feet and
gave us blisters. The guides and servants wore the same sort of
shoe as Krishna or, more commonly, nothing at all.

"Where do you live?" my father asked, and Krishna replied
with the name of a village ten miles away where we'd stopped
on the way down. There were sundari trees of secondary interest and a population of storks. The people took excellent
care of their cows, minding their illnesses with tenderness and
painting their horns blue. "How did you get here, then?" my father asked, looking for a donkey or pony.

"I walked, Curator Sahib," Krishna said. That was what
made me look at him more closely. I'd heard a respectful tone
with the thin edge of challenge. His kurta had remained without a crease. As we drank tea, my father read Krishna's letters,
which were freshly folded and, like his clothing, immaculate.
"Well," said my father, glancing up, "you're welcome to join us
if you like."

Later I stole a look at these letters, which my father had put on the desk in his tent. They were from Indian and English professors and spoke of "Mr. Banerjee's sensitivity of judgement" and "patience with the most exacting of laboratory tasks." "A good fellow." "An eye for the odd detail."

At the very juncture when we all knew he'd never need help again, my father acquired the best research assistant he'd ever had. I loved to watch Krishna work and to hear the careful authority in his voice when he spoke to the helpers at the camp and the boys guiding the boats. He had a gift for spotting schools of fish that indicated a particularly healthy group of mangroves. He noticed crocodiles when even the boatmen didn't. His handkerchiefs were stunningly white. At the end of the day, when all the rest of us were smeared in mud and had balled our own into hot, wet rags, his was still neatly folded. Dust and sweat seemed to settle on him evenly, so that although his kurta grew slightly more wrinkled and dirty, it seemed as if he had managed its degree of disorder himself. He refused to be paid. He walked every day back and forth to our camp. He said he could work for the next two weeks, until it was time for him to visit family in Calcutta. He would place my tea on the table next to my folding chair, though after his initial greeting, he did not speak to me. It was to my father that he directed his attention.

But he was alert to almost everything. He saved the cook from a tiger leaping from a tree to make off with perhaps just the fish, but perhaps the cook as well. A guard had been sent to inspect the lower branches before the meal, and the horses, usually sensitive to intruders, had been calm. Then the tiger jumped. It seems odd that orange is a good color for camouflage, but in the jungle, it is. I was by my tent when I saw the animal. At the last second, it missed the cook, who pivoted on his heels and screamed. My father had the only rifle in the company, and he went to reach for it, but Krishna found it first.

The animal turned to snarl and charge when Krishna raised the rifle and shot its paw. It screamed as well, with a shrillness I had not thought to link to tigers, and tore into the brush, barely making a sound. Ten feet long, not including its tail. It did not die. The next day, Deepak Pandit and his men traced its path through the underbrush, but they found no body. I don't think Krishna meant to do more than wound it. If he had wanted to kill it, he would have.

"Well done, Mr. Banerjee. Poor cook," said my father, coming over to take the rifle back. An Indian man holding his gun made him nervous, which Krishna noticed. His hands were shaking. It was the only time I saw nerves get the better of his discipline. No one asked Krishna where he had learned to shoot like that. Everyone in the camp was surprised at the accuracy of his marksmanship. We were quite aware that we were far from Calcutta with a man who shot better than my father.

Krishna made all the helpers slightly uneasy, though my father rather frequently said, "He's quite good, Rose. Mr. Banerjee is quite good." They quoted Tagore to each other, Krishna an advocate, my father a detractor, though quite careful to keep his critique polite. When Tagore died, in 1941, the shops had closed for days as people mourned. Thousands attended the poet's cremation on Nimtola Ghat, and the streets were choked with millions of flower petals. But once my father and Krishna left poetry aside, they argued volubly: about the accuracy of local maps, the reliability of this village leader or that, the exact process of desalinization that the mangroves used. Even the origins of the local goddess, Banbibi. It was said she'd been abandoned by her mother and raised by tigers, and that she provided protection to all who lived in the forest, tiger and human alike. Krishna said historical evidence existed to support the claim that she'd been an actual person. My father scoffed at this idea, claiming she was a manifestation of Annapurna, the harvest goddess, mixed with some animist deity of the region. But they stayed away from politics, from the war, from Indian independence. They were scientists with a range of interests, their work and conversation said. They had far older and more consuming problems on their hands. The plants were so much quieter, subtler, and more mysterious than most people. I grew sweaty and stained. My father turned brown. Krishna stayed clean. Ten days later my father said he felt a storm coming, and Krishna said good-bye and walked off into the trees, towards his village or Calcutta he didn't say. There was no closing ceremony, my father would have been galled by such a display, but we all knew—the assistants, Deepak Pandit, and I—that my father's work in the Sundarbans was over. The servants folded the tents, my father thanked and paid the local people who had helped him, and our rather dirty group returned to the edge of the jungle to find the jeep stripped of its doors and wheels. It was the first time in twenty years that anyone had dared to harm one of my father's vehicles. He stared at the ravaged car and said only, "Back to the horses, Rose." It turned out he had been wrong about the storm. The weather grew hotter and drier. That year, monsoon was far too late.

David and I have agreed to meet in Portland to go and see the children at their camp. I've asked Sam to take care of the dogs while I'm gone. David wasn't pleased when he heard. I'd told him about Sam's troubles. He made me promise not to give the boy the keys to the house, and I'd agreed, though neither of us pointed out that if anyone wanted to get into the cottage, all they'd need was a strong shoe to kick down the door. This evening, I showed Sam the animals' blankets in the shed and how much food to give them. He didn't pay close enough attention, and I told him so. I asked him, "What are you good at?"

"Getting stoned," said Sam, staring across at his parents' house.

"How boring," I said, and he looked at me directly.

"Where are you from?" Sam asked.

"India and London," I told him. "And you?"

"Jupiter," Sam answered, still looking at the windows where the curtains were blowing. "Nothing there, just a lot of gas and rocks and gravity."

"Sam," I said, standing up to close the shed door, "you need to go back to school."

"That's hard for people from Jupiter," he said, and reached down to pull Marlow towards him.

I wonder if he'd have been different if he'd seen Japanese troops taking Singapore or lived through Indian heat that would not break. I wonder what it would have done to him to be in Calcutta in the spring of 1943, when famine struck hard and the English did not respond well or quickly and the city was filled not only with soldiers but with dying families. How much do our circumstances shape us, how much of our lives turns out to be shaped by our own stubborn natures? Planting things, I've seen both outcomes. In my own life, as well, I can see the influence of both.

I will never forget, for instance, the hungry people of 1943. It was far worse than the hunger that I'd witnessed just a year before. Tennis stopped entirely. I went to various women's houses to knit bandages, something I did badly. The nuns at my old school gave out rice once a day to the starving on the Maidan, and I helped with their work, and each time I did, I could not sleep. I read the newspaper and went to a few dances at the club because my father said young men needed a girl to dance with before going off to be shot at. They would dance with anyone, those soldiers, even though I was graceless in their arms. At night, my father and I and the servants listened to news reports on the wireless. I knew it was almost over for us. I was useless. I would soon be packed off to England.

Then one afternoon in early May 1943, my father told Muhammad Rashid that Krishna Banerjee would be there for dinner. It was the happiest he'd looked since he'd been in the Sundarbans. He told me to get on a decent frock. Krishna wore a kurta even whiter than the ones I'd seen him in. He called me "memsahib," not "miss," as he had in the mangroves. He brought a garland of marigolds, the old Indian welcome, which was sly of him. I dipped my head at the door and felt the flowers brush my hair and cheek and smelt their strong odour and realised that despite the war, the riots, and the hunger, I had fallen badly in love with Krishna Banerjee.

I remember almost nothing of the dinner except that the lanterns kept sputtering and the electricity faltered because the rains were nearly there and the wind was blowing. Krishna asked me no questions directly. I wished I had known before that evening that I was in love with him because I would have worn a different dress, not one that made me look like such a wrapped package. But I was glad for the silence he offered, and for the inconstant light. It allowed me to imagine the conversations we might have.

Elgar was on the phonograph, both of which were gifts from Aunt Fiona. I remember the smell of curry floating across and through the shuttered windows, the sound of a child crying, a mother hushing it, and the clang and jingle of cow and bicycle bells. The men talked of pneumatophores and alkaline deposits.

Ayah was serving, scuttling about in a way that tried to pretend it was quiet and was actually loud. Later that evening she said, "Mr. Krishna Banerjee is making eyes at you." Her hands were full of mosquito netting, probably worrying a hole into it. She spoke English in case another servant was about. "I am telling Rose Talcott now that she should be very careful around this White Kurta Krishna Banerjee." Then she was gone, taking the lantern with her, and I lay awake listening to the winds push at the shutters and doors, the house creaking like a boat in a gale.

He was staying in Calcutta, he had told my father, not far from our house. He had relatives in Kumartoli, respected statue-makers. I knew exactly who these people were and where they lived. The first showers of monsoon had finally come, and the streets were muddy, and for a few days, people were gloriously happy. Later they grew ill because the arrival of the rains always contaminated the water supply, making monsoon a strange time that mixed festive parties and funeral processions. And this year the famine was gathering force, and the war was in full and horrifying sway. There were brawls in coffee shops. Troops and jeeps clogged Calcutta's broad and narrow streets.

I find myself slightly scornful of Sam, but really I was no better then. One can see men on their way to a horrid swamp in Burma, know about famine, and still follow only the candle of one's need. One makes the rest not matter. Love creates its own narrow channel, its own river of fire. It becomes its own end. I went in search of Krishna Banerjee.

I had only to walk through the street to have word travel through the buildings and the lanes that there was a white girl about, the daughter of the curator, the mangrove man at the museum. Miss Rose. They knew of course that I would be looking for the one person in the neighbourhood who also looked at mangroves. Krishna Banerjee came out of his uncle's house, and, with great ceremony and the attendance of six or seven of his nephews and cousins, showed me the statue-making workshops. We were surrounded by children chattering in Bengali, swinging on Krishna's outstretched hands, running to fetch us cold drinks and then, when the afternoon rain started, extra umbrellas. The statues were huge, too big to put in a kiln. As they dried under thatched mats, cracks ran across their bellies, their cheeks, cracks that the sculptors filled with fresh clay and then painted over. The statues weren't meant to last—they would be smashed and pounded back to dirt and eventually become again what they had started as, the mud that made up the Hooghly's steep banks.

"They're lovely," I said, seeing the bold curves of a goddess meant to resemble some manifestation of Kali.

"No, they are not," said Krishna Banerjee in his perfect English. "And they are not meant to be. You are being the polite British girl. Full of concern for the Indian ways, and it is touching, very touching, but not I would guess particularly honest. Do you like India, Miss Rose of the Swamps, Miss Daughter of the Man with the Last Monocle?"

He was so bold. I had never expected this, though the edge of irony that he'd loosed from the beginning ought to have alerted me. I should have been more sensitive to the signs of rebellion.

But he also irritated me. I did not like that swagger, and I pulled back, the children looking at me, listening to the rough edges of the English in the air. It is so ugly compared to Bengali, has none of its slipperiness, its ability to translate quickly into song. And how dare he assume that I didn't like India, that I saw only what he supposed I saw, because of my father, my skin, my sex.

"Everyone sees beauty differently," I told him, "and I think they are lovely. At the very least they are cheerful and not angry. And yes, if you want to know, I do like India. I like it very much." Which of course sounded all wrong. As if I were saying that I liked it because I was English, because I had been born there and deserved it. That was not at all the way I felt, but it was what came out, the perennial problem with conversation and people, the problem with love.

"But you will be leaving." And I knew he meant leaving in all its forms—the city, the country. "Are you political, Miss Rose?" he asked, looking not at me but out at the river, which we had strolled to. The children were quiet now and beginning to drift in clumps to the bank to find stones to skip on its flat surface. The rain shower ended, though the clouds were still heavy. We closed our umbrellas and stood looking at the water. Despite the eyes I knew were watching us, we were alone, as alone as we could be, which is to say there was no one right there interrupting our talk, which is not to say they weren't observing the space between us—at least three feet—and how much we were speaking.

"I don't know," I told him honestly. It was such an adult question, and I'd had so little practise at being grown-up.

We saw then three sculptors, portly men in their forties, wearing towels wrapped around their heads and dhotis around their waists, hoisting the statue of a *dakini*—one of the minor goddesses who accompany the grand deities—over their heads. She was a uniform grey, not yet painted, and she had dried more evenly than most of the other statues we had seen that day. The men were arguing good-naturedly about when they were going to break for tea and cigarettes, and they paid no attention to us. They were getting their goddess back out into the sun to ready her for the skin of paint, the eyelashes and bright cheeks they were going to give her. Their hands were on her hips, on those small breasts Indian artists through the centuries have prized, and on her slender waist. Ideal proportions, which their dusty fingers were grazing with terrible casualness.

We watched her, and Krishna Banerjee did not have to say a word for me to know that he was telling me that one day soon he would touch me there, there, and there, his clear eyes watching the breasts, waist, and hips of the *dakini* raised above the improvised turbans of the three sweating men on her way to the final stage of her beautification. I knew that underneath her clay she was made of sticks of straw, bound together with string to make the roots of her body. Golden, but easily broken or made to burn.

I came back home and was unable to talk, and Ayah knew instantly that I was holding something to myself. Her suspicions increased when she found out I had sprayed my clothes with lavender water that Aunt Fiona had sent at Christmas. It came in a bottle with an atomiser that forced the perfume out in a triangle of mist. Once Ayah smelt the scent, it was like being in a room with a woman wielding a large broom. A woman trying to smack dust from corners and instead raising small tornadoes. The next morning she was at me to get up, have breakfast, drink tea, comb my hair. Really she was saying, Talk to me, foolish girl, before you bring shame to this household.

I did not know then that Krishna would say the perfume made me smell like the colonel's wife: wide-hipped, floppy-hatted Mrs. Crowley, always greedy for the choice cuts ordered from a halal butcher who suffered when the meat didn't exactly suit. I did not know then, either, that I would hang my clothes in front of the window on every chair or coat rack I could find to let the smells of India back in. Even now, when I smell lavender in a sachet—old lavender, it has to be a faded kind—I feel a horror at having been so young and inexpert and vulnerable to the judgements of others.

Neither Ayah nor I had a glimpse of that yet. Even so, before anything had transpired between me and Krishna, she acted like a grackle with a woman's tongue, a grackle in a sari. I told her that and knew I'd stung her. Usually, after we traded insults—I was often the white cow; the poor, slow girl; or sometimes the slovenly child who will never find a husband—

the tension between us would ease, and we'd be able to get on with the day. With points scored, we could dispense with irritation. But this time she marched out of the room, abusing the English who behaved as if they were missing half their brains. Which they were. As anyone with his eyes open could see. A thick and silly race who fried in the sun and still managed, Kali only knew how, to exert control over Muslims and Hindus. "But not everywhere," she reminded me from the threshold. "There are the princely states, stupid girl. There is Mysore, Kashmir, Hyderabad." (With regents or governors in all of them, I might have pointed out but did not.) "You will never hold on to us. We are *Maha Bharat*. Great India."

I sat against the pillows in my dressing gown and savoured my small resistance even as her rage pierced me. She was mostly right—about me, about England, about the people who tried to keep India in line. But I was seventeen. And for the time being, my secret was still my own, sewn close to me, the way embroidery curved along the hems of my sheets. Another present from Aunt Fiona—good English sheets, she'd written in her looping hand, as if the cotton hadn't in all likelihood come originally from India, as so much cloth then did.

A few years back, my father and I had taken a trip through the south to visit temples. I had seen cotton fields, thousands of bolls glistening row by row. The only colour came from the backs of women bent double as they picked their way through the field. Pink, red, yellow, the brown lengths of their arms and then the white on the tan plants. The cotton was taken on carts to a factory, where it was carded and spun, and then to a mill, where it was woven into sheets that covered bodies all over the empire, some of which had found their way back to me.

We saw the women at the end of their day at the weighing station, and they looked at us without veiling their faces, their hands resting on their loads. From behind the building came the sound of a creaky pump and the splash of water. My father was talking to a man who kept track of how much they picked. The two of them were speaking slowly, my father hobbling along in Tamil, the man trying to practise English. The sun was going down, but enough light was left for me to see the salt lines curved along the pickers' chins. In the dimness, the blood that dotted the cotton from their torn hands appeared black. They watched me, and I watched them back as the men exchanged greetings, information, and thanks, and the birds of the area began to sing again now that the worst of the heat had gone. As the birdsong grew stronger, the light died, and with it the details of the women's faces, though the whites of their eyes still shone. But not their teeth, for they hadn't opened their mouths.

Those sheets and those women are wound into my memories of what it was like to be in love for the first and most terrorizing time, desperate to tell someone and knowing how dangerous it was. I remember, too, the sense of my imminent betrayal of my father and Ayah and their quite separate notions of honour—all the while wrapped inside my Anglo-Indian sheets, smelling both of curry and of soap. All this when Krishna was nothing more than a series of gestures and words, an alluring and essentially imagined person. All this when David was working twenty hours a week at a stationer's in Washington Heights and studying for exams that would let him get scholarships to university. Jews were dying every day in the camps. Indian and British troops were being killed by the Japanese in Burma, and if bullets did not get them, the heat and the malaria were likely to, and all I could think of was Krishna's hands and beautiful hair.

Still, it was impossible to avoid news about the failure of the rice crop and the poor management of the response. Information was filtering into the city itself and not only through the newspapers. Even in Kumartoli people were going hungry. One night my father and I were listening to a wireless report about fighting in the streets and police stations being stoned. He switched it off, and the sound died slowly. "How they expect to live as a nation is quite beyond me. They'll never manage it," he said, the only time he ever spoke of India's independence. "But they are set on trying." Then he told me I was headed to the mountains in three days with Mr. Banerjee and Ayah. He would join us later in the month; he had affairs to settle first.

I had expected that I'd be going—it was a yearly migration—but I'd had no idea that Krishna might be coming, too. I did not realise that he had earned so much of my father's trust. One would have thought the information would thrill me, and it did. But if I were scrupulously honest, I would have to admit my first reaction was disquiet or unease. Whatever there was between us was going to have the opportunity to evolve. We would discover what we had in store for one another.

I am back now from visiting Anna and James, but still alone. David came up for a short while, then went down to Boston. At least we'd both been glad to see the children. They were sun-browned, full of complaints about the rules and the counsellors and the mosquitoes. In short, quite happy. Their ease with paddles and campfires rather confounded us, and they both looked as if they've had access to this kind of pleasure their entire lives, though it's the first time they've been away from us. But even as I saw the pots they'd made and the bunks where they slept, I couldn't stop mulling over the news on the car radio from what I couldn't help thinking of as the real world. We heard about an animal the announcer called "the flight subject."

A pigtailed monkey named Bonnie hooked up to monitors, sensors, and catheters and sent into space in a capsule. I wondered, too, how Sam was doing with the dogs. I knew that I would have to describe to David what I was writing. He would see the medical forms and the number of pages and know it was not a letter to my father.

Driving back, I told him. He listened without turning to look at me, and he let me take my time. His family had survived extreme losses. I think he learned very young to navigate around wounds, staying well away from their margins though conscious of them. I have always understood that this is why he became a doctor. "Well," was all he said. "That's quite an undertaking." We stopped to buy vegetables and he said, as the tomatoes lurched the scale to one side, "Are you sure you have to put it all in?" He knew what I'd answer. But it dismayed him when he got here, all the pages, the typewriter in the centre of the table. He decided, after one evening, most of which he spent listening to a baseball game on a battery-powered radio, to leave me at my work. Before I dropped him at the bus, he said, "Who is it for?"

I didn't exactly know, I admitted. For myself. Maybe for the children. It's not a story for friends, to be twisted like taffy into bits of gossip. What I wish I'd been able to say, but couldn't out of shame, was that I needed to make a record of it, and writing it down was the only way I could think of. "You have to check with me if you ever want to tell Anna and James" was all he said, and then the bus came. He felt that some histories, the small ones at least, were better left lost and unspoken. Opening them up might not be worth it. This was a contradiction, though an understandable one, from a man who insists that the darker pieces of national and foreign policies be aired, but who, when the talk becomes more personal, grows quiet. Like me, he's gotten used to living with the past being mostly walled off.

Anna and James, however, are sensitive to these sealed places. They are sensitive to details in general. They always want the exact word for a thing, its proper name. For roses, breeds of dogs, utensils. "Colander or sieve?" Anna asked me when she was seven, the steam from the peas rising into her curls. "Which one?" she demanded. But when I see them with classmates, they are careful to walk like the others, to speak as they do, to absorb their postures.

Yet they enjoyed the stories we gave them, David more generous on that point than I, as well as the ones in books. David read to the children, and Anna in particular bent into the ritual. Stories grew in her mind like string beans up poles. She got confused sometimes about the line between what happened on the page and what happened in life. She wanted pieces of fairy tales to spill into her day. I'd overheard her telling friends lies about how I'd ridden tigers as a child. But I never stopped her; that would have meant I'd have to correct her version and tell her what Calcutta was really like. And that would have meant answering a host of questions I wasn't willing to entertain. When she asked how David and I met, I told her little more than we first saw each other at the library where I was working. I said that our friendship had developed slowly and that David was very kind. She turned away, disappointed I hadn't created a shinier version of love.

Maybe, too, she couldn't imagine me involved in anything romantic. I'm too tall for her. I've seen her watch me mournfully during parent conferences. Too big, too foreign, too fair-skinned, with the accent that won't be lost. Matching the mother with the small, overworked father who won't stop talking about baseball and maps makes the picture that much more confusing. Even the cutlery is mismatched, tossed together from two families of divergent tastes. David's mother gave us the forks ornamented with roses. My father sent us the ones with handles that look poured, silver so smooth it feels almost like flesh when our hands warm it.

Yet I sense that Anna may profit from her many possible traditions. She'll have a great deal to draw on, though the mix may not strike her as useful for a long time. James may have an easier go of it. He'll choose a single course and adhere to it. He won't let himself get distracted, although he also won't be able to tolerate as much, perhaps. But he'll be happier. Anna already gets stranded in odd places. Once, at Crane's Beach when she was five, she insisted on rubbing her hand against a barnacle until her fingers were bloody—in slight pain but interested at the same time. She drank sips of my tonic water flavoured with lime when she was even smaller, and though the taste made her shiver, she kept coming back. She didn't like the bubbles and the bitterness, we could tell. But she kept saying, "More," her hands around the glass.

Sam, to my relief, took good care of the dogs. They were calm and happy when we returned. Sam looked a little better, but he was distressed that David had left. "Did you have a fight?" he asked, and I told him no, we hadn't, we didn't argue much. Sam and I were in the living room drinking tea. Another chilly day. We could hear the raised voices of his parents even through the closed windows. "They do that all the time," Sam said. "All the time." I didn't say anything. What could I have told him? Marriage is a cold comfort sometimes and more complicated than one ever suspects at the outset. Avoiding each other, as David and I had just done, was just as damaging in its way as what his parents were doing. We sat there for a while until I asked if he'd mind taking the dogs for a long walk. I needed to get working. "What are you writing?" he asked as he unbent from his chair and took his cup to the sink.

"A story," I told him, "about when I was young."

He looked at the typewriter then, the old Royal I'd had since university, the machine on which I'd bashed out my untidy thoughts on Blake and Browning. He said then, with a kind of curiosity in his voice, that it was hard to imagine me as a girl. I told him that it was hard for me, too.

The day that Ayah and I left Calcutta, it was 120 degrees before noon. The birds were silent; the lizards had gone still. Dust hung like dry rain in the streets, and people were made either sullen or openly rageful at the smallest setback. The porters were late. The taxi's tyre got a puncture. My father was feeling ill, though he did not say so. But Ayah and I could tell; he was slightly yellow in the face, more drawn.

Only Krishna seemed comfortable. He arrived precisely on time, and though he daubed his face with a handkerchief, he was spotless in a neat khaki jacket and trousers, not his usual kurta. The clothes emphasized the spare lines of his body and suited him well, which surprised me. I'd thought of him as made for the looseness of Indian men's dress. "It will be cool in the mountains," he said when he saw me looking, and then glanced away and leant down to fiddle with the lock on his single valise. I was unable to look at him directly after that. He acted indifferent towards me, polite but distant, and I wondered if I had imagined that afternoon in the statue-maker's street. I was pleased that he would be far away from me on the train, in a second-class compartment.

Though I loved Calcutta, I was glad to be heading north. The heat was awful in the city, the mood surly. I knew our life there was crashing to a close. More selfishly, I expected the air at seven thousand feet would make my heart less feverish. Perhaps Krishna would look different there among the Nepalis and the Gurkhas. And I was looking forward to the actual train trip, though it would have its discomforts. I do not know what

Indian trains are like now. Crowded, of course, but they always were. Yet both Indians and English were proud of the trains; their tracks and routes had been so hard to engineer. We were on one that was notoriously slow, the best my father could do in a short time. The cars were jammed with soldiers in turbans and regimental colors.

Ayah was in a foul frame of mind. Darjeeling was too cold for her. The fog in the mornings was bad for her lungs. She thought the local rhododendrons unlucky, but when I pressed her as to how exactly they brought ill fortune, she would not say. The tea, she added, was filthy, which made me laugh. It was the same tea that she drank in our house every day, grown right in that region. The poor quality of the water in the mountains ruined it, she insisted. Too few streams for so many people, and nowhere to drill a well. In the tumult of the station, she was still muttering about all this, and my father, feeling unwell and keenly aware of the soldiers, rifles, and officers keeping their men in loose order, barked, "Ayah, stop the chatter," which nettled her further. He, Krishna, and I were relieved when she headed to the women's section in second class, where she would probably spend most of the journey reviling other passengers and pressing sweets on children.

My father and Krishna saw me settled into my own compartment, which seemed to be the only one in the long series of cars that wasn't filled to bursting. I almost wished it was, given the other occupant. An old Englishwoman was asleep there, her Yorkshire terrier a small, damp mop in her lap. "Rose," my father whispered so as not to wake her, "send a telegram to say you've arrived." I knew he wanted to say he was sorry I'd be staying with the Crowleys until our rented cottage was ready. I even knew that he wanted to say that he was worried—about the museum, the mangroves, the war, India, us. Since it was the last time I took that trip north and I was so aware of Krishna, these details are certain in my memory. My father's face was the colour of pale mustard. The brown marbles of the terrier's eyes blinked at us. Krishna stood in the doorway, his suit still perfectly neat, waiting to wish my father good-bye. They shook hands, and Krishna and I agreed to meet outside the ladies' first-class waiting room in New Jaipalguri twelve hours later for the next transfer. Soon after, the train started to shift, wheels screeched, and the Englishwoman woke. She exchanged mumbled greetings with my father and pointedly ignored Krishna. "Safe travels," he said; then they both left the compartment, Krishna to find his seat, my father to get on with his day. He did not turn to wave to me. I saw him walk with dogged precision towards Howrah Station's central hall.

The woman's name was Mrs. Hastings, and she was on her way to see her son, who ran a tea garden near Siliguri. She took me in, dismissed me, and returned her attention to the Yorkie, whose name was Jig. I guessed that she was thinking about the season, the round of parties that enlivened Darjeeling in the summer. Girls went to the hills to dance and flirt and sometimes marry. It was an old trajectory, and Mrs. Hastings assumed I was doing just that, despite the war and the Quit India campaign and the famine. As if those festivities were all still in full swing, which they were not. But a woman such as she would have thought war and the like was men's work, men's worry. According to her assessment, my chances weren't good.

We tacitly agreed in those first minutes to retreat to our own corners. I read my novel, though I do not remember what it was, and I slept, worn out with the heat and the lurching of the train, rolling across Bengal towards the mountains. I woke from time to time to see Mrs. Hastings tempt Jig with sandwich crusts or snap open the stems of her eyeglasses. She had propped herself up so that she didn't have to look out the window, her attention funnelled towards her book, whose title I tried and failed to see.

It was near dusk when I stopped dozing, thanks to Ayah, who appeared at the door of the compartment. I saw her thin face and blazing eyes, and it horrified me that my first reaction was embarrassment. She was screeching in Bengali, and to calm her, I had to go into the corridor. Mrs. Hastings frowned and testily brought Jig to her chest as if to protect him. As if Ayah were intent on harming small dogs. She could not have cared less about the animal. She was simply beside herself. It was too hot where she was. The tea was poison. The women in her section were poor and uneducated, and someone was coughing violently and spreading pestilence. She was dis-traught—but not so much so that she had forgotten to pull her veil across her face. She knew she wasn't allowed to be in the first-class compartment. I wondered how she had made it past the ticket collectors, Indians all of them, fierce enforcers of the class separations the railway insisted on.

People were staring at us through the door windows. Moth-ers with fair children, a minister in a dusty black coat. Ayah and I were speaking in Bengali, and I wondered how many of the onlookers understood us. Only the minister seemed to be following. How had she gotten around the collectors? She was like a pebble that had passed through the sieve into clean rice.

Then came a moment for which I still hate myself: my em-barrassment at her unexpected arrival shifted fully into shame. I knew from years of experience that all she was saying was that she was feeling unwell because of the heat and that she wanted to talk to me, be cheeky, and then she would go back to her seat and feel better. I knew that, yet I said to her, in En-glish, "Ayah, you must go back to your compartment. You are not allowed to be here." For that comment I have no excuses. Not the heat, not the tension, not the war. Not youth, not infat-uation, nothing.

She stood tall, pulled her veil more tautly around her mouth. I saw that she had been waiting for my betrayal for years. She had schooled herself for it. It was how things were, and she was not going to be disappointed by it, nor let it pass unnoticed. "You deserve what you are asking for," she spat in Bengali. "Every scrap of pain you are inviting your way, it will come to you. It is on your face." Her voice dropped as she finished her prophesy, as if it saddened her to have to tell me about my upcoming misery. She turned then and moved back down the corridor, bouncing with her limp and the jerking motion of the train.

I still don't know exactly why I disavowed her. Partly it was Mrs. Hastings's dismissal of my prospects. I was so tired of having the English shake their heads about me, sighing as they sipped their tea. I was tired of men like the eavesdropping minister taking my father aside to warn him of my distance from God and England. I was tired of never living somewhere I could feel entirely at home. The only place I felt comfortable in all of Calcutta was the house in Kumartoli, which did not really belong to us, and which, since my interest in Krishna had caught fire, had begun to feel small.

I also knew that cruelty was the only way I would ever shake Ayah loose. Otherwise we would have kept on being wound around each other's lives as thread hugs a spool. My heart pounded when I spoke the English words aloud, and writing this, it is doing so again. I felt terrible remorse. But I was—and this still appals me—exhilarated.

I believe she was trying to sever things between us, which would account for why she picked the very time and location that made her the most vulnerable to the kind of attack I launched. Attuned as she was to reading events and patterns of status and speech, she must have been aware of how tempted I would be to do what I did. She knew how irritable we were being with each other. And as I've said, she certainly knew that India's submission to what she called, more and more openly, the pale and stupid English, was almost over. It was time to move on.

Then again, something might have happened in her compartment, or she might have seen something that disturbed her. She was upset enough, perhaps, to come and find me, to reassure herself that at least one thing, one person in her world, was going to respond as expected. But I don't think so now. I think she was inviting the end, and she was relieved when I released her in such a way that made it impossible to love me any more.

When Ayah slammed the door, I felt instantly depressed and angry with myself. "Well done, Miss Waldorf," Mrs. Hastings said, and she bent to feed Jig another morsel. He lapped it up, and I wanted to smack them both in the face.

I turned my back to watch a rice paddy shining like liquid mother-of-pearl. The sheen was disturbed from time to time by a buffalo in profile, egrets, the lines of a plough echoed by the lines of a farmer's body—except at his head, which was wrapped in a turban. Beyond the field rose dust from lorries, slow because of the weight of their loads and the condition of the road. They were packed with goods and people and probably soldiers, though I couldn't tell in the fading light. None of the drivers were using headlamps. Wires dipped between the tall lengths of telegraph poles. The scene was that much more impressive since so many of the paddies had failed that year. This one, so admirably fertile, surely had access to irrigation.

It wasn't just those paddies that we English would have admired. It was how the ancient parts of India blended with the modern elements we had brought and championed. The juxtaposition seemed to leave room for what appeared to be the essential India, the India of buffalo, rice, and the old plows, a society shaped thousands of years ago. Undisruptable. Timeless. Able to tolerate our incursions, our insistence on telegraphs and telephones, regular electricity. Look, the placement of the old next to the new seemed to say, there is space for it all. Mrs. Hastings, had she turned from her book, would have appreciated the scene aloud, affirming as it did that we were part of something grand yet real in India. It would have been doubly easy to praise the vista at just that moment, thanks to the absence of the smell of raw sewage.

I had none of that perspective as a seventeen-year-old, and who knows how precise my memory is? I did care for India, and not just for pretty pictures of men plowing. I cared for it because it was familiar in the deepest way possible: as a set of sense impressions I'd known since infancy, a place whose customs I understood and used reflexively. What love I'd known had been in India. And I had just gone and wasted the most precious part of it. I leant back in my seat and felt I might die from ill humour and downheartedness. I couldn't get comfortable on the plush, which was lumpy in places and worn away in others like the fur on a mangy tiger skin. Nothing fit — not my skin on my bones, not my body on the seat, not my hands to my wrists, not me to India or to England. I believed I would never find a place to hold me.

I feel that is still true, though with less adolescent drama. Most people don't have much luck at achieving that secure a fit. I have a family, and that is far more than most people. I have David, Anna, and James. But *having* is an odd verb in this respect. We are next to each other, but it does not lead to completion. We are not Indian that way.

In any case, no amount of love makes it any easier to sit with one's mistakes and missteps, the hurt one has dealt out to others. To feel the weight of one's errors is to feel homeless, bound to nothing but one's own capacity to deliver pain. I have kept hoping that my feelings will not be as strong as they once were. It shocks me to realise that in certain respects they are even stronger. I am more aware now of how cruel I have been. I know, too, it cut Ayah deeply. She wheeled, her anklets sang, she pulled her sari close and stalked, jangling, down the corridor. I never saw her again.

It is late now. I am tired but unable to sleep. I've been up with the dogs, warming them. Sam took them out in his dory earlier; they grew skittish and jumped into the ocean. He was lucky not to have capsized. I glanced up from an early supper when I heard a splash and saw the two animals struggling to shore, their heads just above the water. They were winded and cold, exhausted with the swim and the surprise. As Sam hauled the boat onto the shingle, he kept saying, "I'm so sorry, Mrs. Singer." His eyes were a little wild, and his hair was wet and spreading across his shoulders.

I was furious with myself for not having protected the dogs, and I was curt with Sam and his mother, who raced down to see what had happened. "He's just a boy, Rose," she said, a tiny woman next to her tall son, scrabbling for purchase on the loose rock.

"That's not a good enough defence," I told them, which both is and isn't true. Thinking about whether youth excuses poor judgement has kept me up, as has keeping an eye on the dogs. I rubbed them down with towels and put them by the fire. I gave them extra for dinner and put blankets over them, but they are still shivering. Mostly it is my own shame keeping me up, shame at how I behaved when I was young and lonely. Sam thought he was giving the dogs a treat. He had underestimated their fear. I'm glad David isn't here. I wouldn't know what to say to him about the dogs. I also couldn't write the next part of the story if he were in the cottage with me.

Night fell over the plains. Mrs. Hastings wrapped herself in a large dressing-gown and doused her lamp. It was still stifling. The porter had come by earlier and given us sheets, which were nearly wooden with starch. I unfolded mine and opened the window as wide as I dared. I sensed that Mrs. Hastings was not a woman who slept with open windows. She seemed like someone who would have an entire theory of illness based on exposure to Indian air.

The train ground on, swaying forward. As evening fell, the lights went out in the other compartments and then in the towns. We were fully on the dry and baking plains of Bihar. This year especially, people there were starving on them. I knew that if we had passed in daylight, we would have seen heaped bones of cattle, not to mention families not far from that fate, the children tied in sacks to their mothers' shoulders. Those thin bodies on the failed fields scared me, and I wanted badly not to know they were there. I wanted to see beauty in a landscape that was full of thorns and worry, dust and hunger, war and anger. I also had a more elemental fear, an ancient one: those with luck tend to pull away from those whom it has deserted. We imagine we risk being tainted by the mere sight of those less favoured, as if a twisted spine, an empty stomach, were contagious.

I drifted in and out of sleep, but when, somewhere past Patna, I heard the door of my compartment slide open, I sat straight up. Mrs. Hastings stayed asleep, her snores a lulling buzz. It was Krishna, of course. His hands were full of scraps from the dining car, brought especially to quiet the little dog. Jig began to growl, and my breath stopped. I was sure Mrs. Hastings would wake up.

Krishna gave him something from his palm, and said in a normal voice, "She's almost entirely deaf. I just brought something to comfort it for having such a master." I was too impressed and frightened to dare to speak. I knew why he was there. I knew he had planned this, had probably hopped down from the train at the last busy stop and made a dash on the platform to reach this car. Or he might have bribed a collector or the laundryman to sneak his way in. Things were changing. The Indians knew these trains were theirs and they would run them. Perhaps they'd also looked the other way when Ayah made her way through the corridors.

"How has your evening been, Mr. Banerjee?" I asked, the comment a reflex of politeness, which told me exactly how agitated I was. I could have slapped myself. As if we were sipping tea at a fête for veterans from the Great War. As if I were fully dressed and a band were playing "Rule Britannia" at the Red Fort. "Just lovely, Miss Talcott. And yours?" he answered in a wobbly but accurate imitation of my voice, mincing and too high, but the cadence just right. "Just smashing, miss," he went on, still in falsetto. "The views are most beautiful, and as always, Indian Railways is such a pleasure to ride." He laughed then, a sound he made no effort to quiet or conceal, and I said something like, "Oh shut up, Mr. Banerjee, you'll wake someone."

He didn't reply. He set the pile of scraps by Jig's head and came over to my bunk. What I remember of the next minutes, apart from what happened to my body, was the squeal and lurch of the train, the lapping of the small dog's tongue on the meat Krishna had brought, and the steady pull of Mrs. Hastings's snores as she slept through the kind of abomination that would have filled her with a joyful rage. Yet she missed her opportunity.

The train pushed along, a great length of wood and steel, clanking its slow way towards the Himalayan foothills. I discovered what a man's sweat smelled and tasted like, and a new form of sensation that combined pleasure and fear with pain and sadness, along with a near total disbelief that something so shocking was happening to someone like me. I felt, nearly for the first time, the actual contours of a self. It came as a surprise in the stifling compartment, with the sleeping English only yards away, that I had a body, a face, a taste to offer, and preposterously, that someone as intelligent and handsome as Krishna Banerjee wanted it. I was young enough to hope that it was me in particular that he wanted.

He mapped me out with fierce precision on the berth of that Indian Railways car, a large deaf Englishwoman sleeping straight through his conquest. The hot plains of Bihar rolled past the windows, through which I could, from time to time, hear the bellows of hungry cows and smell both drains and smoke.

It took me years to recognise that as I held Krishna's slender back, I was also thinking of a narrative of love imprinted in my mind. It involved themes that seemed far too bold for the timid father-and-Ayah-bound existence I was leading. According to my novels, life was supposed to be treacherous and vivid and replete with large gestures—but Krishna was rougher than any romantic encounter I'd read about. And silent, except for telling me that I could use some new frocks. So the gap widened between what my books said was possible and what was actually happening to me.

His shoes slid around the floor, the dog scrabbled about for more food, the sheets scratched at my exposed skin, a feeling almost as uncomfortable as what was going on in my body. We knew that we were engaged in an act that neither Indians nor English liked to believe was possible. He could be killed. I could be ruined, that old-fashioned but accurate word. We were courting danger.

There was also this: we each liked the look and smell of the other and had from the first moment. Simple. Old. The wondrous mechanics of nature that impel us to assert our biology, the most basic parts of ourselves. There's a terrific sameness to human bodies all over the world. I remembered at some point the definition of a species, my father's words echoing in my head. A group whose members can mate and produce fertile offspring.

I don't think Krishna stayed more than half an hour, though it was a half-hour that had seemed to last days, given how I played it over and over in my mind. He had only to rearrange his clothes, since he hadn't taken them fully off. Slipping into his shoes, he bent over to pat the dog on the head. The train passed a rare electric light, and he took advantage of the brief glow that filled the compartment to press his index finger to his lips. He crept back to the corridor. He did not kiss me good-bye. He hadn't, I realised, kissed me at all.

There was no chance of sleeping now. I remade the bed, not bothering to be quiet. We were nearing a large town, and lights became more regular, allowing me to notice a small stain on the sheets. It was black, the way the blood from the women's hands in the south had been black in the dim light against their baskets. I used a pair of sewing scissors to cut a ragged hole, and then I took the patch of soiled cotton and threw it out the window. I sat up the rest of the night, horrified at myself and at Krishna and more awake than I think I had ever been. Ravenous, I gnawed on biscuit after biscuit to keep myself from crying or laughing or both. I was on the wrong side of the train for sunrise.

I assumed that all these feelings meant I was in love. I thought they would make me beautiful. Instead, I was shocked to see how tired and bedraggled I looked in the mirror on the wall of the women's WC. My face jumped and trembled with every jolt of the train, but even so, it saddened me to see how little love had improved my looks. I very much wanted to see Ayah, not Krishna Banerjee, who now possessed a kind of power over me that no one else had ever had.

But Ayah was not in New Jaipalguri, where I expected to see her. Instead, the supervisor of the ladies' waiting room had a telegram for me from my father saying that Ayah had felt unwell, had gotten off the train and returned to Calcutta. This meant that she had not told him about our rift and she had, very bravely, travelled alone. Indian women rarely went places by themselves, much less at such an unsettled time, with so many soldiers about. To get back home so quickly, she must have left the train immediately after our horrid scene.

The line was so long at the telegraph office that there wasn't time to cable my father, though I badly wanted to tell him that I was also planning on coming back to Calcutta as soon as possible, even that I had had enough of India and was ready for England. Then Krishna was there, with no expression on his face other than his usual slightly disinterested courtesy. I told him we needn't wait for Ayah; she had gone home. "Disagreeable woman," he said mildly, that openness of opinion the only sign of our increased intimacy.

My courage died when he said this, and I knew I would let him settle me onto the next train for Darjeeling, fulfilling the expectation my father had of me. I sat in a compartment filled this time with women whose children were flushed and cross with the heat. They spilled squash, fought over toy trains, pulled wings from flies. Their mothers cooled themselves with fans improvised from day-old newspapers, the ink smudging their hands. They barely noticed me, glad only, perhaps, that I hadn't come with anyone else in my party. I tried to imagine what it would be like to have children, to have to pry their hands away from window latches and mop up their sticky faces. I couldn't imagine how something as adult and brutal as what Krishna and I had done could result in creatures with such fine hair and so much energy.

The women were far gentler than Mrs. Hastings. They

asked me questions about the Indian Museum. They had seen my father's exhibits on mangroves there and said politely how fascinating they had been. They were eager to share their cooled tea. They were quite kind to the porters. They gave money to the beggar who beseeched us at the station where we changed for the narrow-gauge railway that would take us through the forest to get to the ridge of hills that was Darjeeling. They were even cordial to Krishna when he came to fetch me for this last stage of the trip. They thought him a servant and did not see that he didn't cast down his eyes, hear how good his English was, or admire the quality of his face. I saw, too, that he knew this about all of us—how little we saw. It made him angry, his knuckles gone white and shining against the handle of my heavy bag that I was not supposed to lift myself, though I was inches taller than he.

I just made some Darjeeling tea, which I usually avoid. An old packet, stuck behind a cannister, so it is stale but still recognisable. We had it every morning in Calcutta, Gold Leaf Orange Pekoe, the premium variety that cost a great deal. My father supervised the brewing, heating the pot first with steaming water, then tamping the tea in a silver ball my mother had given him the Christmas before she died. The ball was polished every week. You had to keep at it, my father said, or the tannin would creep up, and it was hard to scrub off. The tea itself is amber, smoky, with an edge of sweetness. It brings back those heady weeks in the town that gave the stuff its name, a place where rhododendrons turn into trees of forty or fifty feet. Their petals were like white and crimson bits of silk. Clouds there cloaked the mountains except at sunrise and sometimes at the end of the day. The roads in the town were steep, and because of the altitude, you needed a hot-water bottle to ward off the nighttime

chill. The tea also brings back an afternoon in rattan chairs listening to Mrs. Crowley rant about Gandhi and what she, per-
sonally, wanted to do to him. It was almost precisely what was
done to him just five years later, in fact: a violent death at the
height of his power. Cup after cup after cup, I drank so much
tea during those four weeks in Darjeeling that I was shaking
from the effects and always needing to find a lavatory. But I
would have been that way no matter what I was drinking—
milky Indian coffee, spiced *chai*, purified water, orangeade. My
father was delayed in Calcutta. Mrs. Crowley presided over
military gatherings, parades, and send-offs, and paid no attention to me. Krishna and I never saw each other during the day.
I spent my time instead with the Englishwomen who, like me,
had headed to the hills to settle into mouldy cottages from
which they could admire rain clouds the size of an English
shire and take milk baths to lighten their freckles. Even then,
during the war, people often mentioned how the views reminded them of the Highlands, though how they squared the
Siva temples and the enormous mountains with Scotland never
made much sense to me. I also strolled the Mall and patted the
ponies. I ran up and down the hillsides, kept track of planes flying overhead, and watched soldiers and pilots swagger through
the streets. During the afternoons I wrote poems and planned
my wedding from under the mosquito netting. At night Krishna
would tiptoe into my room, which was the worst in the house
according to Mrs. Crowley, opening as it did onto a garden
where monkeys gathered. Somehow Krishna never bothered
them when he slipped in through the doors that gave onto their
realm. He quoted the poetry of Mirabai to me. He said she was
a woman who had been a Rajasthani princess in the thirteenth
century. " 'Mira's lord is half lion and half man. She turns herself over to the midnight of his hair.' " I could never get my
hands out of his.

He said the feringhees were horrible, except for me, and he had grand plans for India when we left. I told him he was full of rot about us, you just had to get to know us better, and many other silly things a girl tells her first love. We had to be astoundingly quiet. It is a miracle that no one discovered us.

Then my father arrived. He found me one afternoon at the Crowleys'. I was disheveled and tired and feeling recklessly alive. "Happy" would not have been the word. What I was engaged in was too furtive for pure elation, too illicit. And I felt as well that I was on the brink of hurting too many people. I had written Ayah several letters during that month but not heard back from her. So "happy" does not quite cover the sensation. "Bold" or "vibrant" comes closer. My father sensed the change in me and did not like it. He told me to freshen up and meet him at the Windemere for tea. Then he stalked off to his own room, being more brusque with Mrs. Crowley than I'd have thought possible.

We were settled at a small table on the lawn of the hotel when he told me that I would not be going back to Calcutta again and I was to be sent to England by plane within the next few days. It was probably safer than travelling by boat. He was being posted to Burma. I was to live in London with Aunt Fiona and take some courses to prepare myself for university if I liked. (Later I found out that she supplied the funds for my schooling entirely out of her own pocket. I don't think my father really thought girls were worth that kind of fuss.)

I tried to calm myself by looking at the clouds around the mountains. It was hard to grasp that some of the world's tallest, newest peaks loomed behind blankets of fog. When they were covered with mist, it was almost impossible to remember how huge they were, how implacably tall and jagged.

It was growing cool. I had forgotten to bring a wrap, but he did not notice my shivering. Most of the other people in the

garden had moved indoors. "Rose," he said, looking down into
the valley, "I've only brought one trunk of yours. We had to
pack at the last minute. The house has burnt."

I dropped my teacup, and the brown stain spread on the
skirts of my dress. It was going to rain soon, and the wind had
picked up. Monsoon wasn't far off. These were the earliest of
its showers. He reached down to retrieve the cup from the
lawn. A kitchen fire, he said, had spread to the main house
quite quickly. He and Muhammad Rashid had thrown what
they could into a trunk for me. Keepsakes, he said, some books.
The things on my bureau and in the wardrobe. "We filled it and
then had to toss it out the window to some bearers because it
would have been too slow carrying it down the stairs." He took
out a handkerchief and mopped at his moustache.

"Were people hurt?" I asked, dabbing at the stain and making it worse. "Is Ayah all right?" I thought of her own mother,
and how her chances for a good marriage had been dashed in a
fire. It would not come as a surprise to Ayah that a similar dis-
aster might be visited on the daughter.

"We didn't see her afterwards," he said carefully. "You've
made quite a mess," he added.

"Had she gotten my letters?" I asked.

"I gave them to her," he answered, and told me that she had
stayed in the house after I came to Darjeeling but had quarrelled with everyone. She'd seemed very out of sorts.

It was as close as he came to asking me what happened between me and Ayah on the train. Drizzle spattered from the
sky, but neither of us attempted to go inside. The tea stain
etched a darker line at its border as the liquid soaked in. Ayah's
things were gone, they discovered after the ruins had been
raked through, and no human remains were found. She had
lighted out for somewhere. I wondered if she was back in her
village or if she had found another post in the city, though she

wouldn't have gotten far without letters of recommendation. I wondered if she had started the fire herself or simply not checked it. Perhaps she had used it as an opportunity to leave without the difficulty of making a good-bye.

Much was left standing, my father continued. As he spoke, the shower came and went. It was jarring to sit on the plush, wet lawn and talk of a ruinous fire. "Your library?" I asked. Most of his records were at the museum, but he stored ongoing projects in his desk at home. "Oh gone, quite entirely gone," he said. I felt worse and worse. I kept thinking that if I'd been there to talk to Ayah, she wouldn't have been so tempted to leave such wreckage in her path.

Muhammad Rashid had obtained a good position at the museum, my father told me; he'd been able to see to that. Cook had been sacked because the fire had started in his territory. No one was officially accused. No one had seen it start. I thought my father guessed it was Ayah, but really he blamed himself. He hadn't been paying enough attention. We ought to have left India earlier. All the signs were there. Usually so good at predicting unstable weather, he'd missed something gallingly obvious.

I saw all that darting in his face, but he spoke only of how, in the midst of the chaos, Mr. Rao had driven up with pails of water, not to throw them on the flames, but to save the carp. Badger the horse had been impressively calm. Now he was sold to Mr. Mukherjee, at a price, I suspected from my father's tone, that did not match his worth. There had been no time for bargaining. My father took a large, careful sip of tea. He held his hand out, palm down. There was barely a mist now. "You'd still recognise the house, Rose," he said. Marble is fairly hard to destroy, though like any substance, it will melt and crack in great heat. This fire had been quite quick, quite thorough, eating all the furniture and paper and cloth. Someone could rebuild it after the war and probably would. "The columns stayed put, although they are stained, what with the smoke." A servant came then to clear away the cups. My father stopped talking, not wanting to be overheard. Everything had changed.

That night Krishna did not come to my room. Nor the next. Like Ayah, he had disappeared. A visit while my father was in the house was too risky. A letter left for me might have been discovered. He simply went away. I could not blame him. I knew, even as my imagination had danced in other directions, that it had to be over between us. Besides, I was leaving India. He would have known what my father's arrival with all those crates signalled. Perhaps he wanted to be the first to go. I was so hurried and confused the next two days, I barely had time to miss him. That came later.

Sam slipped a note under the door while I was out. "Dear Mrs. Singer: I overstepped myself with the dogs. I am very sorry." I wrote back and told him the dogs were fine and he was welcome to come by. I left the envelope in their mailbox during a walk. Their house is shuttered. The car is gone. The buoys are clanging loudly, and the lupins are fading. Low tide brought a thick smell of fish today and revealed a great deal of tangled green line. I tried unravelling a knot or two, just to see if I could, but it didn't work. There was nothing for it but to finish writing, even if I need to jump to another piece of the story first. The part about David and how I behaved when I met him.

I had a job handling the periodicals at Harvard's medical school when I first met him. I'd been working there several years, and I liked Boston and Cambridge, all the serious, polite students and the buildings trying so hard to look English. David didn't look like he belonged in such a setting. In the cool

and cavernous library, he looked as if he'd stumbled in by accident or even come there on a dare. He seemed much more like
a man comfortable around a table in a smoky bar—the sort of
place I imagined and did not frequent. David was in a leather
jacket, scruffy in a managed way. If he'd been taller, he would
have been rather alarming. Then he asked me where he could
find the latest *Journal of Neuroblastomas*. The pads of his fingers
were wrinkled, and I knew he was just another boy on his way
to becoming a doctor, endlessly scrubbing up. But he also actually looked at me, which most of them did not.

I heard myself say, "You don't look like you're in medical
school, except of course for your hands." My voice sounded
loud. I was never so forward with men. It came from how he'd
looked at me. It was inviting. He'd wanted to make some kind
of contact.

"What am I supposed to look like?" he asked, pleased I was
talking to him, I could see.

"You've got to wear glasses," I said, "be pale, and cultivate a
squint. Fretful, as if you're waiting for your marks on an exam
about the gallbladder."

I had been alone a long time, and had lost the habit of easy
intercourse with others. I was courteous, perhaps, but sealed
off personal exchanges rather than extend them. My colleagues, also reserved people, respected my silence. Librarians,
after all, appreciate quiet, seek it out and enforce it. The stupidity of this was that I read a great deal and went to films
every weekend to hear characters speak wittily to one another.
I rode the subway for the same reason: to listen to people talking. In England, I had stopped playing tennis. I had done nothing but study, and when I was done with university, I came to
Simmons to learn about libraries. It was a good choice then, all
that brisk categorising of knowledge, but I certainly wasn't
well. Without David I would have spun into the lunacy that af-

flicts people who spend too much time by themselves—having
hay in the brain is the sensation, sick with a sterile sort of loneliness. I cared too much about the way the African violet in my
studio bloomed. I was irritated by overturned dustbins in the
streets. What sent him my direction that day and why I chose
to reach out to him are two of the surprises of my life. The desire to keep living had been leaking away from me.

Yet I was embarrassed that I'd said as much as I had, and
I turned away, telling him a little sharply where to find the
journal. He would not let the conversation lapse, however.
"Actually, I don't want to read about brain tumors. I've been
watching you. I think you're in the wrong job."

Normally, I'd have turned my back on him or made my
English accent stronger. I'd noticed how cowed Americans
could be by an English voice. They thought it the indicator of a
certain kind of education, and they didn't differentiate between
someone from London or from Yorkshire. If I wanted to skirt
some encounter, all I usually had to do was speak a few words
and the person would scuttle. But that morning I had seen a pigeon's shadow on the wall of my bedroom, and it had pinned
me to my bed. The bird made me think of Calcutta and the pigeons that had flown through my room there and the great distance between the girl under mosquito netting and the woman
lying in a single bed. I thought about the idea that the creature
had a more pressing reason to move than I did. All I was was
an Englishwoman with a sombre, rather sordid story, lying under her blankets in a flat north of Harvard Square. The bird
had more energy and purpose. I had eventually dressed and
dragged a comb through my hair, not conscious of doing so, but
doing it nonetheless. When you lose will, at least habit will
keep your arm shrugging into a shirt and force the paste on the
toothbrush.

I was just beginning to inhabit myself again when David
came to the desk. My first customer.

"Where are you from?" he asked, swerving away from his first observation. I could smell his leather jacket, its scent of the tannery.

"India," I said, not England, which is what I usually said. "Calcutta."

He looked at me, assessing, fiddling with a pencil. It was 1955. Just seven years since partition. "What do you remember most about it?" he asked then, the pencil gone still.

"Women dying on sidewalks holding their babies who were still breathing," I said. I can't bear recalling that I used to speak that acerbically to well-intentioned people. My hand started to shake on the counter. I was looking at the bookcases that lined the wall, and I was thinking, They are about to fall down. Someone ought to do something, when he placed his hand on mine. My first thought was, I can't marry a man whose hands are smaller than mine. Such an odd moment. I didn't even know his name, but there I was, marrying him. Without once using the word, I had been turning over the problem of connection day after day, of wanting to become part of someone else's world, a task at which I had so badly fallen short. It was not love I felt, but a bumping up against a likeness. Someone similarly damaged but open.

"That's one of the worst things I've ever heard, Rose. That's your name, isn't it? I got a friend of mine to ask."

"Yes," I told him, and asked his. Then I asked him what my job ought to be, the real one. "I don't know what they're called," he said, "but the person who sits up in the crow's nest and watches for storms."

"I'd never fit," I said, but I liked the picture of me scanning the ocean with a spyglass. Then I found myself telling my supervisor that I was taking a break, and David and I were out in the spring light, the clean May wind.

He took me to a coffee shop where women wore black leotards, which sounds silly now, given what has happened since to women's clothes. They also had headbands that pulled their hair off their faces, so that you had nothing to look at but their jaws and noses. David ordered Turkish coffee for us both and poured so much sugar into the small cups that I heard the spoon scrape on the granules before the heat melted them.

He wasn't staring at the girls. He was staring at me. He had a way of watching me that made me feel pretty, which is not a word women my height often use about themselves. Then he said, "Tell me," looking at the scar on my left palm, ripped there by an Indian thorn, "what you remember. All of it." I came to recognise this tone as one he later adopted with patients. He deferred to pain and always hoped that being solicitous would elicit confidences and intimacy. I think that's what David was after at first with me—a closeness of contact with someone he saw as hurt. I don't think he knew for quite some time how damaged he himself was and how I might be helpful. But it astounded me that day: someone had asked, and I had willingly answered.

I told him what had happened in my life—not just that afternoon, but all through that summer and fall, which were unusually mild. It was the beautiful autumn, in part, that made this possible, providing a gentle backdrop for news that was not. He was cutting up cadavers and wrestling with nausea, with driven classmates, and with the weight of yielding to his father's insistence that he become a doctor. He was a man made for something buoyant, born to parents who cultivated fear and intelligence as means to prevent unpreventable disasters. He's not really a scientist, though he retained medical information with an offhanded precision. "Oh yeah, the islets of Langerhans," he would say, and launch into the intricacies of the pancreas. But not for long. Miles Davis would resurface, or a bottle of Burgundy he was saving for us. Wine and jazz; I was almost too old for it. I liked his fervour for the natural world and for politics. I argued with him, and he liked the pressure of someone pushing back. We shared a common suspicion of the breezy Americans around us, as effervescent and insubstantial as their carbonated drinks. It was enough then, at that time, sitting on the rim of the country and looking in.

Yet I was not quite honest with him. I didn't dare be. I liked him very much and wanted only to present my best side, certain that if the worst were known about me, he would excuse himself from our friendship and I would never see him again.

Then, one afternoon in October, David and I went to Walden Pond, which is now just a few miles from our house. He was not content to let me wander the path and admire the water's clarity. Then as now, you could see through the water the round stones that line the pond's bottom. He wanted to swim.

"I don't have a suit," I told him. I didn't tell him then that I didn't even own one. My body was not one I wanted unveiled. Through the summer, he had waited patiently. He liked talking to me. He said he admired what a serious person I was. He had no idea. I was a sixty-year-old woman compared to the girls I worked with.

"No," I told him. "I do not want you to see me." We were standing near the beach. All the other visitors, as far as we could see, had left. It was late in the afternoon and growing cool. How strange to have had the intuition that I would marry him but still be reluctant to be led towards feeling his skin against my own. I needed that skin, that pressure, the voice and life attached to it, and I had had enough of needing.

That afternoon, I knew we were heading towards something new. I saw him looking at me in that way, although he'd been good about not insisting on it. It had been easy in the years I lived alone to dismiss the other men who had tried.

There hadn't been many, but their impatience allowed me to reject them without qualms. Saying no to David, however, would have had consequences. It would have meant taking a step away from my fate, as Ayah would have said.

But nothing prepared me for watching him strip off his jacket and then his shirt and his shoes. He balled his socks, and he tucked his wallet into the pocket of the leather jacket. "Rose," he said, "let's go swimming."

"It's too cold," I protested. He walked closer to me to keep me from retreating up the beach and back to the parking lot.

"I'll keep you warm," he told me.

"I'm frightened," I admitted.

"I will comfort you," he said.

It was that word. No one had used it since I was a child. I would not let him undress me. I took off only my sweater, stockings, and shoes, not even my skirt. "All right then," I said. The sand ended quickly, and soon we were slipping on the brown stones and splashing each other. Our clothing stuck to our bodies. Quite gradually I grew aware of the breadth of his chest. The water was colder than I had anticipated, and it stuck in silver beads to his arms.

"Rose," he said, "there's no one here. The sun is going down, and we are going to drown if we try to swim like this."

"I can't swim," I told him. "I can't even do the dog paddle."

He stopped. "You can't?" The train passed and made the woods on the other side of the pond shake slightly. The water set up a small rippling. "You brave woman. And you're up to your neck." He sloshed over to me, put his arms around me, and pulled me close to him, and we were cold and warm at once. I felt happy and relieved, for the first time in years, and still I knew I could not fully undress. This was all I was going to allow him. He had no idea how little courage I actually had. I did not think I could afford to have him see me naked. He was training to be a doctor. He would know, unlike most men, how to interpret the marks on my body. He would see that I'd had a child.

Soon after our swim, I told him. Always sympathetic, David was nonetheless taken aback. Partly, I think, because what I'd done was at such odds with how I appeared and spoke. I had changed over the years, I said, and as I talked, I knew it was true that I was different now, that I wanted to be part of the world. He listened to me, held me as I spoke, and did not ask many questions. Perhaps it was a way of protecting himself. But he also felt this way about information: once you know something, you are obliged to behave in light of that knowledge.

Not much later, he asked me for my hand, as he put it, and I accepted. "You were very young and very lonely," he said. "I don't know why, but I get this feeling you're the one I'm supposed to marry." And so we did, in Cambridge, by a justice of the peace. Our parents barely commented, they were that horrified. My father sent a large cheque and a letter saying he hoped matrimony would suit me. Walter and Isabella took the train up from New York in December and looked at me with both kindness and mistrust, an appraisal that's shifted little over the years.

We set out to live with the consequences of old grief without letting ourselves dwell on them. David was keen for children, and I wanted badly to make him happy, to confirm his sense that I was part of something destined for him.

The pregnancies and labours were straightforward. I was told at the time that I was lucky to have such easy ones. The only other person who knew I'd had a child before was the doctor who delivered me, a friend of David's. The new babies helped us in our task of getting on, as did our work, the dogs, the houses. But the children are growing, the dogs are old, the houses well-tended. Nothing needs us as much, and we have started to look at each other with less of a sense of fatedness and more awareness of choice.

All this at a time when the present looks exceedingly bleak. And when people from India have come back into my life and my past is abruptly available to me again. It's tempting to think that news about the old troubles has returned because a crack in current history has made that possible. Since last spring I've caught myself thinking of Anna as my second child and James my third, words I'd always banned before.

I gave birth to a little girl by Krishna in February 1944 in Folkestone, in a home for unwed mothers that Aunt Fiona had found. I thought the nausea I felt when I got to England was from the long trip and the dislocation. I could even blame one missed cycle on that disruption. But not two. Aunt Fiona was incredibly kind. "It's a confused time, my dear," she said to me when she found me being sick one morning. "We are all of us not ourselves." She sighed, helped me up, and said, "A soldier. Some horrible young man who just forced himself on you." She did not want to hear anything else, much less any deviation from her version of the story. My father had not supervised me closely enough, and this is what had happened: her fears had been realised. Her rightness gave her a burnished energy. She did not say a word to my uncle Lawrence. My cousins were away in the country, boarded out to farm families. She managed to keep my condition quite secret, though it's why I don't like to go back to England. I can never be sure who knows what or what was said.

I always stayed in touch with Aunt Fiona, however. She led that household with spirit and verve, if not a great deal of native intelligence. If she decided to take me away and find me a small cottage to live in, as she did, she could. She got me to the home when the time came. She made sure I had everything I needed. She never once reproached me. "It has," she said once, "happened before in the history of the world."

But two things were understood from the beginning. I was never to tell my father. Aunt Fiona may have told him, or he could have heard a family rumour, but he has never behaved any differently with me. In part, this was a great relief. In part, it was horrid, because having the baby changed me drastically, and I couldn't discuss it with the person whom I'd known longer than anyone but Ayah. That uncertainty as to whether he knew was one of the reasons I went to university and then left England for good.

Another reason was that I couldn't bear to be in the same country where my daughter was. That was the second understanding. I was not to keep the baby.

They do not do this now, I am sure. But then, when a child was born who was to be put up for adoption, the mother nursed it for several weeks before it was given to the new family. You stayed with the other girls in the home and took care of your baby, and then a relative came to fetch you once you weren't quite so tired and a bit more back to your normal figure.

I remember that she was beautiful. She looked like her father. She had fairish hair, though she was darker-skinned than most of the other English infants. Her eyes, however, seemed like they would stay blue, and I was shamefully pleased. At that time, birth certificates announced only the mothers' names. The fathers' line could be left blank, and that is what I did, like most of the girls. It was why we were there.

The baby didn't cry much. She waved her hands the way infants do. I was frightened I would drop her. Nurses rustled about. We fed the children, then one of attendants would come and whisk them off. We weren't allowed to spend too much time holding them, for fear we'd become too attached.

What nonsense. I had lived with her inside me for nine months and given birth to her. I had held her and fed her. I would be attached to her for the rest of my life.

I have no idea where she is or who she is or if she is even alive.

Anna looks like her. When I held Anna the first time, it was as if the first daughter had been given back to me. I promised myself to be a mother who wouldn't die. I don't think I knew then that that isn't quite enough. Nor did I know how hard it would be to turn into a person who just loves someone. It had been so dangerous to do that. I'd had so little experience of it. I had Krishna's example, but that was brief and full of passion that had caused me pain and trouble. I remember just how much, because I saw him again recently, which is one of the reasons I decided to start writing.

I had gone to the Gardiner Museum to see the flowers, then decided to walk over to the Museum of Fine Arts. I hadn't been in Boston in ages. It was a whim, a kind of pleasure I rarely allow myself. But it was too hot to garden, and the children wouldn't be back until three. I was in the gallery with the Gauguin paintings when I saw the Indians. What caught my eye was the walk: so distinctive, feet turned slightly outward, deliberate and limber. They weren't looking at the paintings; they were gesturing at the gallery, the lights, the way the room was built. They wore thin cotton shirts and did not look flattened by heat, though it was one of those brutally warm days of late spring. They raised their hands to flick hair or push back spectacles. Indian men visiting Boston. A delegation from Delhi, I thought. Engineers with a hole in their schedule. They stopped in front of one of the Tahiti paintings. Then I heard the rushing flow of Bengali. They were teasing each other. After twenty-five years it was hard to understand, but I grasped enough to know that one man was ribbing the other about the girl in the picture. "That's what you wish your wife looked like, isn't it, Suresh? That would be nice to come home to, wouldn't it?"

Then someone said, "Yes, but can she keep up her end of

the conversation?" and they all laughed, and I looked more closely. The man who had spoken was Krishna Banerjee. He was balding now, bespectacled, and had obviously enjoyed his share of *bhelpuri*, the Calcutta delicacy. The lenses were thick in his frames. I must have moved, because, ever alert, he glanced up and saw me. He stood very still. He knew exactly who I was, as I had known him. He waved at me, barely a gesture, an involuntary lift of the palm. It could have been read as an invitation either to come forward or to stop. It can work both ways in India. Then he turned towards his group with what I have to say was tenderness. I watched him for a few moments. He hung back slightly, wondering, I think, if I was going to approach him.

To say what? I thought as they went to the next gallery. Trade pleasantries about his family and mine? Describe the baby born in Folkestone? Admit I had nearly lost myself after that? Say that for years I could not sleep without nightmares or have a day not split in two by headaches? Certainly if David had been there, I would not have come forward. But I was alone. I could have gone up and said hello and been introduced. Spoken their language rustily in a bad accent. Endured some polite and awkward minutes, halfhearted invitations to tea, Bengalis to the last. He was right. It was better to let the moment pass.

I could guess more or less why he was there. Scientists on an exchange program with botanists in America or some such scheme. He must have been well-placed to earn that sort of honour. He would be living in a decent area of Calcutta, in a flat with his wife, who was a good cook and a good Brahmin. He was spending his days doing science, maybe even at the Indian Museum. He'd negotiated political difficulties with aplomb. In the evening he would see his friends, and they would talk of corruption and elections and then listen to music.

A few days a week, I imagined, he would come home in time to take his daughter on his knee as she told him what she'd done in school. What pleasure it is to have a daughter, he would say, then pass her to his wife for her evening bath.

I saw that he had recognised me, that he had not forgotten me, that he remembered everything, and that it had mattered to him, too. That sort of love, as wide and unnavigable as a flooded river, is hard on children, on family. I had given that kind of emotion to Krishna, and he owned it, fat and bespectacled as he was. None of it meant that he hadn't been brave and lovely and shown me something marvellous. I drove unsteadily home. I did not tell David, of course. There was no way to do so without wounding him, and we'd founded our marriage on not causing each other more pain.

As much as that is possible, which isn't very. Apparently Krishna was to be the one person who would know me as someone capable of gentleness. Krishna's and my affection was a rare thing. For the rest, I had Ayah's model of love, the one devoted to serious scolding and the assertion of authority. It had been very difficult to develop something less dire and to keep myself from returning to the blankness of the years after the first baby came. It took a great deal of will just to stand upright. Besides, what love I had to give might well be treacherous.

My father, it seems to me now, has had much the same sort of problem. He needed his rigidity to manage his work, to deal with me, to handle his own substantial grief at losing a young and cherished wife. I remember him on the Darjeeling airfield at dawn, the only time of the day when the clouds lift long enough to allow for safe passage. "Be cheerful, Rose" was all that he could say. "No long faces." Then, just as I was about to leave, my trunk and valise loaded into the belly of the plane, he added, "Good girl. Chin up," and waved. I didn't see him again for three years. The plane flew to Delhi, and all I recall, because I was shaking with sadness and fear, were the white peaks of Kanchenjunga, five snub teeth that glowed for a short time as the sun hit their eastern face. It took almost a week, on flights filled with soldiers and parachutes and gas masks, to get across Asia to London. I never found out how he managed to arrange it for me. I never got over a fear of flying after that, either. Planes rattle so in the sky. I was in a sort of stupor when I saw Aunt Fiona and Uncle Lawrence in London. It was the end of May, 1943. They were kind and effusive and gave me a comfortable room. My trunk was carried by a pair of boys too young to have been conscripted. The pallor of their skin struck me. I'd never seen white servants before. One of the first things Aunt Fiona said was "Rose, dear, your complexion. It's so swarthy," and she left me with what must have been one of the last jars of cold cream available on Bond Street.

After I had slept for a couple of days, I gathered the strength to unpack. Throughout the trip I had not dared think much about home in Calcutta. Not about the house, Ayah, or Krishna. Instead, I had balled my handkerchief up in knots, sipped awful tea, and eaten a few biscuits. I stared at the night sky as we flew, dark as the land. The cities below had been bombed or blacked out. I took letters from soldiers and promised to post them in London. I said "Thank you" over and over to people who steered me from one plane to the next, people who made sure my old-fashioned trunk and valise made each step of the journey with me. I slept on a folded jumper that did not lose the smell of fuel for a long time after.

I inspected the photographs that Fiona had of my mother with her sisters, all of them in large bows and high collars. Throughout, I felt seasick, at odds, uncertain. It seemed quite fantastic that I was related to them, though you could see the resemblance—my mouth and nose shared out amongst these black-and-white pictures. I experienced not the slightest tug of recognition or connection. It felt impossible to touch what I was most familiar with, until one day I finally forced myself to open the trunk and take out the few clothes my father had saved. My mother's comb had survived, but not the wedding portrait. Then I pulled out a notebook in which I saw Ayah's practise alphabet, the letters small and careful. Below it lay the beads I had broken in the garden, the ones we had restrung and never played with again. I knew that I had not left them on my bureau and desk with all the other odds and ends my father gathered in his haste. She had put them there, knowing I would find them.

I unearthed them in the Concord attic last May when I received a letter, which is the other reason I started writing. It came with a note from Fiona's daughter, a frequent enough occurrence for David not to pay particular attention to it. "This arrived for you, Rose," my cousin wrote, "and we've sent it on. News from old friends?" It was from Sujata, the oldest of Ayah's girls. Padmini and Puja had died, as I knew. Radha lived in Howrah; Sita was studying to be a zoologist.

Sujata was a teacher in the school her mother had founded back in their village. English medium, she told me, and very well respected: the Sri Lakshmi School for Young Ladies. She thought I would want to know that her mother had died recently. The letter had been written in March. Ayah had had an infection of the lungs, and mercifully it had not been a painful illness.

Over the years in England, I wrote to Ayah in her village. I knew only its name and province, and that was all I put on the envelopes, with no certainty she ever received the letters. I used Aunt Fiona's house in London for the return address, which seemed the most permanent one I had. I told Ayah that she had been right about Krishna, that I had found the beads, that I thought she'd started the fire. That I had had a baby. That I was studying hard, trying to get on with things. That my father had settled into work with the journal and we never spoke of India. That I forgot more and more Bengali every day. Writing the letters helped steady me—seeing my trouble march out onto the page and then off, to someone who knew me well. Childish gestures, hopeful ones.

Sujata said that her mother had saved them all, which was how she had found my address. Her mother never had the time to write back, what with running the school and caring for her family. (She made no mention of Mr. Kumar, and I never found out what happened to him.) I answered her right away, including a donation for Sri Lakshmi, and said how glad I was to hear about her family and how sorry I was that Mrs. Kumar had died. But I did not mention that my heart had jolted to read that Ayah, who she said was called Shantiji by her students, had always called me *choto konya*, youngest daughter.

David had found me sitting in the kitchen, unable to make supper. He was tired to the bone; it had been a long and gruelling day for him at hospital—a fire, children with burns. Was I okay, he asked, and I said, "It's nothing, really. I'll be fine." He didn't believe me, but he didn't press and instead pulled sandwich makings from the icebox. I watched him watching me as he sliced tomatoes and spread mayonnaise, but I could not bring myself to tell him. I would have had to hear myself say aloud that the woman who had raised me had died. And it was more than that. I had never called her anything but Ayah—she would have scolded me otherwise. Taking such familiar liberties wasn't done, though we knew so much about one another. I don't think she ever guessed that in my head I'd always called her *Amma*, the Bengali word for mother. I never let it slip, not once. If I had, she would have slapped me hard. But *Amma* was the sound that wrapped around her in my mind, at the core of another old memory, older if less clear than the one about the necklace: her strong hands holding my small, fat ones, guiding me step by step up the broad stone stairs of the house we did not own, whose burning she would later take part in. But then, teaching me to walk, she wasn't thinking of flames. She was making sure I could conquer the smallest, most human of challenges—finding balance on unsteady legs.

I rose early after sleeping badly and saw on the calendar that today is Bastille Day. Revolution. Thronged streets. Aristocrats fleeing in carriages losing wheels on unspeakable roads. I was glad that David had taken his radio. In the car on the way to the store, I heard about fighting in Central America, riots in Northern Ireland. More bombs of course in Vietnam. Between those reports of dire news rose memories of Ayah. The way she braided her hair without needing to look at the progress of the plait. Sucking at her teeth when they pained her and taking another one of my sweets anyhow. With all this racketing about my head, it amazed me I was still in Maine, passing the small houses painted blinding white, returning to the cottage.

I'd just opened the door when I heard a car race into the Ellises' driveway. The tires spun, and the dogs were startled and barked madly. Karen raced over, and I saw that her face was the colour of wax. "Is he here?" she kept asking.

Of course she meant Sam. They'd driven with him to Boston to talk to a doctor, which is why the house has been shuttered and locked. I had wondered if just before he left, Sam hadn't come into the cottage while I was out and read through my pages. A few had been in the wrong place, and something had felt disturbed. The bastard, I had thought—unkindly, I knew, but I was furious. This is terrible, but when I heard that after the appointment Sam had run, I hoped he wouldn't come back, that he'd take what he'd learned about me with him.

I tried to get Karen to sit, to give her a blanket because she was shivering, but she wanted to go next door to see if he had left a note or taken clothes. I could hear her calling "Sam?" Sam?" over and over as she tore through their house. He'd been upset because the monkey in space had died, Karen told me, her teeth nearly chattering. The official cause was reported as ventricular fibrillation, but Karen said that Sam kept shouting, "It was terrified. It had a heart attack because it was terrified." I imagined Sam's narrow back and his long legs running, pushed faster and faster by fear. "I thought he'd come here," Karen kept saying, once she'd finished searching their home. Her hair was flying about, and the dogs swarmed at her knees, their tails wagging, trying to assuage her fright. I didn't dare ask where her husband was and could picture his rage, his dismissal of his disappointing son. "Maybe Sam will be back by tonight," she said again.

"That's right," I agreed. But we both knew he'd been trying to escape all summer and probably before that, and that she might never see him again. Sometimes lost children stay lost, and that did not mean you hadn't done the best you could, that you hadn't given what you had, even if it wasn't what was called for or what soothed. Even so, you had parted with it.

Part Three

Storm of midnight, like a giant child awakened in
the untimely dark, has begun to play and shout.
— Rabindranath Tagore

Anna

June–July 1992 ✣❀✣ Calcutta

I should have seen it coming. At first I thought it was only going to be an affair with Krishna. I never thought of an actual half sister—a baby, the result of a passionate first, maybe only, love. I started reading the last section on the plane from Varanasi, but I couldn't make it through to the end. Once I got to the hotel, I forced myself to finish, and then once I had, I needed to lie down on the bed and cover my head with a pillow. The news was too overcoming, as Abu might have put it. I couldn't help it: I started to imagine Rose's child. She's forty-eight if she's still alive. I see her as tall, with dark skin. She lives with her family in Chester in a pretty detached house. She's got two kids, a husband in real estate. She likes to do watercolors on weekends, and for vacation they go to the Algarve. Then the whole picture shreds. She could be anything, anyone. I don't know her name, if she's got good teeth, if she still has blue eyes. Is she Baptist? Buddhist? An artist, a teacher, a mathematician? Could she find us? Where is she? Rose said the fathers' names weren't on the certificates, but wouldn't the mother be traceable? Rose's name and identity must have been written down somewhere. Kundera says the only immortality is in police files, but hospital records come close. There's got to be a history. Or did Aunt Fiona take care of that as well?

I can't believe not knowing about her daughter hasn't destroyed Rose. But perhaps it has, given how sternly she raised us and how stiffly she's controlled herself. Letting go of that first child closed off something central, a critical valve. She functioned, but never as fully as she might have. She was like the civil servants who returned from India and distressed Aunt Fiona with their need for more sea air than other people. Perhaps that was Dad's great disappointment: he had thought, as he always did, that with love and patience he could help her thrive. But she couldn't recover, entirely. His tactic worked better in medicine, less with a mangled past. The damage had been too severe. Their marriage hadn't been arranged, but it turned into a marriage with its arrangements. He turned to us to lessen his sadness: Red Sox games, bicycle rides, attendance at our plays and games, and that total warmth he gave us whenever we came home, that broad smile. "My children," he'd say over and over, even when James turned into a technocrat and I married the wrong man. "My lovely children."

Rose couldn't fully avail herself of that consolation—James and I provoked too much ambivalence—but she tried as hard as she could, I do believe that. It's clearer now, too, why she never liked going to England and also why she settled so firmly, if strangely, in America. The only place I remember Rose looking entirely comfortable during our one trip together to England was in Kew Gardens. She moved slowly through the great park, examining the bizarre ornamentals, touching bark and leaves, and saying, "Yes, that's a tree that grew in Bengal. It has pink flowers in the spring." Pressing the trunk, leaning close.

It's four in the morning, and I am in a hotel in the center of Calcutta, not far from where the Missionaries of Charity tend orphans and the dying. This city was the part of the trip that concerned friends most, the name itself a source of anxiety. Americans imagine crowds, Marxist riots, flooded subways, slums the size of Boston. The story of the Black Hole still jars, even if people don't remember when it took place or how many were killed. (I had to look it up, too. The incident occurred in 1756; Siraj-ud-daula, a nawab who'd attacked the city, locked British prisoners in a guardroom, where they suffocated one humid June night. The numbers of the dead are disputed; perhaps as many as 123 perished, perhaps as few as 60. A horrid fate. Then you wonder about Indians in British jails, and what happened there.)

But I haven't seen much of the city yet—not the Indian Museum, not the Victoria Memorial, not Rose's old neighborhood, and I haven't called Kartik, Lev's friend. Since reading Rose's pages, I haven't been able to do much more than go out to change a bit of money or find some food. I've only explored near the hotel, which means that I've bumped into the Missionaries quite often as they pick their way steadily though the crowds, not bothering to glance at the uneven pavements. The women are deeply familiar with the broken curbs and sudden drops. Distinctive in their white robes with the blue thread at the edge of the head scarves, they come not only from India but from Africa and Europe. It's curious that no matter what their origin, they look alike. It's less the habit than an eerie smoothness in their faces, the certainty that they are doing good and that God sleeps close to them. They are not so much righteous as focused. They've singled out a purpose and submitted to their calling. They move slowly, not only because of the heat, which has the force of a slap, but because their work—bathing people, dressing wounds, giving medicine—requires that considered pace.

Calcutta's as big and filthy as Delhi, as slow-moving as Varanasi. Sprawling doesn't begin to describe it, but saying that every alley and boulevard is crammed with people might give the right impression. Indians still call streets footpaths, even when thousands of cars, bicycles, and rickshaws block the way. Then you look closer and see people walking near the vehicles; it's always inspiring how many of them do manage without shoes. Shod or not, it requires incredible concentration to thread your way through. If you stop for a second to take in the breadth of the scene, the thickness of the exhaust, the sheer numbers, you'll be mowed down, shoved, or made to lose your bearings. Shoulder to shoulder, elbow to elbow, Calcuttans press steadily onward, in constant physical contact with one another. As in the other cities I've visited, it's very difficult to imagine the British here, though their presence—in the architecture and the occasional street name—is slightly more palpable.

On the other hand, Mother Teresa's portrait hangs everywhere, her face as puckered as a dried apple. You see her in rows of pictures, between Gandhi and Kali, in restaurants and shops. Odd that an Albanian girl should find her way here and be venerated next to a Jain with incredible political instincts and the goddess of destruction. Yet it's no less odd than most stories of immigrants, no matter the direction, from east to west, north to south, which are always stories that combine wonder and disappointment in nearly equal measure. Even as exiles marvel at their luck, they know, too, that their new world could collapse or fall to pieces anytime. But Mother Teresa would probably scoff at this description of her life. God had his vision for her the whole time, she'd say. Even the setbacks were put there by Jesus to test her resolve and make her work harder.

James and Rose arrive in four days. If I joined the Missionaries, I wouldn't have to match the Rose I've known with the one she's revealed to me, as cracked and hard to navigate as a Calcutta street. I've always followed Rose as if I were in moving traffic, doggedly attached to a single perspective, one I could live with. Now she's come to a halt in front of me, and the stillness of the picture, its frailty, make me want to run right back into the choked road.

According to Rose, Dad didn't want to ask too many questions, either, but that wouldn't have meant he didn't believe at heart in reconciliation, even partial reconciliation. Given that the holes in his own history were so glaring—the lost cousins, uncles, grandparents—it probably amazed him that Rose wouldn't want to connect to the pieces available to her. I remember their arguments: Dad stalking around the kitchen, hands raised, Rose frozen as marble at the table, her eyes trained out the window. They were so different, yet they yielded to an intuition that they belonged together. This was a strange contrast to their views on religion, but in India it's clearer to me that we are often more vulnerable than we like to think—to something sensed but not necessarily seen, whether it's the future, love, science, God. Rose and Dad believed both that they'd been fortunate to get to Boston and that they should never forget what they'd seen and where they came from. She leaned into Dad's tolerance for wounded people and responded to that generosity as well as she could. She let him be Isabella and Walter's son. She ironed and burned his shirts. She had his babies. She was probably a good wife in ways I'll never know. She's discussed a great deal, but there are still acres and acres to cover, regions we will never get to. It's a wonder how vast a country a single parent can turn out to be.

Rose is brave, much braver than I knew. She'll have to tell James about all this, if she hasn't already. It's one of the reasons she's coming here. Yet this admiration doesn't stop me from wondering more about how she became the mother my brother and I knew, someone who actively scared us. I keep remembering small moments of meanness. Once, she refused us a night-light in the bathroom because it would waste energy. Another time, she botched James's haircut and was angry when

Dad spent money for a barber to repair the damage. Maybe she feared that if she loved us too much, showed it too boldly, someone would rip us away, as if Durga, Kali, or Indra could dip down from the heavens and scoop up something she had the temerity to claim. She'd mentioned that Ayah would have been surprised to find out how much Indian beliefs had influenced her.

Then again, having had one child taken, she knew that children don't quite belong to parents. Not only can they be taken, they can leave, like Sam, who never did come back. They never found him. A couple of years after he disappeared, the Ellises divorced and sold their house. Karen moved to Santa Fe and from time to time wrote in a perfect hand on embossed stationery to tell Rose about her deep and total loneliness.

Maybe, too, Rose knew she wasn't exactly trustworthy, not only because she'd proved that with her own decisions, but because no one is. She knew—from India, her own life, the way she was raised—that luck and people can turn without notice. One walloping moment of weakness or bad fortune makes room for others, so she would not let us rely on someone who'd already shown she couldn't be counted on.

But then I imagine her in the home for unwed mothers. She would have been eighteen and a half. I picture a newborn in her arms, and a hovering nurse. The Great Wall indeed. By the time her father's colleague called her that, she'd been breached a thousand times.

I'm beginning to understand James's impulse to move to South America. It's tempting to believe that it would be easier to start fresh rather than meet here in the city where Rose was born and have to talk to each other about half sisters, fire, and old loves. I wonder if gathering in Calcutta will prompt other confessions. Maybe James has a child out of wedlock in Rio.

Maybe Rose will tell us Dad had a long-term affair with an attending physician. Right now, I just don't want to know. And all I've got to confess is an abortion after my second year of marriage, an event I've often thought of here in this place filled with babies.

I am having breakfast in a coffee shop near my hotel, and I am watching a group of students argue. Thin, intense young men with floppy hair are yelling at each other, reaching for books to find page numbers, quote references. I've just called Kartik, Lev's friend, and arranged a visit to his shop later today. "Great," he said. "Looking forward to meeting you. Lev said you might call." In the background I heard children wailing and a woman trying to calm them.

I'd had to do something to get out of the hotel and get away from my own memories. Since reading about Rose's first daughter, I have been unable to stop thinking about the child I did not have. It had been shocking to have my pro-choice politics bump up into the emotions and arguments on the other side. Whatever the doctor pulled from my body that winter afternoon was alive. It had been the bud of a being. I'd felt it there, turning into something.

But I knew that I would lose my husband if I had the baby, and that is what started the unraveling of the marriage. Then I lost in every possible way: no baby, tied to never forgiving Mark for being who he was, tied eventually to losing him not just to that girl, but to ambitions too grand for ordinary, child-rumpled love. I didn't tell my family—not only out of shame at the abortion, but shame at the smallness of my marriage, its inability to accommodate disparate visions. From then on, Mark and I proved unable to live in carefully handled compromise, at peace with what we'd given up because it let us stay together. The sum should have been larger, even with its flaws and awkwardness, than our separate, preserved selves.

It would certainly have been easier if Mark had shared my

grief. He was kind enough; he made me soup and brought me flowers. But he wasn't sad. He was terribly relieved because he'd won that skirmish. He moved on crisply, busying himself with new projects, though his hard work came to seem a way to avoid feeling much of anything at all.

I wanted to get over it. My body healed well. But I stopped sleeping through the night. The poems I wrote then were about orchards bred to produce bitter fruit, houses with holes blown through their rooms, old cities lost beneath sidewalks. I wrote, in short, about nothing but wanting to be a mother and the fear I knew came with it now. You could never charm the world into safety for a child, yet you could still want nothing more than to bring a child into it. The amulets and kohl that Indian parents give their babies to fend off evil make a lot of sense to me. The illness, pain, and terror that life delivers are stronger than even a fortress built of money, prayer, and love.

It must have been awful for Rose to stoop down to wipe our faces and think of the other baby. To buy clothes for us and wonder how big the first girl had grown. Still, she did it. Hoed her garden, drove us around to our practices, and even managed to put her story down on paper, because no matter how much she weeded the lettuce or brushed the dogs, what had happened to her had made her ache. It needed a page to spill onto.

But then for more than twenty years she kept silent about it. It took Dad's death and my trip to bring the news back out in the open. Maybe she felt something as human as this: she never knew when she too might be taken away from us, the way Dad had been. Maybe she didn't want us leafing through her papers without her. Maybe she was frightened that we'd never know or that we'd overlook the bundle of pages, and that her story would be lost entirely. She wanted in some way for us to be aware of what had gone on and of who she had been. It caught me hard, how much she must love us, if you think of love as terrible honesty, an exposure of your darkest self and then a standing still.

She's let me in on so much. The old flame returning. And he was a thickset man of middle age whom she recognized from behind. She remembered the way he lifted his hand. He also knew immediately who she was. It had been twenty-six years since he'd seen her, and I get the sense that part of her could have walked right back to him. Turned it all over to the midnight of his thinning hair. *Bhalobasa*. But it wasn't just seeing Krishna that got her writing, or even the grief for Ayah.

She was thinking of that baby as she wrote, not just me and James, as she had day after day, so the pages became something addressed to all of her children, two known, one not. Two available to her, interested but skittish, wary of her imperious ways. It had hurt, trying to get too close. The other was oblivious, making tea somewhere maybe, fiddling with the loose hem of her dress, pouring milk for a tired child, having no idea she was the object of such passionate concern and pressing love.

Here in the coffee shop, two of the students are standing now and shouting at each other. They've slammed their books shut, and they gesture angrily at the waiter to bring the bill. They throw some rupees on the table and storm out into the stunning heat. I wonder what it was they'd been debating. Economics, biology, political theory. Something they cared about. No matter how abstractly they'd begun, the conversation had gotten personal, grown bitter. For a moment after they left, all the other customers stopped talking, taking in the enmity, noticing the empty space the two men left.

I've just come back from an evening with Kartik and his family. It was calming to get out of my room and to walk into the thicket of people on the street, to be just another person with my own set of troubles, propped up next to the other twelve million living here. The pleasures of not mattering in a huge city. The thought of going back to New York to be one among many came as a comfort, not as a threat of isolation. I am looking forward to its dance of faces and language, to sitting in the usual mix of everyone in a jolting subway car, looking and listening. Perhaps I'll be more aware of the work that has gone into fashioning our separate and most likely incompatible versions of life in America, the country's great, complicated gift, the chance to make that word mean almost anything. "American" is marvelously, frighteningly, an adjective as mutable as a tide line, a sky.

Walking out of my hotel, I noticed a sign hanging on a window front that said HAPPY MONSOON FROM POPY UMBRELLAS. The first showers have started: low, heavy clouds are starting to clump up in the east in the afternoon, and the rain brings a blessed temporary coolness. To avoid getting soaked, I took a rickshaw to Kartik's. They are still pulled by people here. I couldn't find a cab, and the driver seemed desperate. He was impossibly thin. I got off after a few blocks and paid him double what he'd asked. I couldn't bear to watch him struggle. He had prominent cheekbones, wrists like a girl's. His gums had receded so that his teeth resembled white guitar pegs with wide gaps between them. He wiped his forehead with a rag. After stashing his money in a fold of his dhoti, he wheeled his rickshaw off.

From the taxi I found at last, I kept watching children. Babies are everywhere, crying, laughing, being passed from arm to arm. In India there's no shame in a crying child; people simply try to make the child happier. Everything's acceptable. Babies on the backs of motorcycles. Babies in bicycle rickshaws. Babies screaming in trains. Of course there's trouble, Indian parents seem to say. That's just in the world. They know better than most people how many obstacles can crop up in a child's life. But we have places to go, they seem to say. The children need to see their grandparents. We're going on pilgrimage.

Kartik embodies this attitude with a delicate grace. He's married to a beautiful woman named Bharati. They have three children, from two to nine. He came back to India, he said, because he missed the weather, then he laughed. He and Bharati asked after Lev, hoped he wasn't going off the deep end. "Not yet," I said, "he's still reading Dick Francis," and we agreed this was a good sign. We could have broached something more then—I saw Bharati look at me closely—but all of us decided to enjoy the lightness that monsoon seems to bring, to keep things simpler, as much as this is possible in India. We went to the shop where Kartik sells his statues, all elegant, traditional forms. Gods and goddesses are subtly worked in gray schist. Some are bold and large, the others miniature beauties. I was drawn to the small ones, which we looked at while sitting in a room on whose floor was a thin mattress covered in Indian cloth. "That's my brother's stuff," Kartik said. "He does the hard ones."

I asked where he was. At his wife's family's, Bharati said. "They lost a baby a few months ago. They are visiting for a ceremony at her parents' place." She said it calmly, and I didn't want to ask more. I picked up a gorgeous piece, a tiny rendition of dancing Krishna and his consort Radha. "When did he make this?" I asked. "A couple of weeks ago," Kartik said. Krishna's love of trickery and pleasure were evident in the soft lines the man had shaped with an eye that refused to be entirely informed by grief. In the meantime, Kartik and Bharati's kids were spilling like talkative water around us.

Kartik invited me to go to a magic show tomorrow. "Come with the kids," he said. "They're glad to see an American."

"Disneyland," cried the oldest, who still remembered. It was the first time it had felt quite safe to be American in India. We talked of both countries. They still love Berkeley. Kartik looked dreamy at the mention of Chez Panisse, and they might go back to California sometime, but for now they've chosen Calcutta for their children and their extended family. Like Amit Patel, the man I met on the flight over, they were open to a lot of possible combinations, willing to handle the complications that arose.

Before I left, Kartik said he'd take me to visit Kumartoli to see if we could find Rose's house. They had no idea how the tea, children, and beautiful sculptures had helped. On the way to get a taxi with Kartik, a transformer failed. Years were shaved away from the century. Merchants stuck candles in gunnysacks of rice. The small gleam of light cast short shadows and made the grains shimmer. Televisions died. Little shops turned from lockers shiny with packets of nuts and candies into narrow caves. But voices didn't lift with surprise. People were used to this sort of disruption and had ways to handle it. Flashlights were switched on, and we watched a young man shimmy up an electric pole to fiddle with a profoundly dangerous-looking tangle of wires. A cascade of blue and white sparks showered onlookers, the man laughed, shielded his eyes, then slid back to the ground to some appreciative laughter. A moment later, light flooded again onto the street and people leaned over to blow out the candles.

I woke early this morning and decided to try to find Rose's street myself. I wanted to spare Kartik the trouble, and I didn't quite trust myself to talk about Rose. Cotton Street was fairly easy to find. I even saw some of the statue-makers, who were painting a large blue Siva when I saw them. But Grandfather was probably wrong. The house hadn't been rebuilt, or if it was, it had been torn down again. I think I saw the remnants of a gate, though the statues and the gardens are gone. The astrologer, too. "I am looking for the stone lions," I said to an elderly man with glasses.

"Lions?" he asked. "Not for a long time, madam. That was many years ago. Not here now." In place of the house with its gardens and its carp stood four tall cement buildings, their terraces draped in drying saris.

I wondered if Rose will be disappointed when she comes here, if she decides to make the visit. I tried too to imagine her as a girl, walking in a stiff dress down the crowded street, and I could barely conjure the picture. It was hard to see her moving freely here. Maybe she hadn't. Maybe she'd always walked that upright, that conscious of who she was and how she didn't fit, because she had to be.

I asked the man to indicate the way to the river, and he did, with a motion that chopped the space in front of his body with his forearm. Walking through narrow streets, surrounded by children in school uniforms, I thought of the kids who'd watched Krishna and Rose as they began their courtship. I wondered where her school was, and the Kali shrine. I didn't see one, but that was probably because I didn't know where or how to look. No lepers there at any rate. The kids followed me gleefully, and I started to yield to their giddy good humor. It is almost impossible not to, they are so curious. I was more interesting to them than getting to class, and we chattered at each other companionably until I came to the Hooghly, which was broad and brown.

Brickmakers with tall, smoking kilns make their wares here, using mud from the banks. Houses were built to the edge of the river. Women came out from one of these to say hello and invited me in by scooping their arms in the air, as if I were water being steered toward shore. When I smiled and nodded to a bench by a tiny shrine to Ganesh, they understood and brought tea out. Three weeks ago I would have said no and hurried on, suspicious and frightened at the closeness of the contact. Today I'm grateful for the company. They talked in Bengali and fingered my rings and my satchel's strap. They were curious, too, about my hair, which, to their pleasure, I took out of its braid. It's finally clean; the hotel I'm in has hot water a couple hours a day. It's not dissimilar to theirs, if not quite as deeply black. We sat there, the women and the children and I, in the sun by the river that had flooded on the day Rose was born. Mutually unintelligible. I thought of Lev and his precise, excellent Hindi, which he'd taken the time to learn well. The exact words didn't matter right then, though of course they would if I stayed, if I tried to be part of someone's life.

Two of the young women, giggling the entire time, braided my hair into something tight and intricate. They brought out a mirror, but they were shaking so with laughter it reflected mostly river and edge of an ear. I couldn't see what I looked like until I got back to the hotel. I never could have created something so elaborate without the assistance of many hands. It's a kind of woven crown, and at the back they'd threaded in a strand of frangipani, the white bells shining against the dark plaits.

I came to India hungry for change. And it met me at every step, just not in ways I had imagined or thought possible. I had thought exposure to its people would open in me an answer about how to live, and it has, but not abstractly—it got personal, as it had to. I got touched at the bone. I don't know what the consequences of all this will be, but once you invite change in, no matter the country or circumstances, you're blown wider than you thought possible. The self has a lot farther to travel than it usually dares.

It is late, and I am writing from Kartik and Bharati's. Today Kartik and his children and I went to the magic show set up as part of a carnival on the Maidan. The whole family liked my braids. Their little girl tucked the flowers in more firmly. "That's wedding hair," Kartik said.

The show was a celebration less of sleight of hand than of technology that allowed the boy who was serving as emcee to hear his voice at twenty times its normal volume. We paid five rupees each for a seat on a folding chair and took our place among the families in the audience. Dust rose in tired spirals from the velvet curtains framing the plywood stage. It was three in the afternoon, and the green plastic roof was propped up, like the stage, with scaffolding made of bamboo poles. The sun beating through it tinted me the color of algae. The Indians ate from picnic hampers and scolded children running up the center aisle.

Finally the magician and his assistant emerged. He wore a sequined maharaja's jacket whose edges did not quite meet over his belly. His mustache was his most impressive feature: swooping and silky, like a crow caught in mustache form. It glistened even in the aquarium green of the light. His assistant, who wore an orange sari and sneakers, was also plump, as if between shows they consoled themselves with sweets for the thinness of their magic. We could hear the squeak of the soles on the plywood between the emcee's comments.

It was the least magical magic I had ever seen. The boy with the microphone cried out in Bengali as the magician sawed his bored assistant in half and plucked scarves from her prominent ear. They made no attempt to look animated as they rolled out their repertoire of tricks. The assistant looked very far away, as if contemplating a failed love or a fight with a sister, her heart and eyes focused on some domestic disappointment. The boy who provided the narrative had much more fun than they did, and every now and then gave the act its only unnerving note:

he had a horror-house laugh, pitched first high as a giggle, that ended in a low shriek. Everyone reacted to it, especially the five children who had crept in under the plastic sheet that made a side wall.

They seemed to be between six and ten years old, three boys and two girls, all of them in rags—pants with torn hems, dresses that had once been bright yellow and pink. Their hair was in tangles that had started to thicken into mats. The boys were missing teeth. They had the wildness and need about them of beggar children and would probably have descended on us if we'd been on the street. But they were entranced with the show: they couldn't stop staring, hands in their mouths. All of it mesmerized them, especially the rabbit with red eyes that was pulled from a Sikh's stiff turban. They laughed, quietly, because they did not wish to be seen. Their bodies were tensed for flight. The oldest or at least the tallest was scanning the audience for any adult who would shriek at them and make them scatter.

I caught sight then of the man who had taken our money at the makeshift entrance. He frowned, about to wave his hands and shout, and I found myself standing and saying, "No, sir, please, let them stay. I will pay for them." I pulled out a hundred-rupee bill, at least seventy-five rupees too many, and pressed its faded red into his palm. The magic show continued, the emcee laughing his maniacal laugh, the assistant contemplating her disappointment, the magician extracting coins from his wide sleeve.

Several Indian families saw what I had done, and the adults whispered among themselves. Their children stared open-mouthed at me, round calves banging the struts of their folding chairs. Kartik and I looked at each other. He shrugged. "Why not?" he said. "Why shouldn't they have some fun?"

I patted the seats next to me, and the children climbed up

cautiously. The girl in the yellow dress sat next to me. She said something, and I shook my head to mime my lack of comprehension. Kartik said, "I think she wants to know your name."

"Anna," I told her, and she repeated it, its syllables perhaps familiar to her from her own language. It wasn't a common word anymore, just a piece of change, a sixteenth of a rupee, a calculation that the British often used, complaining of being overcharged by one or two. She smiled, and I saw that her front teeth were gone.

"What is her name?" I asked Kartik, and he translated. "Sarina." The oldest boy, the lookout, shook his head at her. Don't talk, he indicated. We weren't to be trusted; he knew the limits of charity and didn't want to accustom his band to bigger expectations, broader exchanges. He had settled himself into a chair, not quite relaxed, because nothing in his life would allow him to lose vigilance, but he was watching the show. He was eager for that rabbit and the bored assistant. So was Sarina. I found my arm around the back of her chair, as if to protect her gaze from interruption. She was enjoying herself. She believed in what she was seeing.

Kartik whispered, "They are street children, Anna. They'll want money afterward."

"I know," I told him. "It's okay."

He nodded back, and then, with no warning, the show was over. The magician took off his sequined jacket in front of us, making no effort to hide his transition from indifferent artist to overfed man. The assistant left the stage and a few moments later returned with a laden tray. She unpeeled a banana with the greatest enthusiasm we had seen her exhibit so far. The emcee put down his mike and wrapped its cord around the base with a practiced, happy gesture. He was about the same age as the street boys, but taller and fuller in the body. He had a job and food. His hair gleamed with oil, and he watched the assistant devour the rest of her banana with a patient fondness. A family of sorts, a troupe on tour. The tray was full of steaming tea and other dishes, and they settled on the platform to eat, in front of the case in which the assistant had been sawed in half. They scooped up small pillows of rice, not losing a single grain.

Kartik and I both noticed that the children watched this even more intently than they had the magic show. A commotion broke out. The people on the stage barely looked up, but the collector charged down the aisle, shooing off the children I'd bought tickets for. Kartik chastised him, but he had to make sure his own kids were all right. The three boys ran. They were gone so fast I couldn't have said how they'd left, and the older girl went with them. But the small one had stayed, too frightened by the man's angry voice and too focused on the food in front of her.

Which is how I found myself, an hour later, with Kartik and his three kids in a restaurant near Sudder Street with a street child in my lap, waiting for a meal. The children sucked at Limcas through narrow straws that collapsed in on themselves. Kartik was watching me speculatively. "Thank you," I told him, for about the fourth time.

"Stop it," he said, waving away the gratitude. "It's normal to feed a hungry kid." Sarina concentrated on the sweet drink. Kartik's three watched her as they drank their own sodas. The restaurant walls were a pale flaking blue, and the space was lighted with a flickering fluorescent tube. The doorway was hung with plastic beads that made a soft clatter as customers passed through. A fan whirred with little effect in the corner where the cashier sat fingering rupee notes. Receipts fluttered on a spike that pierced their centers. For some reason I couldn't stop staring at the rounded arm of the cashier, the skin of his wrist pressing the edges of his too-tight watch strap.

The waiter was a slender boy of effortless beauty. He scattered flies from the rims of our glasses with delicate snaps of his dishrag that left the creatures spinning on their backs. "Getting practice at sending them to the next life," Kartik said. Finally the food came, and the children dove in. But after a couple of minutes, all of us stopped to watch Sarina. She ate as if she were praying, if you define prayer as a stripping away to essentials, to an awareness of real need. Her cheeks were pouched with chapati and dal. Her jaw worked with steady intensity. She hunched over the silver disk of her plate so as not to drop a speck of curried eggplant on the table's worn top. She was eating as if she might not eat again, and she wasn't going to waste a scrap, either of the meal or of her charm as she worked carefully from one platter of vegetables to the next.

"Thirty thousand a day," said Kartik, his arm around his youngest.

"Thirty thousand what?" I asked.

"Children dead," he answered. "Around the world, from various causes. Diarrhea. Malaria. Malnutrition. Accidents. Mostly preventable."

Inside the restaurant, the fan whirred, the cashier counted, the flies were flicked to their next incarnation, and we watched Sarina eat. Kartik murmured something to her. She stopped to sip some water. "Slow down," he was telling her. "We will get you more." She kept chewing as she looked at him. She did not smile. She was assessing him. Then something even more basic than hunger took over. Her body, overwhelmed with food, needed sleep, and I could see her eyes start to sink shut. She swished off a fly, and soon she had drooped in my arms, warm and filthy, her belly rounding out with rice and lentils. I arranged her so she would be comfortable and found my fingers running through her hair.

"Careful. There are probably lice," Kartik said. He saw me

looking at her, the protective tug I gave her skirt. "She might also have rickets, worms, and God knows what else. Her vision, hearing should be checked. There's no question of her having been to school." He waved to the waiter for the bill and would not let me pay. "You don't have any idea what you're getting into."

We were close enough to walk back to Kartik's house and did so even though an afternoon storm was threatening. I carried Sarina, and he took his youngest. The older boys were quiet and held each other's hands. It was the last thing I expected when I woke up this morning, to grow attached to a child's scraped knee, a dal-smeared cheek, a back that I could glimpse through a tear in a dress.

I'm writing again from Kartik and Bharati's, where I've spent the last two days. It is very late. Sarina is still with me, and right now she is curled up tightly, as if to escape the cold. But it is breathtakingly hot, and I think she must have learned to pull into her body because she's needed to protect herself and also because she has not had room to sprawl. She lay herself out on the bed like a star after her bath the first night she was here, and the length of her limbs seemed to surprise her. Damp and curly-headed, she did not speak, flexing her fingers and toes. She kept looking at her fingernails, which I had trimmed, as if in wonder at finding no grime below them. At night, however, the old habits must take over, and she balls herself up.

The first night, she slept for twelve hours. I spent much of that time in a chair, just looking at her, wanting to be there to comfort her if she woke. Bharati, after her shock at seeing a street child invited into her house, recovered quickly. She gave us sheets, towels, and soap, and helped me wash the child to get off the worst of the grime. She touched the matted curls with a finger and said, "Yes, well, it's to be expected. We'll get them tomorrow. Don't sleep next to her, Anna." Kartik had been right about the lice.

When she woke, Kartik and I took her to the bathroom. The shower at his house is a drain in the floor, and the water that comes from the fixture is cold and fitful. The space was lit by a single bulb and smelled of Dettol and drains, the old Indian battle. But the tile was new and green, and Kartik saw me noticing. He'd done it himself, he said. Quicker than waiting for contractors. You could hear the water descending from a cistern on the roof. "Not too much," Kartik said. "It's different when monsoon really gets here, but right now, we should be careful." He had an immediate sense of the proportion he could assume for his family, measured in relation to all the others in this building who had the good fortune to have indoor plumbing. Neighbors were a bristling fact of life. One minute too long, and Kartik would hear of nothing else for days.

Sarina was in such wonder. Although Kartik said nothing, I sensed that he too wanted to prolong her happiness. It was hard not to be generous with the water. She had probably not seen many showers, much less had one. She was used to washing while dressed, in puddles, ditches, or, if she was lucky, at street-corner pumps. Despite the novelty, she seemed quite at ease. She opened her mouth to drink and started to laugh. Her dress was soaked through, and it clung to her like a thin shawl.

Kartik bent to take it off her so we could wash her hair and body, but when he undid the safety pin that held it together, the entire thing ripped. She started to scream, and the sound echoed in the tiled room. Kartik tried to hush her, speaking Hindi, hoping it might be more familiar than Bengali, since he thought she was from Bihar. The boys had sounded Bihari. "We'll get you a new dress," he told her. "We'll find you something clean."

She wanted her old dress. As she cried, her hair grew wet, and as more dirt washed from her, we could see that her skin was paler than it had been. We could see too how wide her eyes were when she was fully awake and frightened, and how far she'd had to retreat into herself to stay alive. That dress was part of being alive, and she was not going to give it up easily.

Kartik rolled the scrap into a yellow fist of dripping fabric and gave it back to the sobbing child. Sarina stood there in the water, her hair streaming to her shoulders, and neither of us could bring ourselves to pull her from it. We soaped her head to toe, and she crowed with the pleasure of the mild bubbles, still holding her dress, then holding it out so it too could be washed. Indian soap doesn't froth much, but it was enough for her. She didn't seem to mind the strong nit-killing shampoo. When Kartik told her it was time to come out, we had to hold her together, Kartik to lift her slight nakedness, me to wrap her in a rough terry towel, and I felt, for a few seconds, the luckiest of women in the most improvised and temporary of families. We were soaked and breathing hard with the exertion.

Sarina ate another couple of huge meals and slept again like the dead. Again I watched her in her dreams and entertained a vision of our returning to Varanasi to live with Lev. I could see the three of us on the ghats, eating peanuts and tossing the shells to the goats. Drinking *lassis* and playing cards as summer rain hammered down on a tin roof. Teaching Sarina English with chalk letters on the steps leading down to the holy water. Lev and I relaxed and doting. Not exactly nonsense, I knew, but a very partial truth. No illnesses, lost tempers, no cultural collisions or disapproval snaking through the picture. But at least it was a vision, a place to steer toward. When I'd asked myself what I wanted in Varanasi, the answer had been mostly cloud. This was something to aim at.

Yesterday evening after supper, Kartik and Bharati pa-

tiently explained what they thought best. They knew a good
orphanage, run by Swiss nuns in cooperation with the Indian
government. It was small, and they had friends on the board.
The children were matched with families in Geneva. Kind, they
both said, very kind, looking at me looking at Sarina playing
with a spinning top one of the boys let her have. She was too
still for a child her age. The first step, Bharati explained, was to
make sure she was actually an orphan. She might have been
sold by her parents or indentured. They would have to be as
clear as possible about that; there'd been problems in the past.
In the meantime, there were good doctors. They would make
sure she had plenty to eat. She would go to school.

The top stopped twirling. I set it up again for her, but she
came to my lap. She was wearing a dress that had belonged to
Kartik and Bharati's niece, but she kept the yellow rag next to
her. She had let me cut her hair, getting most of the mats out,
and she was like a shorn lamb now. Her curls were a lightish
brown and fine. My own hair was back in a braid, the crown
the women made too fragile to last long.

"Are they very religious?" I asked. "The Swiss nuns?"

"Just a couple of crosses around and a little hymn singing.
They don't even wear habits," Kartik said. "Protestants. Indians don't get Protestants. Catholics, High Anglicans, Syrian
Orthodox. We need a big show for it to make sense." He was
trying to make me laugh. They'd made an appointment for the
next afternoon, the same day Rose and James were coming.
Just then their older son shouted at the younger, and their fists
flew. Cries erupted, and parents dashed over to soothe feelings,
pour cups of mango juice, and return a plastic truck, minus a
fender, now much more like a real Indian truck, to its rightful
owner. But the first commotion ignited a second, and their little
daughter started to wail, too, which set Sarina off, and all of us
had our arms full of small, upset bodies, the air full of English

and Bengali ways of saying "hush." Nothing is more crowded
than family life. As my hands ruffled hair and tickled bellies, I
badly wanted the chance to be part of something so densely oc-
cupied, something with edges so tight. People arranging themselves so they could stay together.

As the boys calmed down and settled back to their games
and we pulled our clothes straight and poured more tea, it came
to me that this profoundly physical closeness had frightened
Rose. All that intimacy, all that shared air. She'd have known
how leprosy, the wearing down of nerves and skin, had been
transmitted. Ayah had told her when she was seven the details
of her real mother's death and did not pause to offer comfort or
promise that she at least would try to stay. Her father smashed
her face and did not stop to ask what India had done to her.

The thought of Rose sat as close as a scarf on my neck as we
went to the orphanage. Sarina held my hand tightly as we
walked into the neat compound. Kartik and Bharati had told
her she would be going to a new place. She knew enough to
mistrust change, and she looked around with her thumb in her
mouth, her other hand wrapped in mine, her body stuck tight
to my side. The Residence for Children was in a quiet southern
district. We'd passed a park nearby, and it was full of kids'
voices, with a pagoda, of all things, and a stand of bamboo. The
children from the orphanage were taken there every afternoon,
the pale, self-possessed nuns told us. A tamarind tree swayed in
the center of the courtyard where they met us, and we were all
patterned in the fringed shadows its leaves cast on our arms
and faces.

Kartik had been wrong; the nuns did wear habits, just ones
modified for the intensity of Indian heat. The women had on
jumpers of pale gray summer flannel, with round-collared
shirts. Their hair was pulled back under kerchiefs. Crosses
hung around their necks with solid, brass severity. Their eyes

were startlingly blue, not like Lev's smoky eyes, but the blue of shadows on snow. Sarina couldn't stop looking at the women, their skin, their faces, the way their crosses bumped their meager chests. She might also have been listening to their Bengali, fluent but cramped and made angular by their original accents. The administrator, a fastidious young Indian who clearly wanted to hurry us through the good-byes, told us that Sarina would be well taken care of. It would be tricky tracing her background, since so little was known, which meant, she implied, tugging at her sari, that it might be easier for her to find a placement. She did not say home.

"How long do they stay here?" I asked, and looked up at the windows filled with intent young faces and palms pressed on the screens. I wanted suddenly to see the wards. I thought of Rose's worry about nights filled with coughing, narrow beds made up with sheets of rough cotton. Sarina glanced up as well. I wondered how long the baby who was my sister had had to stay in such a place. If she'd ever gotten out of one. Sarina gripped my hand more tightly, both to apply pressure and to signal fury.

"As long as they need to," the administrator said, watching Sarina watch the windows. I guessed but could not of course say for sure that the young administrator was assessing her attractiveness, the darkness of her skin tone, her dental health, the ease or difficulty of the next step: getting someone to take and hold on to her. The tamarind tree shivered. Thickened clouds blew past. Monsoon was really here. It was time to go. Kartik could sense my wanting to stay, to see where Sarina would be living. He was aware that it was dangerous to let me linger. I knew that, too. I knelt down and started to unwrap my fingers from Sarina's.

The youngest nun crouched down to tickle the girl, but she pulled her hand from mine and squirmed away. She stood apart from all of us, abruptly a tiny column of energy, the fiercest I'd ever seen her. She was shaking, and then the ferocity slipped, and she began to cry, not the imitative fuss she'd made in the general whirl of Kartik and Bharati's family, but with a grief that was far harsher, filled with much more fear and much more pain. A howling, deeply human, not an animal sound at all. She was keening. She knew we were giving her up. She looked at us, her small fists in knots, and sobbed in her borrowed dress, her cropped hair tossed by the quickening wind.

I kneeled down to kiss and hold her. She let me, leaning toward me, shaking in my arms, still so thin, her heart a rabbit in her chest. Her tears dampened my shirt. "Darling," I told her, "you will find people to live with—a mother, a father, sisters. You will have a house and toys and books. Your people will tell you stories. You will be loved. I promise." But she would not stop crying, and although I know she did not understand my literal words, she knew I was describing something I could not guarantee. A safe purchase. A steady affection. A tie that would not come undone or be clipped when it became inconvenient. An assurance of having people to care for her when they already so patently had not. She knew. She already knew all that, and it enraged her. Hold on to that, I told the close curves of her ear as I kissed her temple. You will be stronger for it. You are your own people. A country, inviolate.

Yet even as I said it, I knew it wasn't true. Not for her, for me, for any of us. Open borders, long unfenced sections of the self are how we touch each other. It's how we have to be, though it's an arrangement that invites along with closeness nothing but the deepest sadness, the greatest risk of loss. The possibility of one opens the way for the inevitable incursion of the other.

Kartik said, gently, with the kindness of the best of fathers, like mine, "Anna, you need to let her go." He helped me stand;

he bent down himself to kiss Sarina good-bye. Bharati also kissed her and took out a necklace from her bag that she clasped around Sarina's neck. She pressed her forehead against the girl's and looked her in the eyes, her large hands cupping the sharp chin. Throughout, the nuns stood to the side, watching impassively, not inured to such a scene but not prey to its emotions, either. They knew their next move — getting the child to the stairwell, the dormitory, the playroom. They came to take Sarina's hand, but she stood her ground and kept wailing. She would not let herself be distracted by offers of food or pleasure. Good girl, I thought as I headed to the doorway, forcing myself to look toward the street, conscious of the first drops of the afternoon storm. Don't get bossed around by those Swiss. Show them who you are. Just before we walked out of the compound, I turned to see her. She had not stopped crying. She had not budged. Even from a distance I could tell she was looking at me, resisting having her hand caught up in another white woman's. She did not wave.

One two, buckle my shoe, I'd whispered to her that morning as I put sandals on her callused feet. She had looked at them, not entirely pleased. They might have been her first pair. She scuffed the soles cautiously on the ground, listening to the scrape and drag of rubber on concrete. She'd helped choose them at the market, though I think she was surprised they were actually for her. I hummed the tune again. It was a rhyme my mother must have sung to me. Where else would I have learned it?

James and Rose arrived at three in the morning the day we dropped Sarina at the Residence for Children, and I've traveled from a wailing child to the Oberoi in twelve hours. I am too jarred by all that's happened in the last few days to sleep. My brother's in a room next door; Rose and I are installed in this one, which is green and silver and silent, except for the rain smacking the air conditioner. They are both exhausted from the flight, naturally enough. The Oberoi is colossally posh, with its high ceilings, inlaid marble, locks that work. It's like an entirely different version of India from any I have yet seen, and a vivid contrast to orphans, prim nuns, sparsely treed courtyards. Here I've seen limousines and women in saris of gold cloth and truly large men with Rolexes, bodyguards, and lots of jewelry. Rose was startled at its grandeur, but she was so tired she didn't have the energy to protest the opulence. She was asleep in minutes, saying as she lay down, "Such a long trip." I've just tucked a blanket around her. She's breathing steadily, turned away from me.

I've finished the journal I brought from home and have started using a notebook I bought in Varanasi. Fibers of wood are visible in the paper, and the rules waver. Indians around the country are probably writing themes in ones just like this, or solving math problems, or figuring out interest payments, or calculating the odds for test matches. Anything can happen in one of these. On the cover, Sarina drew some circles with a ballpoint I gave her, which she could barely hold. The circles themselves aren't quite certain, more like amoebas, but she enjoyed the slippery motion of the nib over the paper.

I haven't told Rose about her yet, or about anything really. We're going to meet Kartik and Bharati for dinner tomorrow. James faxed the Sri Lakshmi school and has arranged a time to go and meet Sujata. She had let him know, James said, that they were very busy just now with repairs to the main building and the addition of a science wing, but they would be receiving visitors on Thursday afternoons. "Lots of shyness, nodding, and tea," Rose said, but you could tell she was looking forward to it. She had specially asked James to organize the visit. "Just to see what it's like," she added—as close as she got to saying she wanted to see where Ayah came from and to meet her daughter.

Overall, Rose has seemed a little disoriented. In the taxi on the way in from the airport she kept patting at her hair and saying, "I don't recognize any of this. It's gotten so enormous," and, "Good Lord, they drive badly," as she gripped the door handle, not, as I might have thought, with disappointment, but with wonder. "I've got no idea where we are," she kept saying, staring at the tumble of houses and shops, the sidewalks overflowing even at 4 a.m.

I'd been at the airport since midnight, fueled with tea and anxiety, wondering how we were going to spend our ten days together. We had no itinerary so far. That seemed the best way to approach things; we'd see what evolved. Bharati and Kartik gave me lots of ideas, though they discouraged a visit to the Sundarbans. I looked up the region in my guidebook, and now's the worst time to go. It's hot and wet, the time of year the Bay of Bengal brews cyclones. Most of it, too, belongs, to Bangladesh, which didn't exist when Rose lived here or even wrote her story down, born as it was two years later in a war. Apparently it's a partition that makes little sense geographically; thanks to the swampy deltas, it's impossible to tell where one country should start and another end. It's all part of the same landmass. People speak the same language. A few man-eating tigers still live and hunt there, however, no matter which country's border they've managed to swim across. These days they're defended against with contraptions that look like fencing masks, which villagers wear on the backs of their heads. Tigers like to sink their mouths around that spot where the spinal cord pokes for a moment from the hard curve of the skull down through the vertebrae. Just an inch or two that evolution hasn't yet protected. Instant paralysis, the most efficient way to kill. Apart from the weather, I don't think it's the right time to heighten any fears.

Kartik and Bharati agreed. They had even refused to let me go back to my hotel after we had taken Sarina to the orphanage. "It's not Indian to be sad all by yourself. It's not done," Kartik teased, and I let them lure me to their kitchen and into making a meal with them. Part Indian, part American, to appease Ravi, the oldest boy, who missed good potato chips and real Coke. I chopped up baking chocolate and made some nearly inedible cookies. Kartik met with a customer for some new projects, while Bharati and I put the children to bed.

She told me she had given up work for now. Computers could wait. Children inhaled your time, and besides, in Calcutta everything took twice as long as it had in California. She shifted a pillow below Ravi's head. The delays didn't seem to bother her much. She was obviously glad to be back home. What she was saying, I think, was that even when it was difficult or perturbing, it was where she understood herself best. Her confidence was quite unlike Amit Patel's. Nothing brassy or aimed outward in it, but something she slipped into, like a skin.

She asked me what I did, and I said that I wrote grants at a women's nonprofit, but I needed to find more time to do what I really liked, which was writing poems. I remembered the girls on the train, their delight in Tennyson. "Not fancy ones," I said, "and they won't cure AIDS," but just then it felt like it might be enough to examine and describe, line by line, what I thought and saw. A poet's basic job: clear, precise notation of complexity in language as revealing as Indian sunlight. Responding to what the world showed you and then pushing back out into that world, changed by what you'd seen. I sensed, though I did not say it, that there was room in that work for a child. That the two responsibilities might weave well around each other.

Metaphor and diapers, Legos underfoot and the construction of angular and delicate ideas. Practicality and abstraction, each making the other possible.

It was no less likely than many combinations, and it wasn't gunrunning or drug dealing. No matter how high-minded your choices or behavior, the shadow worlds, the shadow actions, always exist: we're always implicated in them, even distantly, through inattention, the actions of governments, ignorance. Little arrived in a life, not coffee, not butter, without someone's labor that often shaded directly into exploitation. Worse, the inequities seemed intractable. No sort of purity was attainable, and to pursue it was to risk believing in sets of impossible rules, the scorning and punishment of those who did not agree. For me, being human would always involve the braiding of contradictions: being feisty but jealous, liberal but stingy, intelligent but stubborn, all at once.

Poems, computers, sculpture, tending lepers, bathing children, renouncing worldly possessions—the possibilities are dizzying. If you're lucky enough to know what it is you're deeply suited to, you might as well step toward it. It's another manifestation of faith, perhaps in something as slight, miraculous, and inconstant as your own abilities. Bharati and I listened to the sounds of traffic in the road. "Curing is one thing," she said finally. "Helping people is something else." And assistance arrived in the humblest of forms: an unexpected orange in a palm, a baseball card that featured Jesus, a promise spelled across the skin.

Rain spattered the windows, and we closed the shutters. Downstairs, Bharati and Kartik ordered a taxi for me, said they'd see me the next evening, and waited in their door until I was on my way.

The storm had delayed the flights, and when I went to the Asok Sugar See Off Shack, a convenience store in the terminal, all its compact umbrellas had been sold. I had a hard time caring that I was going to get wet. Monsoon relaxes people. "Finally, the rainy season," a woman sighed. A man turned to tell me, "We have been waiting a long time for this." The damp breeze came through the doors every time someone walked in, arms open to the water, shirt or sari dripping. Young men shook the water off themselves, laughing. But that's not all there is to monsoon. The paper yesterday had an article about a flash flood that killed thirty people. A picture showed a man's body draped across telephone wires, tangled there like a large, sodden bird. Rose mentioned that sort of event in the taxi. "Monsoon," she said. "We loved it when it rained. But the cyclones came then. And people died and died." In our room, she took off her jacket and laid it on the desk. She sat on the edge of a chair, as straight as she could on a cushion that gave under her weight. "Well," she said, "we made it." She looked at me.

"Thank you," I said, still on the other side of the room, glad to have my arms full of her bags. Conscious that I was using the phrase correctly, out of deep gratitude and not conditioned politeness.

"It smells the same. I can't believe I remember that, but I do. Smoke and people." She was also saying, No more now, what I'm doing is strange and difficult. I need to do it slowly. I will start with the outside and go in. As I hoisted her suitcase to the closet, I realized I wasn't waiting for more conversation. We'd have room and time to talk if we wanted. Mostly I'd just been waiting for Rose to be here, with her beautiful old face and her large-knuckled hands. My mother, a person who always stayed. "You look tired," I told her, and went to a bed to pull down a cover. "Come lie down. It's been a long day."

"Yes, it has." She sighed. "Thank you, Anna," she said as she lay down. She didn't ask me to, but I sat down next to her and smoothed her hair. "It's a mess, isn't it?" she said into the pillow, already half asleep. But she did not tell me not to touch it.

Rose and James's plane had been announced at last, and passengers had started to straggle down the long corridor, slumped and addled in just the way I'd been only three weeks earlier. The usual knots of family, some excited for their visit, some more cautious. I had spotted both James and Rose before they saw me. James was looking at a young girl in a blue *salwar kameez*, her hair in two shining plaits to her waist. A tremendously fat man waddled past him with a briefcase in each hand. Another man in a fez, another in a Sikh's high turban with three sons—all in black caps that covered the topknots of their hair—being coaxed along in front of him. The Sikh father clucked at his boys and swatted their thin shoulders with vigorous affection. I could see James trying to take it all in. He looked confused, he looked pleased, and I realized she had told him. He was touching Rose on the shoulder, not really holding her but guiding or steering, and not even that—it was gentler. Then I understood. It was reciprocal. The contact for both of them was comforting.

Rose leaned in to say something to him, and he nodded, and I thought, It was a long flight, and they've been talking. She had told him the essentials, that there is another sister. "You'd better know what you're doing," he said as we checked in, and held me hard, just as glad to see me as I was to see him. It was reassuring that his hair was a mess and his socks were still slumping around his ankles. He wasn't fully restored to himself yet, either. Not that discovering he had a half sister somewhere on the planet would help; if anything, it would complicate matters tremendously. But it was good that he knew, it seemed to me, though it didn't mean it was knowledge we'd act on. Rose had given her up. She was her own person. She might have no interest in us. She might, too, have tried to find us and failed. It was a long story. It needed to be approached slowly, the possibility that there was another boundary to our family.

I saw Rose glancing around, gathering Calcutta back in, taken aback. Fish tanks gloomy with algae lined the hallway. James and Rose both looked surprised to find them there: the oddness of fish and planes so close to one another. She and James had to steer around children tapping at the glass. Neither of them had caught sight of me yet; the people I'd been waiting with were reuniting with relatives and friends, and the chattering crowd blocked my family's view. The women threw themselves into each other's arms, the men said hello with handshakes that started at the palm and progressed until they were almost holding elbows. Most were smiling and talking instantly in that Indian mix of local language strung with bits of English. "Dead tired," I heard, and "Bloody long trip."

Rose was looking at a large painting hung on the wall of the waiting area, a picture of a Bengal tiger. I saw her point at it and nudge James to look. She seemed older, more frail, even slightly stooped. She was moving less confidently. I tensed when I first saw her, as if sighting something important and rare. And she was—she was my mother. I had often treated time with Rose like time in a temple, as if I were sighting the deity, experiencing darshan. Yet the scale was different now, the arrangements had changed. She cast a shadow still, but it was the same size as mine. We were the same height. I could look straight into her eyes. Then she noticed me.

She raised a hand and waved, and I could see that it pained her to lift her arm. The seats on those planes are too small for people like us. She was coming unbent after being cramped in a narrow space. She gave her bag to James and then came walking quickly toward me. Even hunched, she was so much taller than most of the other passengers. They were expecting her to be more deliberate. She'd seemed elderly and uncertain just a moment before.

I had to stand there at the barricade; the guards, thin men with mustaches and ancient rifles, would not let me pass. I had to wait as she came toward me, moving with clear purpose but conscious of the Indians in her path, alerting them to her passage, speaking Bengali, saying, "So sorry; it's my daughter." *Konya*. I heard the word and knew it from her story. The other travelers let her press forward, people who also hadn't seen their relatives in a long time, because that was why we were all here, to acknowledge the pull of family, light or strong. "Anna," she said, "my girl." Her skin smelled as it always had, of lemon and earth.

I'd wanted to call her something other than her first name. But when I held her scratched hands and then her broad shoulders, all that came out was "Rose," a word that has thorns and grace combined.

She just moved in her sleep, and I went over to tug the blanket back in place. Her hair is in a tangle on the pillow, and it is whiter than I remembered. I smoothed the strands from her face. It isn't what we are called that needs to change, as much as the ability to imagine one another, large women that we are, more largely. The world is big enough for all of us. It has to be.

Acknowledgments

I would like to thank the John Simon Guggenheim Memorial Foundation and the National Endowment for the Arts for generous grants that allowed me the time to work on this novel. The College of Liberal Arts and the Graduate School at the University of New Hampshire, not to mention my colleagues in the English Department, also gave me indispensable support. My students deserve as well my real appreciation for their good questions and their ability to keep me thinking hard about writing. I have found at UNH a home for my working and writing life, a gift for which I am deeply grateful.

Elisabeth Sifton turned her extraordinary eye to the manuscript with a precision, compassion, and profound thoughtfulness that influenced the book in the most fruitful of ways: I could not have finished the novel without her clear, wise guidance. No writer could be luckier in editors. Thanks are owed as well to Danny Mulligan for his calm, efficient help and to Maxine Bartow, whose admirably thorough copyediting improved the book greatly.

Ginger Barber's faith in my work has made, from the beginning, every difference in the world. No one is more willing to read and comment on even a cursory draft. Her patience, honesty, and insight assisted me enormously at every step of writing and revising this book.

Kathleen Toomey Jabs discovered information about India that I would never have found on my own, and Dara Magnon also provided critical help with research. Sy Montgomery's *Spell of the Tiger: The Man-Eaters of Sundarbans* was a fascinating introduction to the Sundarbans, and Diana Eck's marvelous book *Banaras: City of Light* was instrumental to learning about Varanasi. It should be noted, however, that all mistakes are mine and that the India I have written about here is an India of my imagination.

The staff at the Ohrstrom Library at St. Paul's School gave me a safe haven for my work as well as access to beautiful space and an excellent collection.

My readers—Malin Ely Clyde, Evelyn Hitchcock, Mekeel McBride, Louise White, and Mimi White—were unstinting with their kindness, friendship, and helpful advice. Rebecca Brewster, Rebecca Carman, Michelle Hartha, Anna Holder, Donna Torney, and Mary Nell Wegner provided vital encouragement on this project, as did my loving parents, brother, and sister. Everyone at the Children's Learning Center also has my respect and gratitude; without their assistance, I would not have had the time to write.

I would also like to thank the Tulsi family, Devendra Pandit, and Mia Stallone for their hospitality in Varanasi.

Finally, my travel companions in India, Brad and Toby Choyt, are closer to the heart of this book than anyone else. Their curiosity, bravery, tolerance, appetite for adventure, and ability to unearth Punjabi *dhabas* in the most unlikely of places made our journeys across the country the amazing experiences that they were. To them: Thank you, the Indian way.